Wire Pulling Sailors

robertbolumburu@protonmail.com

Wire Pulling Sailors

A Cornucopian Tale

Chapters

These books are dedicated to Blind Boy Grunt, Bobby Allen and the Jack of Hearts.

—More of an outlaw than you ever were

Book One: Bile

In the deep discovery of the Subterranean world, a shallow part would satisfie some enquirers; who, if two or three yards were open to the surface, would not care to rake the bowels of Potosi

1. Scope

Somewhere under Woorish—last outpost of the Glum Valley, saddling a dingle on Woorish Hill and remotely conscious of the spread, incessant city—were a half dozen eyes: incidental eyes, unobtrusive, like the hearts of birds; except that, inexplicably, they touched a nerve, passed over a grave, pressed the strata like the fabled pea, and the entire creaking valley slept lopsided.

A headtorch clicked, held in hand. A beam broke the dark. Small on issue, big on trajectory, it ignored the nearby, went straight for the profound. Where the beam went, a tunnel followed, passing into distance. Then the circle closed, and close things came to browse: a shoe, a ladder, a traffic bollard. But as soon as they shaped, they were shattered; the beam sprang upon a face. It was a bony, strong-set face: brow like a flag; large, unremarkable eyes, blue-grey; big teeth, which, in time of problem, would prey upon the lip. The mouth was primed, wide and well-appointed. It could gurn and grimace, spurn and scorn; carry questions, formulate solutions. It could smile pragmatism, cackle approbation, collapse to horse-laughter; but it never beamed.

The beam moved, as if discomfited, throwing the nose into unwonted speculations. It was a strong nose, with a bit of bridge, and the nostrils basked in their glory. The hair, haloing the forehead, was mousy, pointy, a little longer than short, with a certain stray grace at the neck. Neck was lean and boned; back broad; legs went longly into night. The whole was neither handsome nor uninteresting, an extraordinary mixture of lank and lithe, web and spider, professorial squints and leonine movements. Wire limbs, taut from pull-ups, climb-offs and other athletic wranglings, stretched and groped through his motions. Long fingers, and truant; bane of many a chemical, cliff-face, manhole-cover. To himself he was *Tantalus*, an enigmatic designation, straddling ancient myth and contemporary pulp. To his enemies he was *Crow*, which was at once erosion and allusion: the former from his surname, which was Kroner; the latter to his apocalyptic looks. For there was something of *Compt* about *Crow*, of which none were more aware than those whom a *Compt* would find wanting; whose own names, were they not careful, would sink to the bottom and drop right out—or, if you were Bjørn Bjørnsen, *off*. To his friends he was *Magnus*, and Jude and Harper, who stood with him now in the

alarming tunnel, held those who called him *Mags* in
high suspicion.

'—Not to say *dudgeon*,' said Jude.

Harper touched the ceiling. 'Could have fooled
me.'

They laughed silently.

'Are we all ready, are we all determined?' said
Magnus, looming in, torch still lashing up his face.
They looked like El Greco's *Fable*, staring at the
bulb, right into its spectral wire, as if they preferred
light itself to the world it enabled. But, if Magnus
was the Incendiary—and this was indisputable—
who then was the Monkey? Jude, whose nose was
fine, whose hair was auburn, whose general pallor
incarnadined on demand (his own or others'),
would have been quick to judge, were it not for the
fact that El Greco's fine, auburn, incarnadine Man
was also a presumptuous boor. Squeezed between
him and the Monkey, Jude was unsure which to go
for. Neither represented the allegorical jackpot. He
bit his lip, rejected the entire comparison.
Nevertheless, his cheek looked as if something had
pressed it and found something other than bone.

The Incendiary saw it. 'No *general
unwillingness?*' he leered. A hard, humourless leer.
The Incarnadine Man had been known to possess
general-unwillingness in scrapes of various kinds,
in particular when jumping onto rope-swings from
great heights. 'It's not that I can't do it, or am

3

horribly *afraid* of it,' he had said, recoiling from the word *afraid*, 'merely that I have a—' and he thought for a space, '—general *unwillingness*.' Of which, afterwards, he was often suspected.

The Incendiary shook a fist, quietly hyperbolic. *The Incarnadine Man* blanched for lack of options, then exhaled, acknowledging the gibe. 'Yes,' he said, solemnly, to the good auspices of the expedition. *The Monkey* glanced at him, arch but approving, like a middle-man twice-remunerated. He pushed his lips out and pointed to the onslaught of darkness. *The Incendiary* was indubitably leader, but that was nothing in itself. What gave the expedition *gusto*—or, *The Incarnadine Man* might have argued, *desperation*—was the willingness. And a particular willingness at that. *The Monkey*, *The Incarnadine Man*, neither spoke *The Incendiary*'s language. Nothing about them smacked of the active or progressive, though they cheerfully could have. They didn't even know the rules of *Magic: The Gathering* (though they understood *Talisman* profoundly). Yet they were *The Incendiary*'s protégés, enticed to the hive of action from the wastes of idlesse. Not that they saw it that way. Certainly they took pride in a friendly barter, bluffly trafficking with the empirical. But, if to *The Incendiary* they were a mission, it was sufficient to them that he was more than fiction. *The Monkey* and *Incarnadine Man* despised the fiction that was *all* fiction. However slovenly the bounds of metaphor, they were disambiguated by *The Incendiary*. And for this relief much thanks—though not so much that *The Incarnadine Man* could not withdraw both thanks and bounds at a moment's notice.

Now, for instance. 'Behold!' barked *The Incendiary*, walking off, torch trained on the ground. 'The Dreamers dreameth!' His voice dropped, not so much for distance as effect. 'Roll up your loins, men. Gird your unctuous sleeves!' In the puddle of light fell ten fingers, two legs, the silhouettes of rucksack straps.

'I grant you,' said Jude, with the burr of biding time. 'Your Dreamer is a fungoid slob—a Lard, as any one of Stan, Goodhead, Turner, Moore or Melvyn Browne could have told you. But then, it can't be denied, your Man of Action is a deluded myope. A Mole if you will. A *Man That Was Used Up*, sometime during the Kickapoo campaign, constantly denying what the Dreamer has long since grown bored of recurrently dreaming: namely, that the empire will fall *any century now*. No, I maintain,' he maintained. 'Speak softly—not mincingly, mark you, but with the mutter of discontent—and carry a *big metaphor*.'

Harper's smile bypassed the eye, went internal, fell on an empty stomach. He gulped. Nothing is worse than a night without sleep. Not that you'd have known it was night. It might have been prancing broad day on the earth above them, with the sun on the wheat and starlings splitting the light. But it was night. Not addicted day, its risks and speculations; not even meagre evening, its soft hypotheses; but sober, bankrupt night. The wee hours. Cold and sealed, and the bets all off.

Harper caught up. 'Magnus,' he said, bending near his wrist. 'Light your watch a second.'

'It's after midnight. But time is best forgotten. For the PRESENT.'

Jude considered this proposition. 'On the contrary,' he demurred. 'If *time*—your bog-standard hours, minutes and seconds, *Greenwich Mean* and *British Summer* both—has any pertinence at all—and what does it have if not a paltry, pedantic *pertinence?*—it is to the wary, neurotic present. Past and future do all the best forgetting. Which, of course, is why they are cursed with remembrance. *Ha!*' he coldly yelled. 'Forgetfulness is a double edged *sword!*'—this last with a shriek, so that his voice ran down the interiors and they glowed, appreciative.

Magnus watched the progress of that voice. 'Fact is,' he said, 'there's no telling where on earth this grave goes; whom or what she cradles; why she exists at all; and where, again, she opens to the air. We've seen with our own eyes a few of her sister-tunnels, and, above them, their manholes, stations,

6

chimneys, and the like, but whether this one—
which I'd say looks to be the mother of the lot—is
connected to those is something I can't fathom.
Until now, that is! Now, we're fathoming. Now
we're plumbing depths. Got any questions, qualms,
doubts, perturbations? Employ them, squeeze 'em,
SCOPE 'EM OUT!'

Magnus seemed to have rehearsed some of what
he was saying. Or perhaps he always thought in
declamatory terms. But, unusually, Jude was not
looking askance. He was looking dreadful, straight
down the tunnel. Where was the wit in the
situation, belly soft for incision? Night in a vault
under Woorish Hill was no time for it. Wit here
was all Magnus', in the form of competence.

They put the ladder behind them. The air was
dank. The smallest litter of water escaped down the
side. Footsteps were scuffed or crunching, loud if
you listened. The tunnel floor was gravel and
cement, cooped up by blacker walls. The torchlight
was low, with protective backswell, but
occasionally Magnus would throw it in the void and
be met by sudden loss—the beam, lance-like,
signifying itself.

They observed it blankly. 'Yes,' remarked Jude,
'that's what Shakespeare overlooked. The *real*
idiocy is the tale that signifies *itself*. A tale which
signifies nothing can be riotously entertaining.'

7

'What's more, a poor player is a superb prop,' said Harper. 'Brecht was right: let his poverty express itself.'

'Yet he is nothing,' announced Magnus, 'to the WALKING SHADOW.' And he strode ahead, working defiantly with his arms, consigning our yesterdays like so many mounds of earth. 'Swallow your tongues, men,' he continued. 'I've a fancy we're set on an encounter with the great Glum Reservoir. By my observations, I should say we are descending on a line more or less parallel to the surface, perhaps a fraction steeper in the long term. And, by my CALCULATIONS, if the course remains good to fair as now, we'll pass into the parish of St Swithen's, Meal Common, green jurisdiction of the Reverend Hannah, sleeping sublimely between the flower farm and The Carp and Bell, in, ooh, about half an hour.'

He paused, as if examining doubt itself. He was a game, not an elegant, orator. 'I wouldn't count on tea and cakes though. It might be a while before we find an end to this monotony, this AUTONOMY of pipeline—.'

The last words trailed with him. Jude and Harper were left alone, eyeing him, each other, the discrepancy between word and deed. Naturally the discrepancy was an exact one. Magnus was no deceiver. But how to define *discrepancy*, this was the thing that niggled. And then there was *exact*.

Jude could also have raised questions of *between*, but he thought that would be taking it too far.

'Ignominy, more like,' he observed.

'Same difference,' said Harper, mixing conspiracy with conciliation. They looked back. A mere sheen showed the point of entry. They imagined it was the ladder, imagined their way up it, the bright rungs ringing. Up they imagined, in the long steel stairwell, shuddering, flung with spray. Up again imagining, on strong golden rope, through a hole where the skylight should be. From there it would be too easy: the retarded stars, the gullible moon, the impressionable heap of Woorish ridge. Downhill all the way, from pathy prevarications, through fieldy reliefs, to triumphs on Lostwater Road. Then a prodigious swoop down Heathen Hill, to feast on Meal Common as on so much defenceless prey. What need imagination? All this they projected, as if it had already happened. But they moved toward *The Incendiary*'s diminishing figure as if it were a lure on a fishline, or—when the torch jogged and he flared into limb and shadow—Medusa speculating in her lair.

*

Maybe it was five minutes, maybe ten; somewhere down the line they stood still. Magnus had turned off the torch. He wanted to train his ears. They

9

gathered close, as if the collective ear were greater than its parts. But only their breath was, and it collided on the collective ear. Magnus grimaced, extracted himself. A tiny noise extracted itself too, climbing up to meet his skinny listening.

'Water, gentlemen,' he whispered. His whisper was a rasp. 'Here we strike black gold—in this our only-available Hades!' A white finger pointed to the noise. 'Real elemental rebellion!' he boasted. 'Actual brother's blood, self-daylighting, levelled to the sight of men.' Five fingers elongated. 'Childe Harold, what did he say, beholding black Acheron?' Magnus threw up eyebrows, like one who dabbles. '"Close shamed Elysium's gates, my *shade shall seek for none!"*'

It was an ostentatious citation, daring scepticism. When it came to verse, Magnus liked grace and surface, thought them the match of any depth. If those elegant Lords, Byron and Tennyson, were the keystones of his arch, the likes of Longfellow, Poe and Alfred Noyes were its plaster pilasters, impressed by a well-meaning grandmother upon his mental pantheon. Shakespeare was a different thing: a barbarian, hard to argue with; a visceral force you either liked or lumped. He used rude throwbacks of tools, all thrust and brunt, and a blow could shake the foundations. If you weren't careful your pantheon would be bulldozed down. Magnus liked more intricate machinery—with

10

bells, wheels, handles. Rhymes and words, to him, were so many brackets and hinges. Eat them, you'd get indigestion.

Jude and Harper stood there, uncomfortably summoned. To them, citation was both shame and triumph. Shame in convenience, triumph in aptitude. Between them it was code and sign of friendship. But they were stumped by Magnus's gimlet eyes and gauntlet-theatricals. Jude had also been stumped many times by Alistair Hobbes off the bowling of Benjamin McCormack Kepperly-Lie, but that was a different issue. What made the two stumpings similar was that now, as then, he took a long time to accept the umpire's arbitration. Once he had, however, he trundled up the other end to try a little swing of his own, saying: 'What Magnus fails to realise, is that the *whole point* of his Longfellows, Poes and Alfred "irksome" Noyes's, with all their monotonous arabesques, is that behind them—*behind*, mark you—are hollow puritanical abstentions, where words are cast away. I'm not convinced any of them actually believe in language. No, Magnus, try as he might, is an apologist for depth, and of the worst, because *clandestine*, kind.'

This time the wind wasn't with him. Swing as he would, his deliveries went harmlessly wide, rolling down the tunnel in the direction of long leg. There were only two options open: concede or return—to the start, the station, all those known, dumbly-countable, quantities. Naturally they conceded, though closer to return concession cannot be. From the dark centre came the stir of purpose. A lethal chill. They were made, they thought, for the free air, a frugal *flânerie*. Careless variations on cheap routines. Here they smelled the death of both; smelled cold cash and deep expenses. Here were untold reserves, gold deposits, markets crashing and resurrecting like silent forests. Staring ahead, they saw spiralling debts, at unspeakable interests. Few things were as unspeakable as interest.

'I suspect,' said Magnus, 'we shall run alongside this water channel, coinciding with it at intervals.' He ran his finger on the wall, as if solicitous. He was entirely present. Not in his warm home, not with his father on some nightflight to Tahiti, not even on the Woorish hillside, descending in the moon. It was as if the wall and his body were one. You could not say this of them. Their minds were elsewhere and out. Not with opposites—they were not so dedicated—but with medium terms and rational grounds. Facts were things you crossed and brushed by. You saluted the fact, gripped then dismissed it, with aristocratic hand. Etiquette had the measure of all. This casual aesthetic was the soul of the rational, and a world away from Magnus's *rationale*. For Magnus, things made were to be unmade and, if necessary, prodded with sticks. He could die down here. However lightly he wore it, in some idiotic plot of this senseless hole, he was ready to wrestle his Nemesis.

Some years later, Harper would visit the vast marble quarries in Carrara, bleak in the mountain depths. The quarries were white in the moon, staring on the Mediterranean. Harper scrambled up the path to an escarpment, went into a cave and emerged in an amphitheatre—a great, tall hole in the mountain, a hundred yards wide and high, containing the stars. Trails of fireflies hung along the cliffs and bushes in the ledges. On the ground were stones and small boulders and, under the cliff, on the left, a natural shelf. You could have crept in and lain down, topped with a hundred feet of rock. You could come there to die, where death was plain as day. You could turn to stone, not even perfectly fitting, and all one as if twenty fathoms deep.

They were not that deep now, but deep enough. Jude scraped a trainer on the concrete, falling silent. Like Robert Johnson's, Jude's mind was a red light, aware of its own warning. His *general unwillingness* peered like a St. Bernard down the ladder, with a barrel of brandy round its neck. It took many forms, his *general unwillingness*. A car rusting in a field, junk in a spare-room, an elaborate fish-hook cut adrift. Always it was like one of those non-functioning barometers people have on the wall, silently adjudicating. Unwillingness was the

13

source of all his wit. He might have written an Ode to it.

They stepped and scuffed on, depending on who they were, for what seemed an eternity, 'but was, in fact,' observed Jude, 'about half an hour—giving us to wonder if eternity has been somewhat *overrated*—or indeed if the universe is anything more than a particularly *crepuscular* tunnel, perhaps a few hours walk from end to end.' They walked in single file: Magnus, Harper, Jude, fallen again into silence. But Jude had a word for that too, and pronounced it to the nearest ears, nestled under wool-hat and curls. 'Restless silences,' he considered, 'are the proof, that Magnus's apparently profound *scopings*, far from psychic enquiries of any kind, are very material and mundane *schemes*. You see, a restless silence is *annoying*, sir. Anomalous. Out of place. One feels, in it, the oppressive necessity to *suspend one's disbelief*. In fact, I wouldn't be at all surprised if the whole *suspension of disbelief* palaver arose from the need to dispel a restless silence. No, give me the *hateful incredible* any day. With the emphasis on the *hateful*, obviously.' To Jude, there were few things in this world so vile as the suspension of disbelief. He said it again. '*The suspension of disbelief.*' And when it had sunk in he followed with, 'And *those who wield it*.' He wielded a suspended disbelief through the air. 'What is more bourgeois, what more disbelieving, than that tepid suspension, that languid gaze, sailing through the air upon wire and harness? *Continually* unsettled by a tail man, an inappropriate gesture, some burst of bombast from the back.'

'Keep up in the rear there!' blurted Magnus from his point of light.

'Because, Magnus's scoping is *emphatically* unsymbolic. *Disappointingly* inapplicable. Far from finding its centre at any given point, its centre is very definitely the point where you can say *this is the centre*—'

'—and *the worst*, presumably.'

'—And start looking for the exit.'

Jude paused, but he was for qualifying his view of restless silences. 'Not that I condemn the *restless silence*,' he continued. 'On the contrary, if anything has ever set us apart it has been an absolute investment in the *restless silence*, which requires so much more of an investment, precisely because it is so *restless*.' In pronouncing this word, he exploited its proximity to *rustles*, only then immediately to sally round and scorn anyone who held this proximity—or its exploitation—of the slightest value. 'Proximity—and *exploitation*, which is its natural consequence—are overrated,' he pointed out. 'If you think about any of these things for a moment—you are lost.'

15

This plunged them into silence again. Ahead of them, Magnus did not appear lost at all. His definite centre was somewhere round the hem of the Glum reservoir, and to that point they wandered inconsolable.

'We—this water-course we're running with,' started Harper. 'Where is it going?'

'Appears to be running to the reservoir, or near it, probably to the Pump House. I don't know frankly.'

'But, it's not sewage?'

'Hah! Take a smell, man. What do you think?'

'I suppose not'.

'I reckon with you. This is mother's milk stuff. You could cup this in your hand and drink it like a baby. Nothing but a good feeble reek. Bit of moss and slime maybe, but not much more than your ordinary stream accumulates. This is the prime swim and travelling USQUE on the rock right here. I expect with a little of this in our throats we'd enspirit ourselves no end.'

Magnus collected the water to his mouth, and it trickled meekly in. Harper, wanting water more than meekness, stooped to the same and trickled it too. But Jude had no truck with it, suspecting trickery. Time enough for that: in the sun of the city, on the paves and walkways, by the passers-by, girls in their boots and shoes. Then he'd truckle all he liked. Truck or treat. Or both, he wasn't fussy. He still had a trickle or two up his sleeve. 'Right

16

here. In the locker. A bit of eyebrow. A suggestion of leg. A prod, a protrusion of foot. At my disposal.' And he protruded his foot to prove it. 'Kick 'em in the shins, sir. A little bit of impeding. Get my retaliation in first. Nn, the odd professional foul. They love it.'

At the moment, though, Jude was unusually pragmatic. He gathered up his trousers and followed the two in front, directly interested in the point when he would walk out and his time would be his own. Besides, he suspected Magnus had water in his rucksack—'so still *less* call for these abysmal theatrics'. He eyed the rucksack. 'To say nothing of *food*: the flaw to all logic. And then again, the logic of *flaws*.' Jude had little time for food. He had not eaten since early that afternoon, when he had sat alone in the glassy kitchen, rain on the skylights, picking through a plate of his mother's *vol-au-vents*. A man was never going to get away from his mother. At every turn, when it was most desirable that he should, she and his traitorous stomach (in collusion from the beginning) would cook up a plot to rein him in. Cunning deployments of pulses. Sly sallies of asparagus. Open the fridge—BOOM!—a vegetable casserole! It was military. She knew all the epochs of the body, had them reckoned by sleeping rhythms. Communal savours, digestive seditions; the plea of appetite and the spurn of mind. All these she had the measure of. The house was staked out and every surface exploited to advantage. She knew where to stock and where leave bare, where a door should close on the scent of fruitcake, and open to the smell of toast, how to imply pate or suggest sun-dried tomato. These and other arcane maternal knowledges she did not fail to prosecute, and Jude for his part would play along, if only because not doing so would mean death.

'—An overreaction at the best of times,' he muttered, still moving. Generosity was incumbent upon you because you disdained overreaction. Life flourished precisely by process of elimination. Where everything must be disdained you are left with love. Was this how Dante operated? Paradise was the end of an exasperated sigh. Jude sighed that sigh now, but it was not an involved sigh, investing in the world, taking everything too personally. It was the blow out of hope and ego, troubles the water a moment, then is gone. It unleashes lips, replaces them with hardly a private thought. The head is hung, ambition spent; the eye returned to the object. It is true, there was still the small burrowing beast of a private thought in Jude's mind, but even that was obvious and acknowledged, so harmless. It was comic too, so that Jude was buoyed in his surrender with the inside smile of Sphinx.

18

This sigh he sighed, smile he permitted. Meanwhile they walked. Harper was in tune with the sigh. He understood exactly where it came from, had sighed that same sigh. Magnus did not approve of the sigh, but it was better where it could be seen. A true surrender—which involves no sigh—that Magnus would have approved of. At the same time, what would Jude's complete loss of ego have meant for the mission? They had to keep an end-point in mind, even though they had to invest in the depths at hand. Otherwise, even if they got out, what purpose would it serve? It had to serve some practical purpose, or it returned to vanity again. Magnus foresaw these things, kept a close eye on the spending and spooling of ego. Let it out far enough, not so far it disappears. He had never been a fisherman—flouted the rules of the reservoir fishing grounds—but in this respect was a skilful angler.

'These things are built to last' he observed, gazing up as they inducted themselves into the valley. 'But people don't come here much. You don't see too many signs of traffic. We're safe as houses.' They passed loose rubble at the floor's sides, a piece of puddled newspaper, streaks of rust and colour down the walls, counter-running the upsurge of torchlight. 'Everything here has a direction, a movement to it,' observed Magnus. 'This significant torch, these sounds—and the tunnel runs its course either way, or stretches out supine in either direction, any rate invoking movement. Then the walls run with colours, and the stream, now lost to us, flows its line and channel. That ladder we came down had its purpose and connective facility. It was, if you like, less about ITSELF than what is done BY it. It was that very GOING. This gradient, indeed, does not stay on the level but slopes down, ever adjusting, so that the adjustment is the level. Only that illegible piece of pap there stays pooling the water and running out of ideas. Fie! Fie on't! 'Tis an unweeded garden runs to seed—rank unbodied habiliment.'

He picked up the sodden strip with the ink blurred all over. At the top, the words *Even Chronic* sprawled unevenly; underneath, what once was a headline: *Joy iding O he Rise: Ca t eft outb eak in Sin ils.* 'What are we reading?' scoffed Magnus; '"words, words, words"—that what they say?'

'In all *likelihood,*' said a morose Jude, wishing for an end to the haranguing. And sure enough, one came, in the shape of a grid, locked into the tunnel's circle. There was no way past. In the middle of the grid was a barred gate, also locked and chained.

'Hah, what nonsense is this?' murmured Magnus, fingering the lock, feeling down the side of the irons. And unpacking a large spanner, he loosened bolt by bolt, until the grid was wrenched to the floor. 'The immovable object?' said the leader. 'Impossible!' They scattered like rabbits, now here, now there—on one side then the other, subtle, irrelevant, turning up like the numbers of dice.

Leaping a large puddle, which Magnus had the measure of in his *cross-terrain* trainer-boots, but for which Jude found himself better equipped in his *all-stars*, and Harper, better still, in his long *silver shadows*, they rejoined the water-course, to the point that the two channels became one. The tunnel had narrowed. Now it reached in to control the water and slipped its ceiling to a height at which only Jude was comfortable.

Touching to the sides, they passed a dark minute. Harper was unnerved. He wanted a return to surfaces, to breathe the upper air. 'Magnus,' he said. 'There's no chance this tunnel could be some kind of emergency outlet, in the case of flood, somewhere for the lake water to spill?'

A chuckle came from the light. 'I doubt it! Why up here, why so big, why the merger with this stream? No, I've a mind they've other ways of dealing with such things.'

'But if it were, of course, and we were here, we would drown in a vast upcoming tide.'

'Yes—HAH HAH—that is exactly what would happen.' Magnus threw back his head and shards of laughter flew this way and that in the darkness. He paid scant attention to backsliders. Harper knew this. A less than immaculate irony would not be long tolerated. He fell silent, but only for a minute, because the torch revealed another semicircular grate, where the wall fell away and the tunnel became a channel for the stream.

'Well,' said Jude, above the grown noise, 'looks like the end of the road.'

Harper looked at Magnus. Both Jude and Harper were thinking aporia, gazing on that growing vista where the torchlight bounded. They knew Magnus' mind, but they didn't want him to act on it. 'Because what good is a *mind?*' insisted Jude, 'if you're going to *act* on it all the time? It might as well be a muscle.' He looked back where they'd come.

'End of the road—' said Magnus. There was something like hunger in his accents. He strode into the stream, splashing as he went. Arms like penknife appurtenances, whipped all kinds of instruments from his bag. Jude lingered, hoping in his obvious secret heart that, if the screwdrivers met the challenge of the grate, water would prove a more complex problem. 'Because here's the thing, sir. Problematic, unorthodox—downright *weird*— as Magnus thinks he is (and he does, sir, oh he *does*, loosening screws like there's no tomorrow), *water,* much as I hate to say it, is *weirder*. Water, sir, is *sheer lunacy*.' This he communicated to the foregoing Harper, who, turning a hundred and sixty of your flirtatious degrees, retorted:

Ne mæg werig mod　　wyrde wiðstondan
ne se hrio hyge　　helpe gefremman

Jude blushed. 'You're a Wyrde Sister,' he said sombrely, slopping after, soggying his *all-stars*.

'Christ, if this isn't a wrecked will right here!' yelled Magnus, indicating the grate. The roar seemed disproportionate to the water. You had to speak in bursts. 'But hope won't help us—heal this inhibition!' He was projecting forward, as if to the tunnel. 'No, fire's met with fire—and wreck with wreck!' And, twisting his mouth, he cranked up the equipment.

Harper looked on, holding the torch for Magnus, but the grate was a blur of bars. You could feel the water teasing the air, running off with it, and his spirit went there too, flowing to the void as if to kinship. 'Wreck with wreck?' he was echoing. Magnus' outlook wasn't just ascetic, it was futile somehow, based wholly on hard lines. Harper drifted off. He had begun to think of Ruth Murphy, Harriet Morris, Alicia Long, when 'Now listen!' shouted Magnus turning from his work. 'My guess is this. We're nearly at the bottom of Woorish! This plunge into darkness—can't last long or strongly! We know we've been descending for a while! We

23

know the valley floor—can't be far away! We know there must be points—where they can access the water! My guess is this water—isn't running too hard! Despite the noise! Hah hah hah! I'm thinking we make a dive for it!'

He looked to the east, he looked to the west, saw a Thomas at both poles, poking his finger into Truth. Harper poked his finger in the stream. It was shallow. The tunnel looked a jagged slide, cut with shadows, made for a man to vanish in; but it was impossible you could drown there, unless you lost consciousness. He took the torch back from Magnus, knelt in the tunnel and lit the inside. The tunnel plunged at eighty degrees.

'What happens—if we can't get out?'

'We're not going in empty handed!' With a motion, Magnus clawed Jude into the picture. 'Good God man—are we stupid! Rope! Rope!' He pulled one from his rucksack. 'Did you think—I'd send you to your deaths? It'll be a walk in the park! Listen! I'm going first! Scope it out a little! You two stay here! Harper—give me that torch! You take mine! Keep shining it down the tunnel! If you hear me holler—pull me up! Though I doubt you'll be able to hear much! I'm taking a handful of stones!' He exhibited the surprising stones. 'If I throw a stone back up—I need pulling out! If I'm out of stone's reach! I'll have to go it alone! But if

I'm longer than five minutes!—Jude, you time me!—pull me out anyway!'

Jude nodded solemnly, putting his watch to the beam. It was five to two. Magnus always gave the impression of being very careful about his safety procedures. Jude wondered if it was more for their benefit than his. He doubted the efficacy of throwing stones up tunnels. On the other hand, aesthetically and rationally speaking (which were the same thing), it appealed greatly, and he respected Magnus for thinking of it. A more sophisticated mode of communication—some system of levers, jerks or codified whistles, acquired in the climbing fraternity—he would have highly suspected.

Magnus blinked. 'After all!' he barked. 'Isn't your Father the Lord of Time!' No one laughed, but it was a successful mollification of Jude, whose father did indeed preside over *Greenwich Mean Time* and *British Summer Time* too.

'Fantastic!' said Magnus. And, wedging the grate against its frame of railings, he constructed the fastest knot fingers can tie. Jude watched it grow in his hands, till it glowed with the light of creation. Slowly Magnus left off it, keeping his hands in position as he retracted them. Then he turned from it, jerked the rope several times, and attached himself expertly to its other end. His face was screwed in athletic concentration. Now and then his front teeth would search into the darkness for the lip below. He said nothing. Finally he crouched inside the tunnel mouth, attached to the dismantled door, torchlight bathing his face.

'Comrades!' he said. 'Commend me to thy God!'

And with a brief scrape of boot, he was gone.

Jude and Harper shivered. Harper was well-clothed, in t-shirt and jumper beneath a brown, paint-flecked jacket. Jude shunned the accretion of layers. He permitted the cold the way a lord allows a gypsy on his land. Nevertheless, both felt a chill. Miles and hours underground in the middle of the night have a way of stealing from you. They part-faced each other, with staring eyes, grim mouths, like *Hamlet's* watchmen waiting for the Ghost.

It was amazing how little time it took them to start discussing girls.

'I saw that Morris yesterday!' began Harper.

'Inevitably! Inevitably!' shouted his friend. 'Because she's a complete mole! You cannot help but see her—if only for the fact—that she almost certainly cannot see you!'

They chuckled delightedly at this wee-hour aphorism.

'She was rolling round town! near Charlotte Park! Which, as coincidence would have it—was pretty much what I was doing!'

'The result I suspect—being inexplicable mutual sympathy!'

'A smile was the extent—of her mutuality!'

'But a mischievous smile—I'll warrant!'

'Mischief—was in it!'

'Something must have been!' said Jude, slapping the concrete wall, in a gesture of pure cronyism. 'Something explosive, by God! Something potentially fatal to Coventry and Dresden!'

'All those girls were an arsenal! Ingrid Holland! Miche Winkemann! Heather Baker! A dam-bust waiting to happen!'

'Yes, if the English girl has anything—and it's not certain she has—it's an old-fashioned military vigour! A cheerful propensity to kiss and flatten! Colonising and liberating by turns! I don't speak of the Falklands! I *won't* speak of the Gulf War! But certainly, one senses—the Second World War— could have been decided earlier—and unanimously!—merely by dropping the Hollands, Winkemanns, Bakers of their day—all over Berlin, Hamburg, Hiroshima! Flakkers and cannoners the world over—looking up, levelling their guns! White in the face! Banners of black parachutes! Cream of English colleges! Floating down, hockey-sticks at the ready! Squadrons of sexual precocity! A ruck, a maul, a pillow-fight later—it would be shake hands and form a tunnel!'

They shuffled their feet victoriously. Both were recalling a high summer evening, with the daisies flocking the lawns. Jude and Harper had sat on a bank overlooking a virgin playing-field, recalling the virgins who had played it.

'There was the frisbee sir!' An arm was arced. 'And there went Ingrid Holland—pell-mell and sweating.'

'And there—Beckie Greenidge—green and itchy.' They were warmed by firs, crowding to the slope they sat on. There was no one around. From across the field, where the river and the copse-wood was, they watched the shadows lengthen alarmingly. Soon the field was filled with grey.

'Look at that,' said Jude, pointing. 'Like—water—filling up a container.'

They never forgot his brilliant simile.

Behind them, the torchlight crackled in the gulf, as if they were standing with their backs to a small fire. But it was a cold light, and the dark of the tunnel was right in their faces. Like Robert Frost, all out of doors looked in on them. Or was that all indoors looked out? Just as they stood in perplexity, a small stone rattled into the conundrum, sounding sharp above the water.

Jude bent down, troll-like, and eyed the fancy. He wanted to have recourse to the stone if necessary. 'An entirely successful communication system!' he frowned. Pitching themselves against the weight, they hauled up the exultant, clambering Magnus through ten metres of hole.

'Men!' he cried, launching, breathless, from the rim, 'It isn't long! Ten metres or so—then you touch down! It opens into a cavern!' With branching hands he included them. 'Listen here! I'm going back in! You follow!' Magnus' was a fast persistence in the face of all disgruntlement: he was already into details before Jude's could show. Anyway, to show disgruntlement would have required bellowing—'a measure,' Jude thought, 'disgruntlement is disinclined to take—almost by definition.'

'Different system! This time—when the stone comes—that means I'm down! I'll detach myself— and you pull up the rope!' He snaked a finger at Jude. 'Then you attach yourself! Make sure it's secure! And go for it! Harper, we'll swap torches again!' He wrapped his round his head. 'You shine yours for Jude! We'll shine mine from below! Then the same procedure with you! First the stone! Then pull up the rope—attach yourself—lower yourself down! We'll have to leave the rope here!'

He took the stone from Jude and squeezed it in his palm. Trust me!' he added. 'There won't be any problem!'

Jude nodded acquiescence. Then, with a goofy cackle, Magnus was gone—and the cackle converted into noise.

Three minutes passed. Jude was taking extra care holding the rope, face flecked with spray. Finally the stone came trotting to his feet. He pocketed it like one predestined. Harper sensed his fear, saw the method in Magnus' madness. Jude could not be entirely trusted to the darkness of last-place—least of all by himself. With a fallible expression, concentrating hard, Jude pulled the wet rope and tied it round his waist, recalling a formative acquaintance with the reef-knot. Then, gingerly as his hair, he crouched into the tunnel and let himself down. His face was grim. His green eyes looked out a last time.

Harper peered on the flood. His own eyes mixed light and water. He crouched to the railings, cheek to his armpit. Then he waited, pouring moist breath on the metal, murmuring:

> *Forðon domgeorne*   *dreorigne oft*
> *In hyra breostcofan*   *bindað fæste*

Jude did not hear. He was plunging through a vertical shower shot with unnatural radiances, pummelling *all-stars* against oblivious walls. *This* was sensation, life where least expected. He gasped, like the desert rose, gulped, blew water, shrieked his own continuance. All he could see was electric light, a knife trained on waters, flashing up to sculpt the stone dunes, lead him to wellsprings.

30

2. Ignominy

The Yew Lawn was a terraced seventeenth-century cottage, product of the Dimly quarries, and lodging for quarriers. The name was presumptuous, not the house. It was all slanting, cluttered-up oblongs of narrow passages and boxy rooms. Low ceilings, rugged carpeted floors, tapered the perspectives. The conspicuous exception to its crowded economy was a brilliant modern conservatory, all glass and panelling, with fitted cat-flap. When it wasn't night, or wet, the conservatory surveyed the lawn in question. The yew in question had finally fallen on that lawn, and there it remained, first for climbing-frame, later, garden-feature and conversation-piece.

Backing onto the conservatory was a kitchen: a shaded room, outshone. But a skylight kept the spaces fanned and dried, and the radio was a soft flame for war-heroes. You sat by it, eating cereal, when no one else was in. You observed it; it grew on the eye. You wore an air of solemnity.

The kitchen fronted on a dining-room-cum-parlour. This was the house's central space; a jack-of-all-trades sort of room. Walled and flagged with stone, a large hearth occupied most of one wall, hung with adornments. There was a window-seat with flowery cushion; next to that a wicker chair. There was the oak dresser, with its plates, its brass, its photographs. There were the pinewood table and chairs. There was the waist-high rhomboid book-stand with the collector's edition of *The Hobbit*. And there was the curious, ironic, print of the wrestlers, dismembered by Cubism, garish in the grey. It was a room you passed through on your way to other places, unless, again, no one else was in, when you dwelled there—incidentally perhaps, or making a point of it—fixing your eye upon the frozen hearth.

You might be on your way to the living-room, a softer affair, fat with the usual furniture. Or you might be on your way to the hall, up the stairwell: a different proposition; a dark thought. You might pause in that hall, might stop to consider that flagstoned floor, unobtrusive closet, high stool, marble-topped table, trapdoor in ceiling for the lowering of coffins.

You took those carpeted, spiral stairs. Each creaked underfoot. You looked along that passage, bowed like a ropebridge. You looked straight into that spare room, so poorly lit, so crammed with cardboard, books, blankets, a little plastic jukebox. You were aware of the bedroom beside it, a room you knew too well. You were further aware of the staircase to the attic, because the bedroom there, like Poe's heaven, bent above you, ran all the way behind you and sat like a black widow on the house. It also slept the proprietors, when they were in.

Your eye ran back along the corridor, to the bathroom beside you. A seaweed-coloured room, with a ponderous basin, ornate mirror, solid Victorian bathtub, two large brass taps for the hot and cold. You liked it there, could spend hours, drag a radio cable under the door, listen to football commentary on those rainy December evenings when the season's hopes were said to founder amidst all manner of *fixture congestion*, meeting an inglorious end in the *top versus bottom encounter*. You sympathised with those seasonal hopes, but you had news for them. Life wasn't so bad on the sea-bottom. You could lie back, languorous, in your masts and rigging, watching the topsails baffle the tide, listening to others tell your selfsame tale.

Consciously, halfheartedly, you had forgotten one room, the next one along, behind its oaken seal. You hesitated outside. What made you hesitate? Love? Fear? Both these impostors? The fact was, you had no idea if anyone was in. You lifted the iron latch, nudged the door ajar.

Inside was a perfect bed: low, wooden, white-sheeted, white-quilted. It had a new-washed stiffness, almost uncreased. A mathematical calm. Look longer, however, and it was marked with crooked shades, such as Sorolla's sails show, and those shawls and towels he spreads athwart the evening. A ridge, in particular, ran the length of it, where you supposed a body was. Your suspicions were confirmed by a nose sharply jutting. Above the nose: two closed, feminine eyes—in a pale face—so gentle, it might have been not sleep, but death, had stolen in. Above the eyes, careless ginger hair. No curtains ever for this occupant. Sun carved the wall and floor, preserving the air of orderly latitude.

But you had shattered it, by coming in, by observing at all. It was not your fault. It was five in the afternoon. You were not to know Jude had been out on the town with Alistair Hobbes, peacefully ensconced in the Marsh Wharf Cafe, drinking tea, discussing cricket, women and America, subjects on which, vigorously licking his lips, Alistair discoursed energetically, though increasingly pessimistically, as the night wore on. Subjects for which Alistair felt a certain responsibility. Subjects, indeed, in which he had a certain *investment*, and about which, so long as Alistair was footing the bill, and so long as he was the only ride home, Jude deigned not to shatter his illusions. You were not to know that, entering Meal Common, just after midnight, Jude had requested Alistair drop him at Harper's, and quietly shattered his illusions with a careless remark about *Duckworth-Lewis*. That he sidled into the night, leaving Alistair at the wheel, trapped between laughter and offence, opting for some copious licking. That he had thrown a handful of stones at a window, woken Harper, walked with him as far as the crossroads of Stubblow Sack, continued alone a couple of miles, arrived home, pushed open the door, entered the premises, wondered if anyone was in. Had sat in the kitchen, eaten cereal, heard the shipping forecast, wandered upstairs, found himself sleepless, spent the hours till dawn reading *Asterix The Legionary* between bouts of the Chatwin biography. But now you had woken him. You had shattered his illusions. And, in turn, had you not shattered somewhat of your own? You dropped an envelope on the floor and made to leave. Even so, there was a kink in the ridge.

'Who is it?' The voice was muffled.

'Piers.'

'And?'

'A letter for you. Fr-from Magnus, I take it.'

'*Why* do you take it?'

'It-it has his name and address on the back of the envelope.' Piers spoke assertively, peculiarly sanguine in the face of some hard-luck events. Yet there was humility too, as if assertiveness were a device, to avoid bringing shame on the family.

The eyes flickered. Someone—a lover, had there been one—bending over—would have seen the lightest of veins around them, reproduced on the lids—until they opened, took in the room, saw no one there at all. Piers had left. Jude rose, took up the letter and, transformed into a moody, square-shaped object, descended the stairs in his boxers, to the cold-floored hall. He paced the stone, as if there were no such cold thing, through the parlour, into the kitchen where the tiles were warm. Opening the envelope with a cruel finger, he perused it over orange juice:

> *Jude. 8:30 p.m., my house. For a soiree celebrating jointly the day of my birth and the exhumation and removal to Winchester Cathedral of the corpse of St. Swithin, some thousand odd years ago. To be followed by an Expedition, by routes of my devising. One condition only: you must come apparelled as a Creature of the Night, upon pain of Rejection at the Door.*
>
> *Tantalus.*

Jude chewed, tight-lipped on his muesli, put the note to a sly side. He was thinking about Magnus, his *penchant* for hyperbole, melodrama, above all for *fancy-dress*. As if Jude had not already proven his tolerance—nay, his *mastery*—of the form, when

36

he stunned them all with his portrayal of *The Sorceress*. Still Magnus persisted with his ritual humiliations. How long must he be indulged? How long must Jude keep his eyes glued to the door? He huffed and he puffed and he put down his bowl, stalked upstairs to the spare-room, where he rooted out a skull-mask, pulled it on with a weary blow before the mirror in Piers' room.

The skull looked unconfidently at him, with those twitchy interior eyes. You heard its bound breath, felt it condensing, as if inside the mouth. It had been a long time. The mask looked the same, but did it feel it? Never go back, wasn't that what they said? The mask felt this in all its profundity. Many a slip twixt cup and lip. A stitch in time saves nine. The mask felt these things too, though less acutely. Jude pushed back the mask, watching himself now. There he was, right there. The old green bashful eyes. The harsh superior nose. That strained expectant mouth, flirting with itself. Magnus had to be careful his strange mummeries—laudable in themselves—did not become something altogether more worthy. After all, Magnus was a scientist; an exponent of progress, peeler of layers, pursuer of proofs. What he valued—*believed in*, naïve as it seemed—was power, willpower, *will-to-power*. What he practised was *realpolitik*, in all its mundane deceit, and to those ends he assumed the cloak, the dagger, the signet ring; all manner of

Gothic paraphernalia; the spider his familiar, the serpent his idol. Brittle postures all. Ever and anon the superb appearance would slip and show a tawdry motive. No, beneath the constant costuming, Jude suspected something didactic at work, some compliance aimed at, the *unwillingness* to which, to Magnus, indicated vanity, self-interest, even an outmoded interest in *authenticity*. Jude was offended. One day this trick of telling you what you already knew, knowing you knew it, pretending that he didn't, was going to rebound on Magnus. The exemplary and instructive were incompatible. Magnus wanted to have his cake and eat it too. To see *and* be seen. Jude was not persuaded. He pounded down the passage, then up the other side. Where was his brother? Hadn't he been here? Was there never anyone in? He lay down for a minute, in the bathroom, amid mauve and maroon, and when he awoke the evening sun stuck in the knobbled glass. He gasped, as if gravity had got him, rose easily from the floor and went downstairs, taking up a scythe in the hall.

It was a fine evening when he set out, unnoticing he had closed the door. The hill fell underfoot, then gathered him in hem, as if it were a milkmaid and he a spate of blackberries—a judicious comparison, if you pardoned the pun. Not that Jude did, of course. Not that he was not a purveyor of puns. On the contrary—on the *contrary*. Every bit as the next man—with a nod toward Latterly, where the Next Man very likely resided. But a pun petitioning pardon must naturally be refused one, *on that ground alone*. He trod the ground firmly, regarding the yellow fields. Immediately—*immediately*—the petition arose, it must be denied. It invoked, *desired*, its own denial. The petition, he mused, *wanted to die*. Jude despised a petition—and if attached to a pardon, so much the worse for it.

He beat the road before him, to the junction. He looked left, right, left again. Right looked good, he had to admit: a wide road like an upturned palm, shining in the evening. But it looked long, too, unwinding into an arm. Eventually it would hit the Meal-to-Dovecombe reservoir road. If it were not careful, lissom length would become stunning monotony. No, Jude was a southpaw. He went left, past Bullish Lake, to the nooks and corners, cribs and hulks of the Marching hills, which neither time nor space could adequately invade—frequently coming a cropper on some barbed wire and bramble collaboration.

Such a collaboration caught his eye now. He stood, relishing the silent road, assessing the young blackberries with something like fellow-feeling. The blackberry spurned your green, started up a sprung red, between sweet and poison; waxed black and surly, opted for the hood; at last, owned the lane, crookbacked in virility. The comparison *was* a judicious one. For he *was* a spate, a spray, a *flourish*, if you will—though he *wouldn't*—yet, whether or not, he *was*—of ecclesiastical blackberries. Spiteful, urgent, cussed—staining of mouth and pricking of thumb, as Fran Peters could confirm.

Vapour moved off the lake. The hill welled beneath him, toward *Fourpoints Farm*. This was, he could not help but remember, where Nemmins lived, and, apparently, continued to do so. Jude had been not helping to remember this for many years now, as he supposed had Nemmins—though one could not assert the same of Nemmins' mother, who, if rumour had it right, was *barking*. As if to vindicate rumour, a jolly double-barking went up from the farm. If Nemmins' father had ceased as a going concern—if Nemmins himself had never been one—the *Fourpoints* dogs were both going and concerning, and the one inciting the other. Jude was both of them too. Not so much, though, that he did not observe the *Stop Bullish Expansion* signs; that he did not observe it would be the first time a Nemmins had stopped expansion of any kind; that he did not see the ambivalent silhouette in the upstairs window—which, however, made him both of them the more. Soon he was into deep ruts and cuttings, hillside scoops, arched sun-blent branches. He worked his way up, till, emerging in Marching, he took the bent steep to right and touched the level on Shingle Hill.

Jude sucked the air. He liked Shingle Hill. Rather, he liked its *road*. It was a noble, solemn road, along the ridge-line, unrolling through hedges. There were views to vales either side, scored by water-courses. To the right, broad fields deepened to a gulley, crossed by two vast water-pipes which jumped out of the hill on one side and, a hundred feet later, leapt into the next. To the left, less exalted fields led to the Meal, and its shaded fall. The Meal. It was a self-indulgent stream at the best of times, murmuring along as if hoping to be noticed hoping not to be noticed. Feeding perfectly the little ego that was Meal Common, and its modestly ambitious inhabitants.

It was an estimable evening, and the sun was warm. Jude was under the impression that he was equitably strolling, but few could have kept up with his military march. Including the sun, which, bowed and beaten, sank beneath Carp House. He began his own descent, sharply into Meal. The village seemed to gather, humbly, at the tower of St Swithen's. Of course, there was nothing humble about it, as Jude knew well. St Swithen's was a token gesture. Meal, like Washington, was a *bourgeois town*, settled by bankers, lawyers and journalists, replete with watercolours, pantomimes, cake-weight estimations. A place of insular

41

affluence, of *agas*, double-glazing, power-showers; where the toilets bore respectable hallmarks. Jude eyed the Meal side-on, busy in the trees, preparing for entry. The Meal felt all that affluence, sidling among the houses, bent-headed. Perhaps it had humbleness after all. It looked an ignominious thing now. A real earth-inheritor. Was the Meal too good for its Common, or its Common too good for the Meal? Jude wasn't sure. By now he was nearly running into both, so sudden was the descent.

At half-past nine, there was a tapping as of metal at Harper's house: a cheap container of a place, all lightness and transience. Harper was in his element, lightness and transience himself, moving in the big downstairs, where the rooms merged and gloom invested gloom. The curtains were open and a single lamp burned in a corner. He was wearing a sleeping-bag which had accidentally come apart at the bottom; an accident from which his feet profited, shiffle-shaffling about. It was tied around his chest, drawn up on his back over a rucksack stuffed with pillows. On his head was a balaclava. There was a squeaking sound. The sound of fingers being scraped over too much glass. Then a cry, a whimper, a *mewl*. Soft at first, then louder, growing stretched and desperate. Harper shuffled to the kitchen. A tall scythe leaned against the window, looking down a hooked blade. Lower down, a white point announced a nose, and a leer crawled out behind it. A shark-like, downward leer. Ten smaller points signified fingers, pressed to the surface, attendant to hands. The cry became a jabber, crescendoing in a series of sharp yelps, acute recognitions, incomprehensible complaints.

Harper opened the back-door. The night was warm but damp. You could hear church-bells from over the common. The scythe came in, followed at a yard by Jude, with the mien of lord or lady. He was wearing two t-shirts, a skull-mask pushed back on his head, and his eyes had all the seeming of a very conscious procrastination.

'Late.'

Jude leaned the scythe in the corner. 'If you're going to be late, you might as well be *really* late. Getting there when the whole thing's almost over. Anticipating—*undermining*—everybody.'

'Damp.' Harper snuffed the air, closed the door.

Jude studied the cupboard-handles. 'Damp coming past *Bullish Lake*,' he said, as if the lake had a competitor. 'An empty damp—the emptiness of lakes. But warm work, sir, coming up the hill. Not,' he mused, selecting one handle from the many, 'that one pays *any attention* to meteorological conditions, lest they *immediately* become the work, therefore the *weakness*, of imagination.' He came up with a jar of peanut butter, pushing it over the surface like a queen to *d4*. The challenge was explicit. 'No sir, the black tunnel of trees—before the crossroads. The *black tunnel*. And then—*then*—once you've *gained* the hill, the illogical *rushing of branches*, on what was a windless evening. And, finally, plummeting, quicker and darker than you'd like, into Meal Common, the *cast-iron fear* of headlights. Do not,' he said, pointing a breadknife, 'underestimate your twin, incestuous car-headlights, sir. Do not underestimate the *abominable fear*—infinitely worse than all the Unknown can throw at you—of the *absolutely predictable*. You know exactly—*exactly*—what's coming. You even know *exactly* how long it is going to take to reach you. Its sheer mundaneness is not the least surprise. And yet—and yet.' He manoeuvred the breadboard over, began work on the loaf. '*Terrifying*. Because anything—and I mean *anything*—that it could possibly do you have *entirely* anticipated. The desperation of this *wanting it to know*. The *unfathomable rage* of the walker for the car. The walker, pressed into the hedge, staring at the headlights—a madman—ha!—*possessed* with the *entirely accurate prediction*.' He put a slice in the toaster and locked the spring. 'The Kepperly-Lie?'

'—Cited a prior engagement.'

'Oh *did he?* He *cited* it, with special citation marks, no doubt, around the words *prior* and *engagement*. After all, he's a stickler for

44

chronology.' Jude slid another knife from the cutlery-drawer, raised his eyebrows. He needed to buy some time. 'Big Quentin?'

Harper looked up. 'Putting the finishing-touches, I think.'

'Quentin will forever be putting the peremptory—*pre-emptive* even—*finishing-touches* to some masterplan or other. One last Night of the Long Knives. One last bout of Red Terror before we shut up shop. One last—ha!—one last Final Solution before the problem is expunged. And the epicentre of all of this grubby touching and putting will *always be* Quentin's bedroom. Just ask his girlfriend.'

'Maria?'

'Oh is that her name?' Up sprang the toast. 'Greek you say?' Slyly he swathed it in peanut butter. Like Socrates he deployed distraction, indulging his interlocutor, asking questions to which he knew the answers. 'Hang on, what was the name of your *española?*'

Harper nodded, knowing what Socrates was up to, humouring him as so many had before. 'Maria,' he acquiesced.

'Crumbs. Avé Maria.'

While Jude spread his old-woman's delicate mouth, Quentin zealously descended the staircase, shouting about taking his name in vain. He was dressed darkly, with a black, curly wig, which

45

merely extended the premise of his hair. Some effort at a veil was draped over his nose and mouth, which, notwithstanding, bellowed forth all kinds of inconsistencies as if emboldened by disguise. Except that, every now and again, the veil was disturbed by some accident of bombast, and partially disclosed a lip or pristine tooth. Or else it would drop altogether and he would busy again in affixing it. No one knew whom he was supposed to be.

But it was too late to ascertain. Jude took up the scythe. Harper an electric-fan, a pair of sunglasses, a skateboard, and long cardboard-roll, capped with paper, which he tied in place on his nose. They clattered through the hall, out the door, stood in the air. Harper lay on the skateboard, turned on the fan and held it in his face. Then they rolled and they walked up the darkened lane, down Sandal Street and into Welsh Lane at *The Horse's Mouth*. They were just turning into the Kroners' house, when out of the night came Saint on his bike, narrowly avoiding crashing into Harper. He had been held up by a patrol near the Freely-Lowe farm: an unheard-of event. They wanted to know why he was near the Carp Hill water station, wearing a Russian hat. They asked him where he was going. He told them 'bell-ringing at St. Swithen's'; the hat was to 'protect his ears'. In the last resort Saint could be trusted; it was just, as Jude opined, that in all the middle resorts he would be *completely unreliable*—of which, however, his trustworthiness was not the gainsayer but the culmination.

'I am The Goat!' he seethed. 'When you least expect me, EXPECT me!' He was wearing a sheepskin jacket. The hat was from Red Square. Neither fooled anyone. Saint was a mosquito, easily squashed with the implication of slipper. But, flimsy like the mosquito in defence, he was gifted with its incisive attack. His aimed punch could crumple a man over his ribcage as if it took one to know one. Its source was the powerful empathy of fear. And yet fear was a capricious mistress. He had a phobia of spiders, but a philia of fire. Rather than kill the thing he loved, he loved the thing would kill him.

Harper didn't mind spiders, looked kindly upon them; but he blithely murdered mosquitoes and didn't care for flies, which were both definition and refutation of evil, according as evil really was banal. But in terms of fear—irrational flinching fear—for him there was the jellyfish, the balloon, the computer. Harper was oppressed by formlessness. Jude was similar in this respect, but counted also snakes among his enemies. For Quentin, hens; for Magnus, large, rapacious dogs, of the kind which guard private property. These were their neuroses in a nutshell, in which they could not be bounded without bad dreams.

47

The four of them ranged around the doorbell, Harper leaning on the brick-façade, Saint still shaking from the ride. 'There's your Meal Common for you,' said Jude looking up. 'Blight of the nineteen-and-eighties. Everywhere you look: chipboard and linoleum, plaster and polystyrene, brick-face, wood-stain, imitation-marble. Did I forget double-glazing, rubber-joining, plastic electric fires? The sooner they burn the better.' He wafted his hand a-down the lane. Dimly, strictly speaking, was in another valley, the Cooley. The Glum was actually three valleys, the concave of limestone hills, in whose vast bottoms were two large reservoirs: Bullish and Glum. Bullish's was over a hundred years old. Glum's was not yet fifty. Each of the valleys was subdivided into valleys, intersected by hills. Few knew where one stopped and another started.

'As opposed to your Dimly,' said Harper, 'with its Greek villas, its prize-winning village hall.'

'What could be more original than a Greek villa?'

They rang the doorbell.

'Higher Marching has a prize-winning village hall,' offered Saint.

'And a prize-winning drama club to fill it.' No friend to the theatre, Jude had put behind him an early outing in *The Crucible*. Now he was venom and steel, and Harper, who had trod the boards, felt the barb.

48

'As opposed to the swish of shuttlecocks.'

'Yes, yes,' sighed Jude, like one tidying the dead from the field. 'Instead of the ecstasies of *psychodrama*, we are ruled with a rod of graphite and a cheating line-call. Both, of course, emanating from my mother, like some baroque aureole. Which is precisely what makes Dimly more hardcore than your paltry parishes.'

The door was eventually opened by Daniel Drake, fresh from a discussion with Magnus' grandfather on a subject close to his heart: World War II. Close to his own heart, Drake wore a leather waistcoat; a shirt showed chest-hair and a gold medallion. But it was no disguise.

'Drake again,' said Jude, 'exempted from *apparently everything* on account of those most specious of excuses: distance and time. Which would appear, arbitrarily enough, to equal *speed*.'

'If you divide the first by the second,' said Drake, robustly literal.

They entered a porch smelling of warm rotwood. Jude scuffed his *all-stars* on the mat. Quentin crammed in behind, sceptical of entrance. On the right, Saint hunkered by a shoe-stand. On the left, Harper crouched on a trunk, untying his shoelaces on a copy of *The Evening Chronicle*. *Rumours Of War* said the headline. *And Wars That Have Been* added the sub-heading; and, aided by maps and diagrams, the article proceeded to speculate wildly not only upon a war on Terror and a war on Poverty, but upon the Second and First World Wars as well; also the Peninsula Wars, the Hundred Years War, and the Jacobite rebellions. '*Stuh*, a liberal application of the word *War*,' said Quentin, clucking his lips, perusing and scorning the article according as Harper shuffled his feet; here flattening the Cairngorms, there revealing the entire Pyrenees—concealing them again with a length of sock. Quentin was getting in everybody's way. He bent and straightened and bent again, unlacing his walking boots, putting a gloved finger to his eye to remove an imaginary lash.

Reservoir Fire Could Be Arson, Police Say was the *Chronicle's* eye-catching side-column. Harper bent his head, reading all about it. Apparently the Pump House fire had set in motion the Bullish expansion plans. Like an experienced skier, his eye rode a wrinkle straight to the bottom column. *'Beast of Broody' Sighted Again*, it said. Releasing a fold with a foot, he gave it a gander. A beast was loose on the Sinfils, had been spotted twice in Broody. Speculation was rife. Some said a panther, some said a puma; 'same difference' said some. Beside the now quite-downtrodden *Chronicle* lay some baffling but familiar objects, equally portentous and useless. One was a bomb, presented to Magnus' father by the Air Force. *Colin Kroner*, it read, and: *A 13 N 391 DMS*. On the other side:

VF-121 BEST BOMBER. The other was some kind of steel spool or cable-anchor. It was a foot and a half long, on a broad base—crook-necked like a cobra. A hammer-head bent down, two grooves for cables between the neck and ears. On its flat face, an inscription: *For Wire Pulling Sailors*. Nobody had yet established whether punctuation would help. No one knew if sailors pulled wire, or wire, sailors—or what it was all *for*.

For a while they dithered in the porch, disputing personal space, putting the finishing touches on footwear. Mrs Drake and the Kroners came to the door, laughing and marvelling. Mr Kroner had a German joke for them, about dogs and sausages. '*Mein Hund isst kein Fleisch!*' he roared. 'HAH! *Mein Hund isst kein Fleisch!* HAH! HAH HAH HAH HAH HAH!' Then, just like that, Magnus materialised, commanding the doorway with an angular posture. He was wearing a crocodile-head, but otherwise resembled a former incarnation, *The Lord of Death*. In one pocket, a telescope, in the other, an hourglass; at his hip, a video camera, and his silence bespoke a plan. Even Drake was caught unawares, in the middle of a critique of old *PoW* conventions, of which Quentin was an admirer. But *The Crocodile* put the kybosh on that. 'You're late,' he said. He gave them an ultimatum, shrugged, and was gone down the drive, leaving a large wake in

51

the porch. Outside the world was black and the curves in the glass like waves.

Drake was out after him. Eager to pursue, *The Invisible Worm That Flies In The Night In The Howling Storm* laced his pumps again, shooting only a cursory glance at the bottom of *The Minerva*, rival to the *Chronicle*. *Water Board Enforce Hose Ban* said the footer. *Reservoir levels hit record low*. *The Invisible Worm* averted his eyes, and his body followed. *The Grim Reaper* loped slowly after. Lastly—and, in a very real sense, *leastly*, commented *The Grim Reaper*—came *Messrs The Veil* and *Goat*, the last hopping with his shoe. Six makeshift customers, straggling in the dark.

It was a warm, cloudy night, but the cloud was broken and a radiance clothed them. Music trailed from *The Horse's Mouth*. A car shot by them out of Swithen's Lane. The ford was flooding lazily the street. They left their footprints in the water and siphoned off down a green alley, following the Meal to the main road where *The Carp and Bell* was audible. They crossed by the garage and disappeared down an alley, through a housing-estate to a long, dark road, overshadowed with trees. The reservoir road. Here they hugged verge, copses, hedgerows, anything that wasn't road, throwing themselves aside when the cars flew by. Then a savage curse and the conversation would start up again. 'The car,' said *The Grim Reaper*, as they rounded a bend, 'is—in the fullest sense of the word—an *idiot*. And what must man be who has given himself up to this idiot, unconditionally?' There was a breathy silence. 'A pervert.' *The Veil* chuckled, pushing his hands through the air.

'Does anyone know where we're going?' asked *The Goat*.

'You'll see,' was all the answer the mercurial *Crocodile* would give.

'Drake?' said *The Goat*, tugging at his sleeve.

'A-all I know, Saint, is that that rucksack isn't filled with torch, rope and dice for nothing,' said Drake, indicating *The Crocodile*'s habitual appendage. 'Otherwise I'm ignorant as the rest of you.'

Drake, like Magnus, was from East Anglia, where they did things differently. 'Unlike the *Past*' said *The Grim Reaper* morbidly, 'where they did everything differently only insofar as they felt—like a *looming* shadow, mark you—the present's absolute anticipation of *everything*.' The hedges loomed over them, as if concerned who was anticipating whom. *The Veil* did the same. 'Otherwise, they did things exactly as the present does them.' *The Grim Reaper* felt *The Veil*'s hot breath trying to intervene, but he cut it off. 'Not that your present's sense of comfort is not a repulsively misplaced complacency. But your so-called *Past*,' he pronounced, pouting like his mother, 'is an earnest imitation.'

'And yet that IMITATION built THIS!' said *The Crocodile*, sweeping a hand toward the reservoir, which had itself loomed round the corner.

'Yes,' said the philosopher, eyeing the reservoir like an old enemy. 'As earnest an imitation as you could wish to build. Of Bullish, if nothing else. And in that respect typical of Meal Common.'

He turned on the reservoir a disdainful back, turning also from the huge moon which undressed suddenly, above the Backward Mass hills. 'Whereas Bullish Lake, of course, with a full hundred, is verily *old in years*.'

Drawn by his gaze, the others too turned from the reservoir. On the other side, beyond the gate, a drive wound through flowing lawns. At the bottom of the slope was a white, rectangular building, topped by an extra layer, like an unfinished wedding-cake. The top layer, five feet high, was bewindowed all round, as if to shower light on the lower, which, nonetheless, had long windows of its own. All these windows received the summer moon, turning her warm particular to a cold general, remote as word from deed. Like beauty tagged, they flashed in the eyes of the beholders. It was like the kick along a cabaret-line; only here and there were intervals instead of the glance of thigh. The beholders straightened, focused. It was not so glamorous as it seemed. The building was missing half its windows: a galley wall with blanks for portraits. Where the moon should have published its broadsheet reports, they saw only black pages, as if there were a spanner in the printing works.

Thinking this, 'the Pump House,' said *The Invisible Worm*, 'is the ultimate fusion of total transparency and voluptuous opacity.'

'Yes,' said *The Grim Reaper*, 'Trying diligently to remain mysterious, in the midst of abundant ermines. Like all isolationists, giving you the impression that peace is second only to a manicured lawn.' *The Veil* chortled in his joy.

'In which case,' barked *The Crocodile*, 'on both fronts it's been sadly disabused.' He bared his teeth to the building. It looked like a bruised eye in its scorched circle. 'I'd say.'

'Like all isolationists.'

'No, it's in need of the full makeover,' continued *The Crocodile,* pointing to a phalanx of diggers, fork-lifts, cement-mixers, in the trees beyond the lawn. 'And'll get it too, by the look of it.' He stopped where the dam bridged the spillway. The spillway was not much called for at the moment. Its gradations were baked, cracked, festooned with weeds. Moon silvered over lichen, bird-shit, paint-streaks of kinds, far as eye could discern. Near the Pump House, the spillway emptied through a grate and disappeared. Somewhere beyond that, the

Glum reappeared as a river in its own right, rescued from its dissolution in the reservoir, none the gladder for its sojourn.

'That wasn't a fire,' *The Crocodile* was saying. 'It was a freaking INFERNO! Inconceivable! There was nothing really flammable in there, unless you count FLOORBOARDS. The rest was brass and iron. I should know, I've scaled it enough times.' He flexed his hand, gripping, releasing the bridge-railing. 'A sophisticated freaking operation!'

'How did it happen then,' asked *The Invisible Worm*.

'Let's just say it wasn't a dropped fag.' Without looking at him, *The Crocodile* dropped his head toward *The Invisible Worm*. 'Someone used chemicals.' Now he turned to the road. 'Of course, you shouldn't really say such things too LOUDLY, seeing as they haven't yet caught the CULPRIT! Hah-hah-hah! INCONCEIVABLE!'

'What is it?' said *The Veil*, coming to it late. He focused his attention on the building. Still, it didn't seem as if he really wanted to know, or that, knowing, he wouldn't do his utmost to forget.

'What?'

'A Pump-House?'

'That's what I said.'

'Pumping what exactly?' *The Veil* looked sceptical.

'THAT'S THE GOD-DAMN MILLION-DOLLAR QUESTION!'

The Grim Reaper regarded *The Veil*. 'He isn't worth half that,' he said. *The Invisible Worm* bent in half, laughing.

'My guess,' pursued *The Crocodile*, 'is nothing at the moment. Given the state of it.' Leaping over the road, he gripped the opposite rail, bared his teeth to the water. 'Not that you'd know it, though.' He shrugged. 'I suppose we should expect it at midsummer.'

The others drifted over, except *The Veil*, reluctant to leave now he had given the Pump House his attention. 'Why wouldn't you know it?' he called.

'Look this way!' *The Crocodile* threw an arm on the shrunken lake. 'Isn't it a little god-damn LOW?'

The Goat agreed. 'Like a snake's belly.'

'You'd think the Pump House was FULLY OPERATIONAL.'

The road was quiet now; the moon had gone in. *The Veil* came halfway over, keeping the Pump House in sight. 'What do they do with the water?'

'TREATMENT, apparently.' *The Crocodile* shrugged again. 'They run it off for sewage, domestic water, whatever—you've seen the sewage works.' He pointed beyond the Pump House. 'Over there, in those trees.' *The Veil* couldn't say he had. 'You've surely SMELT them!'

'I thought that was compost.' *The Veil* was perturbed by the idea of treated water. He hadn't thought to ask. Perhaps he hadn't wanted to know. He was already making dark calibrations to drink mineral water only.

'You can probably see the manor,' said *The Invisible Worm*, looking over the lake. 'If the moon comes out again. It can't make up its mind.'

'Folly Hall? Th-the Crocodile and I saw it earlier today,' said Drake, squaring up to the railing, touching it with his belly. 'Sc-scarcely credible fucking story about the anchor, though.'

The Veil joined them, wanting to know which scarcely credible story. He looked suspicious, scornful even. Not only was the story scarcely credible but so was the story of the story. In fact, the scarcity of its credibility was so prolific as to put it in danger of becoming credible again. *The Veil*'s was a heavyhanded incredulity, which, *The Grim Reaper* maintained, was exactly why he was so credulous.

'What was it?' continued Drake, breezily. *The Veil* did not daunt him, to *The Veil*'s chagrin. 'A stone anchor. Stolen from the convent of—what was it? Ea-Eanswida? Given to Walter Raleigh by Elizabeth the fucking First!'

'A relation of his,' muttered *The Crocodile*.

'You can see the Ossly bridge too. Over the River Glum, as was. Quite-quite disarming, as sights go.'

'What's this for?' asked sceptical *The Veil*. He leant upon one of the pedestals between the railings, looking disapprovingly at the spillway, which fell from the wide arc of water in another wide arc of steps, like mutually-exclusive parentheses. It was, effectively, an amphitheatre, with a faintly-graded stage, sloping from the audience into a tunnel under the bridge.

The Crocodile bent his head to the problem. 'The SPILLWAY,' he pronounced, 'as the name suggests, 'is the way down which the reservoir SPILLS. Hmh!' He clambered onto the wall. The others followed, standing like bottles in a row. 'Not likely to happen for a while.'

'Unfortunately,' put in *The Invisible Worm*, worming up with him. 'Because I was planning on using this for the Mousetrap scene.' He indicated the amphitheatre. 'When the lake is full, and the water pouring shallow chalices through the laps of the Gods.' He craned round, extending a hand to the Pump House. 'The whole play takes place outdoors. The Glum Valley is our stage and scene. The dam, the Pump House, those copses there—the whole place is Elsinore. We're going to smash the mirror, and view her outmost parts.'

'The Mousetrap,' said Drake with relish. 'A knavish piece of work! The image of a murder, done in Vienna.' Large hands framed imaginary shots. Large stones made spines on the dam. It fell

59

away, further than they had seen it before. At its bottom, the water, permitted to speak, spent its foreshortened tongue—like ghastly Niobe, twice-tortured. So thought *The Invisible Worm*. To *The Veil*, it was the long, turned-out pocket of the Prodigal Son. But to *The Grim Reaper*, it was an Egyptian carpet unrolled before Caesar, from which Cleopatra, like Houdini, had marvellously vanished. 'Ha!—"But she was there a moment ago!" cries Apollodorus for fear.'

They chuckled; but, for his part, *The Veil* did not know which to stare at more: the comparison, Cleopatra or her vanishing. He stood on the wall, gazing at *The Grim Reaper*, wrapped, like Cleopatra, in a threefold marvel.

The Crocodile jumped to the dam. All at once a crowd of coots, ducks, gulls burst squabbling from the stones—a multifoliate rose—drew their different circles in the night and returned to the dam, some further feet away. Too late though. What the flocks had revealed, via their irregular circles, was a side-stepping, goof-grinning prodigal son if ever they'd seen one. One Whom No One Expected. One Whose Name Was Writ On His Birth Certificate. Benjamin McCormack Kepperly-Lie, in a *Juventus* shirt, rod and net in hand.

'Ha! The Lizard Lie!' cried *The Grim Reaper*, jumping down. Everyone jumped down.

'Ohohohono.'

'Found out! Positively discriminated!—incriminated!—by the colour of his shirt!'

'I thought I was safe in there look—gulls and coots together. I was too comfortable with my disguise wasn't I? I have always tended to see things in black-and-white.'

'Is that usual in albinos?' *The Grim Reaper* was harsh. He watched a jogger whiten the faraway dark, making progress toward them.

The Lie put an unconscious hand to his hair. It was pale hair, paler in the moon, come back to compound his error. 'Oh no,' he said. 'I s'pose I've deserved that—exposin' myself in this way. Oh no! Not in that way! Definitely in "this" way, haff-a-haff!' He rocked with difficulty toward them over the large dam-stones. They were cemented together like awkward cobbles, rolling steeply underwater. Ordinarily you only saw the upper stones, but now, like the Lie, they were mostly exposed.

'Just "throwing out my angle" as you might say,' he said, as if they had required explanation. 'Haff-a-haff!' No one laughed. 'No, you can get in trouble, look, fishing here,' he said, coming up. 'Well, fishing anywhere actually—without a permit.' There was a pause. 'I don't have a permit,' he said. He looked blankly from *The Grim Reaper* to *The Invisible Worm*, having espied Harper behind all that invisibility. 'Ohohono! I'm no stranger to trouble am I? It just finds me, doesn't it?

It doesn't have to look very hard, let's be fair! It just walks into the nearest crowd of birds! Haff-a-haff-a, arrgh dear! I've always liked crowds of birds, haven't I, one way or another? One way or another, haff-haff. It doesn't take much to "penetrate" their disguise. Oh no! No, no, not in that way! Ohhh no, that's poor isn't it?' He gazed down the dam road, where a head was jogging on the wall. 'But let's be honest, they've never been much of a disguise have they?' He gestured, wrist cocked, fingers planted on his chest as if his heart were a puppet. 'They've always tended to expose more than they conceal—haff-a-haff, birds I mean! Well, Sarah Kent as well. She wasn't concealin' much, was she, let's be fair! Arrgh no! I've gone too far! Not as far as Sarah Kent though!—But that's another story, haff-a-haff. Ah, dear.'

He shut up as if he'd said too much. *The Crocodile* wasn't listening. He was peering on the reservoir, past the lights. The jogger pounded past, exactly as they had known he would. 'We could see him comin'!' said the Lie. 'Couldn't we, eh, we could see him comin'! Rohohoh no! Ehehah!' There was a flash of teeth. *The Grim Reaper* and *The Invisible Worm* laughed, because they *had* seen it coming, not least because they had been joggers themselves, had forgotten more than anyone would ever know about the aesthetic of the *jog.* The huffing, the puffing, the pounding flesh. 'Yes,' mused *The Invisible Worm*, 'a lesson in the inevitable.'

'Aren't all lessons?' contended *The Grim Reaper*. 'And at the same time,' he pursued, 'what is your Inevitable but an especially earnest Pedantry?'

'There's a lesson for you, for those who'd con it' said *The Crocodile* suddenly. People turned his way and looked out on the water. A quarter of a mile away, something dark cut across the lights. Three feet out of the water were what looked like the battlements of a tower. You could see its teeth silhouetted. Not far from it, a hump protruded. *The Invisible Worm*'s mind was racing. But *The Crocodile*'s was still. It only circled the spot, contemplating.

'The hamlet of Ossly slumbers on the wave. Folly Hall! You said it! A vanity project if ever you saw one. That's right, yield up your sacred anchor, sunder your stones! Farm and field—put out to graze, and the blue level overarched the bridge. From the pulpit they preached fire next time. Hah! The sudden flood quenched their statutes!' He adjusted his head. 'Death's a leveller, isn't that what they say? Read the lines, not between them! There's your lesson!'

'A classic case of building your sand upon the house,' said *The Grim Reaper*. He was bending over the spillway. It was dry and weedy. Pieces of driftwood bedecked it. 'Now, like a repressed memory, we see the house returning.' He practised a careful side-foot pass upon a stone. 'And let's face it, every house is a repressed memory.'

Everybody laughed, particularly *The Veil*, who fell about with his hand on his stomach. People thought *The Veil* may have overreacted, but then *The Veil*'s insistent laughing overcame them and they joined in again. *The Veil* was thinking about Elizabeth I, thinking about *The Grim Reaper*, thinking about the house as repressed memory.

'But which is the more repressed here,' said *The Crocodile*, 'house or *sand*—in your scheme?'

'Well exactly.' *The Grim Reaper* looked neither up nor down. Like Uncle *Toby* he was sideways-on, chewing with his jaw. 'There's a fine line between a cycle of returns and a tedious sequence.' *The Veil* was quiesced by this, pursed his lips, wagged a gloved finger to the shadows.

'Let's hope we haven't crossed it,' said *The Crocodile*, examining a flagpole. It was flying a *Water Board* flag, first raised by the young Elizabeth II, upon the opening of the reservoir, 1953. Underneath a crude metal scutcheon was attached to the pedestal, showing a ship sailing under the lee of a castle, framed by two unicorns rampant. Above the scutcheon were two blue arms, as if sailors' arms. One hand held a blue serpent, a sea-serpent perhaps. The other held a pair of scales.

Under all was the motto: *Virtute et Industria*, as if the two were synonymous.

'Speaking of memories, you remember, Reaper, the amount of water that was flowing through those pipes, not two months ago. Not colossal amounts, perhaps, but well-sufficient. Call to mind the spring just been: hardly a dry one, by any measure! The ford at Meal, come to that—wasn't miserly, was it? Hell, check the rainfall figures! And what do we get? This winking little puddle! You won't need to break your mirror, Worm—it's going to flat out EVAPORATE, HAH HAH HAH!'

The Crocodile grimaced, strode about him. They were on a raised platform, apparently over a hollow in the dam. A control room, perhaps. Two manholes at their feet suggested as much. Poking from the platform were two small pumps, like two kings *zugzwanged*. Inspecting these a minute, *The Crocodile* suddenly threw himself over the platform-side and began scaling down the wall to the amphitheatre.

The Lie looked after him, then back at *The Grim Reaper* as if the coast were clear. 'Speakin' of stories, though, I think you've got some explainin' to do.' He turned to *The Invisible Worm*. Drake and *The Goat* began following *The Crocodile* down the dam. 'Especially Mr. Harlow,' continued the Lie, oblivious. 'I didn't know The Grim Reaper wore two t-shirts and all-star trainers. Mind you, let's

65

face it, it could be worse, couldn't it? He could be dressed as a woman. That's what he did last time, wasn't it? It'll take a lot to explain that away. He'll need all his narrative skill won't he? That silky tongue of his will have to work hard to get out of that one.'

'While, simultaneously, explaining my appearance in women's clothes.'

'Ohh no, I teed you up for that one! Not that that helps much,' he adverted to *The Invisible Worm*. 'He'd still blaze over the bar, wouldn't he? Doesn't matter how many times you explain it, he still thinks it's a conversion doesn't he? I don't know. Mr. Harlow, he's got a chequered past now hasn't he? That's quite a transition took place, isn't it, from rugby to football. Ah dear, Jude never was on first-name terms with the back of the net, was he? They say some people know where the back of the net is. I'm not sure Jude knows where the front of it is, haff-a-haff.' He examined his empty net. 'Does a net have a front? If it has a back it must have a front mustn't it?'

'Perhaps it's only when you catch something,' said *The Invisible Worm*. He felt torn between continuing this conversation and joining *The Crocodile* in the amphitheatre, whose birthday, after all, it was.

'I haven't, have I, to be fair,' accepted the Lie. He looked to the lake. 'Not well-stocked now, look.'

'You should fish Bullish,' said *The Grim Reaper*. 'If the pointless torture and suffocation of aquatic life is your thing. An altogether superior reservoir.'

'It is at the moment. Actually, it was in the past, as well. In point of fact, Bullish is stocked from the Dimly hatchery. They use the original suction tanks, look, to rear trout. But what not a lot of people know is that that same hatchery also supplies us here.' He indicated the water before him. 'Bullish effectively stocks the Glum.'

The Grim Reaper clenched his jaw and nodded, confirmed in almost everything.

'Of course, it's mainly small fry though, haff-a-haff! That's not what Fran Peters told me! Naorrgh, dear.' The Lie's finger went athwart his lip. 'No seriously, time was when those waters were swarmin' with good perch—and trout too. I swear, I've come home some mornins with my net bulgin'—just ask Sarah Kent, ohnooo. Her nets were bulgin' weren't they? Her "fish-nets", you might say. Grrr, she definitely had a back and a front didn't she? She had a side too—two of 'em, haff-a-haff. She was rounded all over—oh no!'

'You're talking about her personality.' *The Invisible Worm* led them by example to the edge.

The Lie looked humbled. 'It was what you might call a rounded personality wasn't it?' he said sensibly. '"Wide horizons" you might say.'

'Oh *might you?*'

'Well you might as well, hadn't you? Haff-a-haff, oh no.' The Lie compressed his lips. He could see *The Invisible Worm* making an abseiling slither to the spillway. 'Seriously though,' he spoke down the wall, 'you're dressed-up aren't you?' He looked none too confident. 'Haff-haff, that much is obvious—I'm very discernin' aren't I? A "discernin' gentleman" you might say. I shouldn't ask, should I? It's a fancy-dress party isn't it?'

The Crocodile growled from the spillway: 'To which you were invited I recall.'

'I was, wasn't I?' The Lie looked bashful. 'No point in tryin' to wriggle off that particular hook, a-haff! Perhaps I should try this one. Mind you, I'm not sure I'd want to wriggle off this 'un! Look at her! Haffa! I spend most of my time tryin' to wriggle onto hooks like that, don't I? Haff-a. Arrgh, no, only in a manner of speaking.'

From the end of his line, he detached an outrageous looking fish hook, comprising a large bare-breasted mermaid, tail tapering both ways to two sharp ends. With a tapering 'Ha!' *The Grim Reaper* took it in hand. 'Ridiculous,' he said. He looked baffled, devoid of sharp ends of any description.

'My uncle gave me that,' said The Lie. He was serious again.

'Oh *really?*'

68

'Really,' said the Lie, baffled in turn. 'Well, it wasn't in fiction was it, haff-a-haff! Ah dear, truth is stranger than fiction, isn't it? It has to be, doesn't it? Truth is real! Haff-a-haff! I mean, what a ridickalous thing to say. "Stranger than fiction". Stranger than fishin', more like. Though, in "truth", there's not much stranger than fishin'.' The Lie reflected—frowned on that reflection. 'What a load—' he dangled. 'Grr, I've read some "strange fiction" in my day. Noooo, no, not that kind of fiction! Haff-a-haff! No, the "other" kind! Haff-a-haff-haff-haff-haff!' His eyebrows waved like an air traffic controller. 'Naaoo, he did, look. A few weeks ago. He's had this dodgy heart, see, and he was clearing his attic, "apportionin'" what you might call the family "heirlooms". I got this.' There was a pause. 'Haff-a-haff-haff! My uncle doesn't like me very much! Haffa-haff haff! I mean, forget the jewels an' the paintings, an' all the old antiques, uncle, I'll settle for that fish hook, haff-a-haff! Maybe I can catch myself an old pair of boots, naaaaooo.' He tailed off. 'No, it was very nice of him. He knows I like fishing, see. Carryin' on a sort of family tradition.'

'To go along with painting, decorating, and drunken balladeering?'

The Lie flared his little nostrils. 'I think they go quite well together,' he said. Then he looked to one side. 'No, I was never really into the whole "painting and decorating" thing, to be fair. That's more Johnny's line. I do have a "penchant" for fishing, though, don't I? I suppose that much must be obvious by now.' His voice was quiet over the spillway.

'Yes,' said *The Grim Reaper*. 'Yes. That much *is obvious by now*.' He weighed the fish-hook in his palm. She was a heavy thing, as fish-hooks went. Not that *The Grim Reaper* had angled, but he imagined as much. Bronze perhaps, or brass. The hooks were ornate; mermaid brown and stained, arms outstretched; between her breasts, a blob of some kind. The whole was curiously wrought, as if to resemble an anchor. 'Ridiculous,' he repeated. What else was there to say? The Lie *had* actually gone too far. Further, at least, than fiction, even if—as the Lie so astutely pointed out—fiction were depressingly familiar. Which it were.

As if seeing *The Grim Reaper*'s conundrum, The Lie spoke for him. 'She's quite old,' he offered. 'But in many ways, possesses all the "modern features".' He chuntered. '"Modern features", ohhh no, that's terrible. It's a bleedin' fish hook, isn't it? A hook's a hook when all's said and done. Haff, it's like sayin' this ball possesses all the modern features of a ball. It's round. Er. Haff, ah dear. "Modern features"! Sarah Kent possessed all the "modern features" didn't she? An' some of the old 'uns too! Haff-a-haff! Most of 'em actually! Haff-a-

70

haff haff! Rrrrgh, I wouldn't mind possessin' some of her features! Ancient or modern, I don't mind, haff-a-haff! She had all the "mod cons" didn't she? Left very little to the imagination, haff-a-haff! Arrrgh, no, I'm doin' it again, aren't I? I'm a "mod con" aren't I? I should just stick to fishin'.'

'Grim Reaper!' barked *The Crocodile*. 'Are you joining us in the spillway? Or do I detect a general unwillingness?'

'You detect a Benjamin McCormack Kepperly-Lie,' said *The Grim Reaper*. 'An unwillingness of a quite *particular* kind.'

'No, she is a beauty though, isn't she?' continued the Lie. 'That's the "barb", the "bend", the "gap", the "shank" and, of course, the "eye".' He looked up. 'Arrrrgh, no! There's a "plethora" of things we could say, aren't there? We don't know where to start with that lot! Haff-a-haff!'

'Ha-ha-ha-ha.'

'No, it's all bronze. Or brass, I'll have to check. What's known as an "artificial lure". Haff-a-haff! No seriously! Haff-a-haff! Arrrgh, no, that's a statement of the obvious, isn't it, if ever I've heard one. Haffa haffa. "Artificial lure" indeed! When was a "lure" not "artificial", that's what I'd like to know! Well, Sarah Kent, possibly. There was nothin' artificial about her, was there? She was as "natural" a "lure" as you could wish to find. Haff-a-haff! Let's face it, this one's a shadow of Sarah

71

Kent in her prime. Or even, haff haff, in her "dotage" come to that. (Snort) let's be honest! I'd take nature over artifice every time, heirloom or no! Of course, they've got one thing in common, haven't they? Or is that two—ohhh no!' The Lie gardened at the wicket. 'They're both "brassy". Aren't they? Ah dear. That's appallin'. Nao, but it's a lovely hook, of course. Quite a "catch", this, to reverse a metaphor.' The Lie looked quizzical. '"Reverse a metaphor"? Arrrgh, no. Can you reverse a metaphor? It's not even a metaphor, is it? It's a fish-hook, isn't it, at the end of the day. I should know. I was just bloody fishing with it.'

'Ha ha ha ha.'

'Not that I caught anything, mind. I just wanted to see if she brought me any luck.' He fell quiet. 'Maybe it is a metaphor after all, ngghhaffahaffahaff! Seriously, though. Here's an interestin' question.' He stood back, pointing at the hook, as if cursing it. 'What would you say it resembled? The whole thing?'

They stood there, overlooking the lake, breeze lifting at their hair. 'Harlow,' said *The Invisible Worm* from below.

'I don't know. A *fleur-de-lys*?' *The Grim Reaper* sneered.

The Lie sniggered. 'Haff-a, a *fleur-de-lys*. Or is that a "*fleur-de-lys*"? I don't know. Haff-a! Depends how you pronounce it, doesn't it! Haff-a-haff-a-haff! I'm a *"fleur-de-lys"*, aren't I? I've got *"fleur"* in abundance, arrrrgh, no.'

'I'm assigning roles,' called *The Invisible Worm*. 'If you have any preferences, speak now.'

'Who's the Dumb-King? Apart from Quentin, obviously.'

'Magnus.'

'Can I stab him in the back with a *fleur-de-lys?*'

'It has potential. Do we have a *fleur-de-lys?*'

The Grim Reaper made sure of a foothold. 'The Lie has,' he said. He held aloft the hook.

'Is the Lie in it, or not?'

'Is he coming to my PARTY or not?' sulked *The Crocodile*.

'I'd already had a prior engagement you see.'

'To go fishing?' *The Grim Reaper* pushed up his mask and threw Drake the scythe. But it didn't mean he wasn't *The Grim Reaper* any more. Far from it. If anything, he was *The Grim Reaper* more than ever. *The Grim Reaper* was tired of the whole *Grim Reaper* rigmarole.

'It was—to go fishing,' confirmed the Lie. 'Here at the reservoir. Exactly as you see me now.'

'By yourself.' *The Grim Reaper* set his body to the wall.

'I don't see anyone else around—except you of course, haff-a-haff!' He looked from *The Grim Reaper* to *The Veil*, conspirators in unwillingness.

'Not that it would have made any difference,' commented *The Veil*, poking the Lie in the ribs—a last poke before he, too, took the plunge, and in some measure compensation for it. 'I seem to remember you came like that to the last party.'

The Crocodile barked: 'You came as THE THING, if memory serves.'

'That's right,' said the Lie, who, though half in awe of *The Crocodile*, was tempted to anarchy at the best of times. 'It was The Thing, wasn't it? At any rate, it was s'posed to be, haff-a-haff!' He stared down at them, hands on knees, silhouetted on the deep blue night. 'Well it was "some-thing" wasn't it? Of that there was no doubt, haff-a-haff! No, it was hard to get up a costume, see, given the time constraints.'

'Oh—*huff!*' said *The Grim Reaper* hitting the bottom with exaggerated pain, taking it out on the Lie. 'It was hard to get up a costume—given the *time constraints!*' He brushed himself down. 'What costume were you planning, then, for The Thing, which time so rudely curtailed?'

'No, it didn't have a tail! Haff-a-haff, arrrgh noo! No, I was goin' to go in my Barcelona shirt, look. But it was in the wash, haff-a-haff! Arrgh dear, I've got a few too many football shirts, haven't I? Anyone might suspect me of being "generous" with my "affections", a "mercenary" so to speak.'

'Sarah Kent, for example?'

74

'I don't think so. Let's be fair, she'd probably think I was an old miser wouldn't she? Come on, she was a generous woman, wasn't she, in every sense of the word. She could lavish her favours with the best of 'em! Arrgh, dear!' The Lie rocked back, looking out of things, until the scutcheon caught his eye. The others were scuffing about the amphitheatre. *The Crocodile* and *The Goat* were examining the tunnel; Drake was on the mainstage; *The Grim Reaper* was beside him, *all-stars* planted, scythe at the end of an outstretched arm. *The Veil* was in the Gods, looking on the water.

A couple of rows beneath his foot, *The Invisible Worm* was seated. 'Yes,' he persisted, looking round at *The Veil*. 'At the moment, you're Polonius. I'm Hamlet of course. You' (*The Grim Reaper*) 'will be doubling Gertrude and Horatio.'

'Oh *really?*' *The Grim Reaper* adjusted his stance not a whit.

'It shouldn't be difficult,' came a voice from on high. 'It shouldn't, should it! He should be used to dressin' up as women by now, haff-a-haff!'

'With the emphasis on Horatio. Because Gertrude turns out to be Horatio in disguise. Hamlet knows this of course—he's not a retard. It's all a big game. He's horsing around with Horatio.'

'As Oedipal a relation as you're likely to find.'

'Who is also aware, of course, that he is playing Hamlet's boon companion, Horatio—at least a piece of him—which naturally causes him to despise Hamlet at times.' *The Invisible Worm* looked arch—too arch. A bit like the spillway tunnel. 'Although not overmuch or he would be falling entirely into his trap.'

'His Mousetrap, if you will,' said *The Crocodile*, bending an ear.

'Ha!' said *The Grim Reaper*. 'So he despises him *in moderation.*'

'Exactly.'

'No, it's easily done.' *The Grim Reaper* drew the hook through the air, as if scratching a blackboard.

'While Hamlet, for his part, is aware of all this, aware of the burden he has placed on himself, exchanging the martyrdom of theatre for the theatre of martyrdom. He's not interested in suffering for his art, he's interested in the art of suffering. At the same time—'

'Ah—at the *same time.*'

'At the same time, he's aware that he's not actually Hamlet at all but Marcellus. Hamlet was last seen in Wittenberg, but he's more of a mythical figure, prominent in anecdote. A cold, strongwilled man. Now that's not bad, that's admirable, and Marcellus feels this—but, although loyal by nature, he feels no great obligation to Hamlet, neither would Hamlet wish him to. So it's really Marcellus who's Horatio's boon companion—but that doesn't stop Horatio feeling exactly the same about him as he would have about Hamlet.'

'No, that's exactly right. A moderate despising is a very liberal sentiment—profligate even. A little goes a long way.'

'Of course,' said *The Veil*, who liked to puncture *The Invisible Worm*'s airy ambitions, 'you realise this has been done before.'

'By Shakespeare.'

'Ha!' said *The Grim Reaper*, getting into character. 'This is what Horatio has suspected all along.'

The Veil scoffed, spurning *The Invisible Worm* with a waft of a gloved hand. 'In any case,' continued the latter, 'We'll be seated here, around the theatre, and assuming the stage as and when we're needed.'

Drake prowled the stage. 'Where will the audience sit in all this?'

'We are the audience.'

'There's no audience? Okay, I like it. Are we going to film it?'

'Of course, if we do,' demurred *The Grim Reaper*, 'it will—I don't say "corrupt" everything, because that were to presume purity—and, of course, there's nothing worse than a purist, except perhaps a *connoisseur*. But it will *enfeeble* it.'

The Crocodile's voice beamed from the tunnel. 'You BETTER frigging film it.' He waved his video-camera. 'You don't have an EXCUSE any more.'

'Hamlet probably would have.'

'Oh!' cried *The Grim Reaper*, 'it's the old "What would Hamlet do?" question.' He seemed to have it in for Hamlet now, sensed a chance of stealing the limelight. But the only lights he stole were headlights, which swept the bridge and dazzled in his scythe.

'Saint, you're down for Ophelia.'

'The *Goat* dresses as no girl.'

'Actually, you don't necessarily need to dress as a girl.'

'I don't care to imagine what you mean.'

'Country matters.'

'The *Goat* dresses as no one but The *Goat*.'

'Ophelia would get a kick out of that, wouldn't she? Haff-a-haff, "a kick out of that". Arrrgh no! that's awful. I'd better be goin', hadn't I, comin' out with comments like that. Of course, I'll need my—'

The Lie straightened up again, a finger on his lip. A door shut quietly. *The Invisible Worm* continued through the roles. Next up was Drake: both Laertes and poisoner. 'Woo't fight?' he said, deflecting the push of *The Veil*. Drake had thespian pretensions of his own (and when, said *The Grim Reaper*, were they anything more?), and he strutted from man to man. 'Woo't fast?' (*The Grim Reaper*). 'Woo't tear thyself?' (*The Invisible Worm*). 'Drink up easel?' (*The Goat*). At the bridge-arch he stopped before the remaining man. 'Eat a crocodile?' he boasted. 'I'll do't!'

The Crocodile, said *The Invisible Worm*, was the dumb-King, looking for all the world like King Hamlet. *The Crocodile* nodded, seemed content with that. *The Grim Reaper* was indicated. Gertrude, *aka* Horatio, was to treble as the dumb-queen.

'Haff-haff-haff, ah dear.'

Rosencrantz and Guildenstern, it turned out, had been done away with, luckily for the Lie who was to be both. They looked around for the Lie, but he had gone from view.

Drake puffed up his chest. 'Claudius?'

'Wotcha!' said a voice, blown from the bridge. There was a man up there but, looking up, it was hard to make him out. The headlights streamed behind, fraying his outline. 'Good evening, chaps,' he said, 'or should I say goodnight, chuckle! What is it, a late-night horror special? Yup? Not a bad place for it. A bit on the exposed side—won't really accommodate an audience, unless you have 'em seated among you—not a bad arrangement, actually—adds a bit of *frisson* to the spectacle!' He rubbed his hands over the railing. They looked like static—some kind of visual noise.

'There won't be an audience.'

79

'Hooper, isn't it, under all that gear? Or should I say "Hotspur", heh? Trouble is, we get an audience, don't we, whether we like it or not? If a tree falls in a forest, eh—eh?'

'What was that?' said *The Grim Reaper*, square in the middle of the stage.

'I said—chuckle. Very clever—the Grim Reaper, is it?—very evocative—still, doesn't really answer the question, does it? If a tree falls in a forest—'

A whisper offstage: 'Another one? Let's hope there's no domino-effect. Haff-a-haff!' There was a pause. 'Seriously, though, trees don't often fall of their own accord, do they? Well, sometimes they do—but let's be honest, it's a bit of a coincidence, isn't it—that falling tree?'

'Yes!' said *The Grim Reaper*, merrily. 'It's a bit of a coincidence!' He stared forcefully at the man. 'What do you say to that?'

The man appeared not to have heard the whisper. He smiled, however, as if in on the joke. The smile fell swiftly. 'Coincidence or not, it's a question isn't it? Give it some thought, gents: if a tree falls in the forest—'

'It would get up,' pursued *The Grim Reaper*, 'and fall louder, just to make sure. You see, what you've got to realise about your tree falling in a forest is that it is *miming*.' He said this last with great force, looking somewhere to the left of him, where the footlights might be. The man heard him though. He leaned down over the fence. 'Josh Harlow, isn't it? Centre-stage, as usual. But I must say, you look a bit stationary there. You need to get a bit of business going! Chivvy it along! *Allez-up!*' He produced an umbrella, as if from his sleeve, cocked a knee, and unfurled it above him. It was a neat thing, Water Board blue, with three *P*s printed on the rim. 'Yup?' said the man, as if proving a point. 'Looks like rain!' And he smacked his lips. 'Eheugh!'

No one moved.

'Humf, you know I think you lot need an audience to get the blood pumping. 'Cause you ain't tearing up trees at the moment, miming or not.' The man folded the umbrella, leant on it, smart but casual. He looked around the spillway. 'Still, you can't deny, it's got a certain *je ne sais quois*, hasn't it? Atmospheric, for sure.'

The mouth of *The Grim Reaper* puckered in the dark. 'Yes, everyone loves an *atmosphere*. It just radiates out of them, *like an enormous fog*, fostering reminiscence. And what could be more titillating than *reminiscence?*'

'Ooh, I like a bit of nostalgia,' said the man with a proletarian swagger. 'I think we all like to wallow, don't we, from time to time? Even you, Josh. It's a kind of melancholy treat, isn't it? Eh, sigh?'

The man seemed very far away, tottering above on fantastic stilts; like *The Wizard of Oz*, cowering behind a curtain. 'Which, like all pleasures,' rejoined *The Grim Reaper*; 'has distinctly *practical* applications.'

'Oh aye?' said the man, who, like the Earl of Warwick, came from whichever northern county was uppermost. 'Do I detect a note of sarcasm? What's that to mean?'

'No. Nothing,' said *The Grim Reaper*. He scuffed the amphitheatre with the sole of his *all-star*. There was no mileage in a conversation with the man, especially when it came down, as it swiftly and inevitably would, to *explaining* yourself. And he would—the man would take great pleasure in teeing you up to insult him, before, pulling the barbs from his flesh, he would shed a tear for humanity, and assign your punishment. He was a bore, unremittingly *concerned* for your welfare. A keen student of the psyche, the man looked behind the disguises to the trauma beneath. If *The Grim Reaper* had anticipated everything, the man had goaded it into the retaliation which made him so sadly smile. That resigned smile would be his death-mask—hovering uncertainly between comedy and tragedy, with courage for neither. Yes, he was an ideal Claudius.

'Come on, yup?' persisted the man. 'Let's be 'avin' you!'

The Grim Reaper stood with his hands inside his sleeves, scythe bolt upright, staring at the ground.

'Let's have no secrets, eh?' What do you mean, practical applications? Mmm? What's it all about?' The man mock-flourished the handle of his umbrella. A car shot over the bridge.

'Well,' he sighed, 'perhaps we'll let it lie. You know you really shouldn't be down there. I'd be happy to chow all evening, get a good crack going, light the midnight oil, this balmy *Swithen's night*, ha. I'm a bit of a night-owl myself. There's nothing like the old lucubrations.' There was a haffing among the birds. 'There's a word for you—look it up when you get home.' He wiggled his hips. In the middle of the bridge, one hand on the railing, he looked like a man who couldn't stand up.

'Speaking of which,' he continued, I should be getting home myself. And so should you gents. I couldn't resist when I saw you—remind me of me daredevil youth, sigh. Still, we can't really have you loitering down there, especially with the culprits at large.' He jerked a thumb at the Pump House. 'The bloodhounds'll be baying before you know it.' He turned and turned again, smacking his lips. 'Terrible job that,' he said.

What was to be done? *The Crocodile* shrugged, began groping up the dam. He was not halfway up before a door slammed and a car pulled away. The others were following behind: Drake, *The Goat*,

83

The Veil, *The Invisible Worm*; lastly, *The Grim Reaper*, having trouble with his scythe. They ranged around the flagpole, spread to the wall, and filed along it; to the right, the dark lake, to left, the darker lawn. The moon was gone in. The Lie too. He had worked his camouflage again, either down the Boat House path, or along the dam, beyond the Outlet Tower. They took the latter way, solemn upon the wall. No one spoke for a hundred yards.

*

'Who was that?' said Drake, harrumphing.

'The Man *Who Would Be King*,' said *The Grim Reaper* acidly. They never forgot this appellation, partly because they had forgotten the man's real name.

'Ah, The Man Who Would Be King,' said *The Invisible Worm*. 'The *Would* is crucial, it being uncertain whether it refers to a desire, or merely a condition.'

'Yes. Like his precious modal verb, lacking a past-tense, he needs all the ambiguity he can muster. How he paces the floor, night after night, sighing: "O that this too too self-explanatory name would melt, thaw, and resolve itself into a dew."'

'Is there any difference between *melt* and *thaw*?'

'That's where the explanatory becomes *self-*explanatory.'

84

They were equal parts mirth and meditation. *The Man Who Would Be King*: the kind of man you knew when you saw him, rubbing gleeful hands, as if he didn't mind anyone knowing who he was. He wore a soft green suit; and those hands were soft. Like Chaplin, every time he crooked a knee or cocked a hoop he was a menace. *The Man Who Would Be King* lived in a state of permanent unease.

'Alas,' cried *The Grim Reaper*. 'His name gives him away!'

'A bit like The Lie,' said *The Goat*, dryly. He wasn't persuaded by The Lie.

'No, *not* like The Lie,' enforced *The Grim Reaper*. 'On the contrary, *he* gives the lie to nothing so much as his own name.' He flipped the mermaid in his palm. 'The Lie is an impossible paradox, perennially jeopardising his own existence. Continually leaving very material traces of that existence, stuck in the flesh of other bodies.' He stuck the hook in the sleeping-bag of *The Invisible Worm*, who had some trouble extricating it, and some more keeping it from the grasp of *The Veil*.

The Crocodile fell into a funk, stalking apart in joyless reverie, hands in his jacket. *The Man Who Would Be King*. Some chance! A pawn if ever he saw one; a sentimentalist, weeping and juggling by turns. Pawns became Queens, it was true—you couldn't put that past him. More often, though, they collaborated, gained control of black squares, white squares, the general centre. Pawns squeezed the spaces. This was what preyed on Magnus. A man like that could make the valley seem small. His very tone was tired, as if the world were too few. Magnus didn't like that tone. Who would? He looked to the lake, as if for ease, midway on the dam wall, while back swung the moon. A shadow slid over the water, plumb in the middle, near the tower of Folly Hall.

'Late for boating, I'd say.'

He uncorked his telescope, leant further than they thought feasible.

'Huh.'

The telescope inched along. So did the shadow. Magnus' teeth looked like the dam wall, falling to a spillway of lip. He saw it clearly: a black row-boat. It moved like mad clockwork, panicking through moon.

'Some bold chancer!' He folded his telescope and the moon with it, in a burst of dry ice. A solemn *sploosh* was heard on the water, stopped like a rebel tongue. Magnus was stopped too, mid-crouch, replacing his telescope. No one spoke. But there was nothing further to hear. Barking an 'Odd!' at no one in particular, he continued along the wall, feeling the vanguard's special disquiet. His men were like lambs to the slaughter, compulsively playful—even Drake, a stride behind, talking with

The Invisible Worm and *The Goat* about films. Drake knew a lot about films. He could get from John Turturro to Orson Welles in six short steps, and leave no one any the wiser. Further behind, *The Veil* was trying to extract from *The Grim Reaper* just how much he knew about the *Book of Daniel*. Drake looked around, but the veil fluttered back into place. Pretty soon it would break against *The Grim Reaper*'s respectful silence, and they would move onto Marvel comics and the Peninsula Wars. They climbed down to the road, past peninsulas of copses between them and the water. 'Madmen—madmen I say—are probably lurking in those copses,' said *The Grim Reaper*, pointing an accusing finger. 'Murderers. Rapists. People who want to be murdered and raped.' A toilet block could be made out in the trees, with lights above the doors. It was particularly the toilet block *The Grim Reaper* found unnerving. 'For, although Lawrence was wrong—deeply, *systemically* wrong—*because* systemically—about *absolutely everything*, yet as chance would have it, he was almost right when he said that a murderable man has a hidden lust to be murdered. The wrongness, of course, being in the hidden. Because it's not hidden. It's transparent—if in nothing else than the way he *hides*.'

'Where does Lawrence say that?' said *The Veil*, attempting, unsuccessfully, to mix doubt with scorn.

The Grim Reaper did not like to say.

'Sounds like something *The Man Who Would Be King* might recommend,' said *The Crocodile*, shrugging.

The Grim Reaper looked sly. 'You're not far wrong,' he said. He wanted them to know: he was potentially treacherous, *at every turn*. Cars roared by them. They slipped and slid along the verge, potentially treacherous at every turn. The lake came into view again, and, near the east bank, Hyde Island. Even without moon they could see the reeds moving. When the road was quiet, they rustled loudly; birds cawed from their nests. Wild geese slept there—early one morning *The Invisible Worm* had trespassed on the lake's far side, field after field, stealing between them like the Angel of the Lord. Now he heard *honks* from the shore. An owl, too, hooted at intervals. It seemed to be on one side of the road, then on the other. Perhaps it was a different owl.

'Ralph Fiennes to Peter Lorre,' *The Goat* was saying.

Drake sucked the air. 'Difficult but not impossible. Okay, okay. Ralph Fiennes was with Sean Connery (once you've got to Connery you can get to anything) in the travesty that was *The*

Avengers remake.' He held up a thumb. 'Sean Connery's in any number of Bond films with Bernard Lee, say *From Russia With Love*—a personal favourite. Bernie Lee and Orson Welles team up in *The Third Man*. Let me see.' He had three fingers raised. 'Of course. *Moby Dick* with Gregory Peck (who I would see in anything). Welles does the preacher cameo.' Up came the ring finger. 'I'm getting there, I'm getting there. I'm seeing the bigger picture. Because, of course, Greg Peck's in *Spellbound* with Ingrid Bergman, and you just know who stars alongside Bergman in *Casablanca*. Peter hot-damn Lorre.' He held up the other triumphant thumb.

'Gentlemen,' began *The Crocodile*, drawn back within the circle.

Because Drake had known *The Crocodile* from youth, and was his accomplice, he was not so mindful of his authority. 'There are prob, probably,' he continued, 'faster ways of getting there. If you accept Hitchcock's cameos—and, really, there's no reason why you shouldn't—then you can leap, leapfrog straight from Connery to Bergman via *Marnie*. Not one of Hitch's best, but check out the theft scene in the office. Au- audacious.' Drake was tall. He swelled in his waistcoat. Magnus climbed a gate, led them offroad, to the reservoir woods. 'Rapists or not,' he said, 'I think we'll be safer HERE.'

But they were thoughtless, content to be led. 'I don't know,' said Drake. 'There, there are probably faster routes,' he repeated, 'but that's good enough for now.'

'Of *course*,' asserted *The Grim Reaper*, who had a store of pointless knowledge of his own. 'Sean Connery was in *The Man Who Would Be King*. I know because it's my mother's *second favourite film*. After *M. Hulot's Holiday*, obviously.' Quite why this was so obvious was a mystery to everyone but *The Grim Reaper*, who only chewed silently on its self-evidence.

'With Michael bloody Caine!' Drake wagged a finger in the air. 'Right right. So you could go through, hold on, hold on. Trevor Howard! In *Kidnapped* or *Battle of* bloody *Britain*.' He fluttered his fingers. 'But that doesn't get us anywhere.'

'Just don't tell Magnus' grandfather.'

'Except back to *The Third Man*.'

'Ha! Just don't tell Magnus' grandfather.'

'He does, however—and this will interest you, Jude, particularly—appear in *Hamlet*, as none other than Horatio. Michael Caine, that is.'

'Ha! Or so you thought!'

'I've got to admit, I watched it last week for prep. A film which, incidentally, features a young Robert Shaw as the gravedigger, who also, of course, stars in *From Russia With Love*. And *Jaws*, for that matter. With,' and he snapped his fingers, 'Roy Scheider (with Connery in the abysmal *Russia House*). Who, I forgot to mention, is also in *A Bridge Too Far* with Michael Caine, who is in Woody Allen's *Hannah and Her Sisters* (and, I regret to say, *Escape to Victory*) with Max von Sydow. Who! quite apart from Allen's favourite film, *The Seventh Seal*, (featuring, as fate would have it, The Grim Reaper himself) happens to feature in *Never Say Never Again*—with Sean Connery. But I suspect,' he said emphatically, 'we're going round in circles.'

'SPEAKING of WHICH—' said *The Crocodile* sententiously, clawing to the right. *The Invisible Worm* started back, then threw himself forward, terrified. 'What do you make of that fire beyond Folly Hall there?' said *The Crocodile*, looking at *The Invisible Worm* in some surprise. He raked a finger southwest, over the reservoir. In the far dark, a tiny red ball bespoke fire.

'There, that's got to be Eanswythe's Knoll.'

'Isn't that where the nunnery was? Eans— Eanswida's?'

The Crocodile shook his ponderous head. 'I'm thinking further over,' he said. 'Towards the Dimly turning. The so-called Coot Bridge. Where the road crosses the reservoir edge.'

'What is it?' said *The Veil*, ready to play the innocent.

'It's a freaking fire, like I said.'

Drake folded his arms. 'A bonfire of some kind I should say.'

'It's early for flaming Bonfire Night isn't it?' *The Crocodile* gawped.

'An ignis fatuus, perhaps? To tempt you to the flood.'

But *The Crocodile* was not for ignis fatui. 'Reaper—Worm—is it ME, or every time we go a-scoping, are we not witness to a FIRE? Last time we were in Dovecombe, for instance! I seem to recall spying FIRE down below!'

They murmured probable but contingent assent.

'Maybe it's the same fire,' said *The Veil*.

'Er, like, *no*,' piped up *The Goat*. 'Fire, like the philosophical river, is never the same twice.' *The Goat*, like Voltaire, was fascinated by fire, and also (unlike Voltaire) used inappropriate Americanisms, which *The Grim Reaper* saw as directly related. 'Only moreso. Because water (nasty, slavish substance) is contained by its vessel.' *The Goat* wet his lips. '*Fire*,' and you could see a small fire in the centre of his pupils, '*eats its vessel—and the fire never saith: It is enough!*' When he was agitated, Americanisms fell from his vocabulary like so much plaster debris, discovering black English nooks and curious Latin crannies. *The Grim Reaper* approved of this discovery, exactly as he hated his *likes* and his *dudes*. As for *The Invisible Worm*, he

92

had seen *The Goat* howl at an Alpine moon, on a snowy fourth-floor window-ledge. He had been on Carp Hill when *The Goat* was borne aloft by a large kite, almost fried by a pylon. *The Goat* could back up his lunacy, if only with more lunacy, falling interchangeably into fire and water.

'Alright, from up there we spy a fire down here. From down here we spy a fire over there,' *The Crocodile* was saying. 'Is it ME or is there a PATTERN developing?'

'There's your repressed memory again.'

'Fire is the opposite of memory. *Fire—is purification!*'

'The opposite of almost everything,' said *The Grim Reaper* thoughtfully.

'The ultimate enemy,' said *The Goat*, licking his lips again, pleased with *The Grim Reaper*'s approval. 'And alive, of course, according to every criterion for life which science can stipulate. Movement? Check.' He held up a cloven hoof. 'Respiration? In- and ex-halation. Sensation? Observe how *Fire* feels for its prey, delects over its banquet, recoils in anguish at the touch of water!' *The Goat* seemed to be speaking from experience. 'Growth? Check. Reproduction. What is more virile? Excretion? Like, rake among the ashes. Lastly—' and *The Goat* held up a seventh cleft, '— nutrition. Throw a little petrol on the pyre. *Nutrimenta eius ignis!* It's alive, alive, you fools!'

93

The Goat outgrabed with his shuddering foreleg, overjoyed with his formula.

'It's typically equivocal of *science*,' said *The Grim Reaper*, practising stepovers with a stone, 'that it doesn't list the most obvious criterion for life, that being death, in the strictly non-Gothic sense of course. A science, moreover, which, observing but not *recognising* death, necessarily remains so much further from *comprehending* resurrection. To which the *per se* of its life-criteria is as distinct as sequence from cycle.'

The Veil was in ecstasies again, chuckling away *ad delirium*. He was like a sloppy dog, indulged with scraps from the table. But the comment had opened a sudden gulf, across which sciences and humanities stared sadly at each other. Only Drake, standing with *The Crocodile* and *The Goat*, saw a perilous path across. He was thinking of defecting from maths to film studies.

'Anyway, like, why wasn't I there, when you saw this fire?' The possession was wearing off, and *The Goat* was reappearing again in his familiar whining guise.

'You were visiting grandparents, of all the god-damn absurdities!' barked *The Crocodile*. *The Goat* shuddered through all his feeble frame. The flame was quenched for now.

'Yes, it's bizarre that you all persist in this primitive sentimental attachment to your blood-relatives.' *The Grim Reaper* turned a haughty pirouette. 'It's not something the Harlows have concerned themselves with in fifteen years.' Another stone fell victim to the drag-back. Someone laughed. *The Veil* was silent again though. He had been spooled back out and was at large in the stream. They continued toward Abbot Staunton. The track kept to the hedge, and the lake receded. Without the gleam of the water, the world grew something darker. Over the hedge, even the traffic had ceased. 'No surprises there,' said *The Grim Reaper*. 'Your traffic, like The Man Who Would Be King, lives permanently in fear of a treacherous *condition*. A narrow lane, a flooded field, even a sleeping policeman troubles it. A spineless, *gutless*, wonder, is your traffic, running, like an ageing central defender, only in straight lines.'

As if to disprove this, a vehicle snaked up behind them—a Water Board van. *The Goat, The Veil, The Invisible Worm* skittered this way and that, as if making to hide. But both *The Grim Reaper* and *The Crocodile* disdained to, hands jammed, heads turning unconcerned as pharaohs. If this was calculated to pacify, it failed. The driver slowed to a halt and three large figures descended. Two were fat—in that packed fashion, passing in the dark for solidity. The other was tall and well-built, jaw like a floating jetty. They left the doors open and cut across the headlights, fat ones in front. The other fell in behind, leaning on the bonnet in the levered shadows. He chewed on a toothpick, inscrutable.

'Alright lads?' said the foremost, rolling in. He wore a truncheon.

No one spoke.

'What's the matter, lost yer tongues?' he joked. 'Mind you, I think I'd a lost my tongue dressed like that.'

'An' yer fuggin' marbles an' all,' put in the second. His voice rose through the sentence, stifled at its apex.

The first turned to *The Grim Reaper*. 'What do ya reckon? My colleague's implyin' you've lost your marbles.'

The Grim Reaper stared away. '*Weell*,' he said. 'I suppose that's our business.'

'Sorry, mate, but I might 'ave to make it *my* business, time being. See you can lose yer marbles anywhere you please—roll 'em all over the road, all I care—but when you lose 'em on private property—an' go searchin' 'em out like some barkin' Bo-Peep, well that's trespass—an' suddenly your marbles's my business.'

'I wasn't aware this *was* private property.' *The Grim Reaper* looked haughty.

'Like, the water is everyone's property?' said *The Goat*.

'You 'eard that late case—Liverpool, I think it was—someone blew up a reservoir. Methane explosion. Nems, you weren't anywhere near Liverpool, were you?'

'Fff, aaahahah!'

'That was everyone's water, weren't it?' continued the watchman.

'It was disused,' said *The Crocodile* dryly. 'Nothing there but bricks.'

'You seem to know a fuckin' lot about it!'

The Crocodile shrugged. 'Literacy,' he muttered.

'Well it int in fiction, is it!' squealed the second. He was red-faced, short-winded, sweaty-shirted. Or was that water? It was hard to tell. Was something worrying him, or was he always like that? It was hard to tell too.

'You're the fuckin' fiction, Nems,' said the leader. 'Fuckin' fairy tale, you are, startin' with "Once upon a time" and windin' up with cold fuckin' porridge. Fuckin' pumpkin pie!' He stared at his colleague, as if not done with this digression. 'When you turn up for work on time—'

'Goodhead was late, I said, pickin' me up—'

'An' dressed fer the occasion—'

'Fell in a puddle, dunt I?'

'You're fallin' in my estimation, mate.' The leader spat. 'First there's that Liverpool job. Then,'—a philosophical tone descended—'there's our little "incident". Nothin' disused about this

97

place, is it?' He cast his eyes beyond the reeds. A breeze swept the tips of them. 'That's important water—soaks a whole city. So best get your facts straight, lads. Before nightfall, you're fine. After nightfall—that's trespass.'

'Oh, I see—after nightfall. Brilliant. Almost *transparent.*'

The third man chuckled. 'What you might call a twilight term,' he said. His voice was low, guarded.

'Almost POETIC,' said *The Crocodile.*

The leader turned to *The Crocodile.* 'Fuckin' crocodile here—talkin' poetry. I think you better get that mask off mate. Someone might get the wrong idea.'

There was a pause. 'What's that then?' said the second.

'You get the wrong idea, don't you, continually. Wrong end of the fuckin' stick.' The leader was a bridge in wind. 'Dunt you? Which is surprisin', frankly, given 'ow you practise.'

There was a scoff from the van. The second responded with an obscene gesture.

'Na, Moore got a right to scoff,' continued the leader. 'Should be in bed, shouldn't 'ee, gettin' in a little practice of 'is own, not that 'ee needs it. An' what's 'ee doin'? Coverin' your retarded arse. What's gon' happen, if we give these fine faggots free passage? All it takes is some monkey ornithologist—big binoculars and tiny eyes—an' we got ourselves a Loch Ness scenario. Cameras, hacks, Americans: crawlin' all over.'

The second scratched his rib, looked round. He had tiny eyes himself, tight with perplexity. 'I didn't know you was an orthinologist,' he rasped.

'Lard,' said the third quietly. He lit a cigarette, blew smoke through the lights.

The Bridge turned to the mummers, eyeing each, amused. But his words went behind him. 'We're makin' a spectacle, int we, Nems.' He smiled. 'You'd think we'd 'ave enough of a spectacle right here, this fuckin' Swithin's night!'

'So come on, enlighten me,' pursued *The Grim Reaper*. 'When is nightfall, exactly, at this time of year?'

Drake did some calculations. 'We're ab-about three weeks past the solstice,' he said. He was always self-assured, inoffensively so.

The Bridge ignored him. 'Nightfall's when the freaks come out—by the look of it.' He swayed again, toward *The Invisible Worm*. 'I'm sorry, mate,' he laughed, 'but what planet did you step off?' He chuckled again. 'I'm sorry, that's fuckin' psychedelic. How d'you expect not to be arrested?'

'By passing the time with nightwatchmen, who have no power of arrest.'

The Bridge clicked his fingers. 'I can 'ave you arrested like that. Or I could just punch your fuckin' lights out.'

'You'll look 'ard for your marbles then,' said *Tight-eyes*. 'Like a fuckin' worm in the night.'

'In which CASE,' coughed *The Crocodile*, 'we shall of course report you to the police.'

'Alright, spread your hands—on the fuckin' van. All of you!' *The Bridge* got lazy with his truncheon. 'You best read up on the rules, boys— fuck knows, they're changin' all the time. We got power to search an' eject trespassers—soon enough, gon' get power to use these 'uns.' He pranged the bonnet. 'They's jus' decoration now, I'll admit it. Self-defence only. But, then again, tell Nems that. Give 'im a stick an' he'll get the wrong end o't. Who's to tell where defence becomes attack? Where "decoration" becomes sommat a mite more practical?'

'Ha! Yes!' said *The Grim Reaper*. 'Who's to tell?' *The Invisible Worm* sniggered.

'Chuckle on, boys. Comes a day, them questions come more 'an rhetorical. That's a national resource, that is. Like nuclear fuckin' power. It don't do to trifle. Now spread 'em, or they'll be tears before bedtime, crocodile or no.'

The watchmen forced their hands on the bonnet, searched them for weed and flammables.

'What's this?' said *The Bridge*, taking a lighter from *The Goat*'s coat pocket. It was the big, chrome kind, butane insert and scrolled mirror surface. On one side was an inscription: *Ignem veni mittere in terram.*

'A lighter.'

'Smoke do you?'

'Er, no.'

'What you usin' it for?'

'A camp-fire.'

'Camp-fire is it? Where you gon' set up camp?' The watchman looked at his colleague. 'Look camp enough already.'

'Hee-hee.' *Tight-eyes* thumped the van.

'On Coal Hill,' said *The Crocodile.*

'Won't be 'ard to start a fire then! Heh-heh.' *The Bridge* pocketed the find. 'That's a "fire hazard" mate.'

'Er, fire is a "fire-hazard"?' *The Goat* sounded incredulous.

'Odd name, isn't it?' mused *The Crocodile*, with a dictatorial chuckle. 'A red-herring, so to speak. When you consider the coal fields were over there.' His large head inclined to Abbot Staunton. 'A short way up the road to Backward Mass.' *The Crocodile* was taking his time, easing into narrative. 'Of course,' he hummed. 'They've mined coal hereabouts, probably from Roman times. But the main fields are—WERE, I should say—in Chancery Fog, Gabbley, Winterton, in that direction. There's no evidence, so far as I can gather, of a mine on Coal Hill.' He cleared his throat, slowly. The speech was obviously a ploy, and all the more disarming for that. 'Could have been some kind of bell-pit, I suppose. Of SHORT DURATION, as they sometimes were. There are one or two suspect DENTS in the surface.' He shrugged. 'Or perhaps they just transported it that way.'

''Ark at the crocodile-man! You'd be a red-herring, mate, if you weren't so fuckin' substantial. Where's your camping equipment? Pegs, utensils, sleeping-bags?'

'Here,' said *The Invisible Worm*, tugging at his sleeping-bag.

'You're a jester aren't you? What's yer name?'

'The Invisible Worm That Flies In The Night In The Howling Storm.'

The Bridge buffeted him in the spine. 'I said what's yer fuckin' name?'

The soubriquet was repeated.

'You got one last fuckin' chance, friend.' The guard took his book out. 'Name?'

The Invisible Worm gave it. The name was written down.

'What's in here?' *The Bridge* tugged at his rucksack.

'A skateboard. And a fan.'

Tight-eyes took his cue. 'And this 'un?' he grunted, lifting the mermaid fish-hook from *The*

Invisible Worm's rucksack. 'Hee hee, Moore, 'ave a gander!' He exhibited it high. 'Fug is this?'

'An ancient *fleur-de-lys*,' said *The Grim Reaper*.

'A potential weapon, what that is,' retorted *Tight-eyes*, annoyed at having his thunder stolen, and by a private joke too. 'Confiscated now. Till further fuggin' notice.' He tucked the hook in his belt.

'Which brings us to that.' *The Bridge* touched the scythe.

'*No*,' said *The Grim Reaper*. He interposed himself between *The Bridge* and scythe.

'Mate, we've got mandates. That's a potential weapon.'

'Not potential.' *The Grim Reaper* stared *The Bridge* full in the face. *The Bridge* looked back. Perhaps his reputation preceded him; perhaps it was the faint toll of a bell in the background; perhaps it was a dim recollection; something to do with Nathan House and a blood-spotted lawn; but *The Grim Reaper* was plausible.

The Bridge jerked a thumb toward *The Quiet One*. 'Listen to 'ee,' he said, relaxing. 'Quite careful wiv his property, innee? What about you?' *The Bridge* plunged a hand in *The Crocodile*'s rucksack. 'What you got in here?'

'Potential WEAPONS.'

The Bridge emptied out torch, rope, harness and karabiners. Six cups and thirty dice scattered on the ground. He scuffed them with a boot. 'A word to

103

your ear,' he said. 'If those are yer weapons, don't get into any fuckin' fights. Heh!' Reaching in to the shoulder he dredged up something from deep.

'A bath towel.' He looked disgusted. 'What ya gonna do with this? Flog each other in the toilets?'

The Crocodile cleared his throat. 'Huc-hum. You never know,' he announced, 'when you're going to need a TOWEL. Hah hah hah.'

This made *The Bridge* meditative. 'You don't, do you?' he pondered. 'You jus' fuckin' don't.' He turned his head. 'Do you, Nems?' He tossed it that way. *Tight-eyes* caught it and started towelling himself down. 'Case you fall in any more puddles. Nems is always needin' towelin' for one reason or another.'

'Hm!'—from the bonnet.

The Bridge explored *The Crocodile*'s person, itemising. 'Keys. String. Screwdriver. Nice camera, Croc. Don't give me reason to confiscate that. Telescope. What are you, a peepin' tom? Nifty though, folds in an' whatnot. Lightweight too. Could use 'em in our arm'ry.' He checked the other pocket. 'Heh, a fuckin' egg-timer. Very sweet. Very cute. An' very fuckin' weird. Alright, stop bendin' over or Nems'll get ideas.'

Tight-eyes lashed out. 'Where's your tent, camp-man?' he squealed, buffeting *The Goat* in the ribs.

'Who needs TENTS?' said *The Crocodile*, tapping his headgear.

'You'll need tents in a minute, my man. Past tents! Heh!' *The Bridge* smacked *The Goat* in turn. 'An' there won't be anything "perfect" about 'em.'

'What if it rains?' *Tight-eyes* was growing intrigued.

'We'll get wet.' *The Crocodile* looked skyward. 'But it doesn't look like rain, does it gentlemen?'

It was a casual statement, but it carried some weight. The guards looked up, looked down, muttered with the reeds. *The Quiet One* stubbed his cigarette, took up the toothpick. *Tight-eyes* looked askance, rubbed one of them. *The Bridge* saw him, pushed *The Goat* away, buttoned his truncheon. 'You got one minute—to get back to the road,' he said, climbing into the passenger seat. 'This path's closed after dark.' They banged their doors, drove slowly through the mummers. *The Bridge* wound down the window, looking back over a propped elbow. 'In a while, crocodile,' he said, and his eyes lingered on *The Grim Reaper*. 'Gon 'member yer face, friend, deathshead or no. Don't think yer mask'll save ya.'

'No.' *The Grim Reaper* huffed, as if an expected outrage had finally come to pass. 'You mistake costume for *disguise*.' The van pulled clear, unheeding. 'Costume is an entirely conscious, not to say *impudent* thing. Disguise—a furtive vanity.' He watched the seething reeds. 'Unless of course it is actually costume.'

The Crocodile gathered his things, moved through the trees, followed by his crew. They were struggling over the fence when *Tight-eyes* cried out:

'An' I wouldn't say that—about the rain!' He was leaning from the back-seat. 'Gon' rain blood! Frogs! Boils!' he yelled. 'In that fuggin' order! One hell of a storm comin'!'

The Invisible Worm raised his electric fan, and it whirred in their direction. ''Member yer faces!' shouted *The Bridge*. 'Don't think I won't now!'

'Hee-hee, 'ow we're not gonna, with a nose like that?!'

They heard the fade of the engine, stood in the quiet of the road.

*

'That was Nemmins,' said *The Invisible Worm*, who had an eye for faces. 'He didn't recognise us.'

'Which?' said Drake. 'The leader?'

'The fat henchman.' *The Goat* was nursing grievances.

'His *brain*,' said *The Grim Reaper*, 'clearly addled by *fear.*'

'Wasn't that Moore, at the back?'

'Who was the leader?'

The Grim Reaper puffed, tired of being everyone's memory, and by proxy—and *only* by proxy—conscience. Why could they not just exert their tiny minds a little more? Or less. Constantly—industriously—repressing what it was easier to remember. 'Walsh,' he said. 'As you *must* remember.'

The Crocodile gurned. 'Remember or not, we've been a little too CONSPICUOUS this evening.' He walked in the dark of the hedges. 'Being spotted twice might be considered CARELESS. Three times is GROSSLY NEGLIGENT.'

'Three times?' queried *The Goat*.

'Benjamin Lie,' said Drake. Then you've got this-this lot and *The Man Who Would Be King*. You'd almost think they were in league.'

The Crocodile looked grumpy. His eyes stared left and right, feigning paranoia.

'No, you *wouldn't*,' said *The Grim Reaper*. He couldn't let it lie; neither a feckless conspiracy-theory, nor a pat aphorism. 'You *wouldn't*. That's the thing about your *carelessness*: it will survive *any number* of trials, never once considering its *insistent* adversaries.'

A white sign wavered in the dark. *Abbot Staunton 1* read one of its branches, pointing to the second road right. First right did not seem to merit mention. *Meal Common 2* read another branch, pointing the way they had come. The last branch pointed off to the left. *Latterly 2* it read, and *Coal Hill 1*.

The Crocodile loped down the unsigned road, parallel to the reservoir. All they heard was, 'and that's the most careless of all'. The moon glanced a moment on reflective material, then he was a long, brown insect on the lane. The others, knowing not the night's purpose, having—except doubting *The Veil*—forgotten it had one, were reminded, meekly following. Straight roads could delude you, but a junction was peremptory. 'An *in*junction indeed,' said *The Grim Reaper* to *The Invisible Worm* softly. They moved with it in their ear.

The road was a ponderous, lightless affair called Pork Lane, a name which, *The Grim Reaper* reminded them, bore no relation to the fact that Ruth Murphy lived at the end of it. The dark was liquid, steeped with verges, hedges, midges, drawing down the eye. Yet the faculties were all awake. The night was precise. It clarified detail, composing daylight's irregular objects. They seemed to walk more quickly than by day, and with half the effort. A large hedge hung on the right, gapped at intervals. Leaning on gates and stiles, they looked for the reservoir, imagining water. All was obscure in the fields. They saw troughs, sheds, a hen-coop of corrugated iron; no water in the immenseness. Over the road, a dog barked from a driveway. Once *The Veil* had assured himself that several meshed bars were between them, he barked back, raising a hand to calm it. Finally he fell to stirring. How, he wanted to know, could the *Reaper* possibly be content with Horatio? Either be the hero or the villain. Either wrest Hamlet from Harper, or give us a Claudius to remember.

'Because your hero is a bland, blond thing,' sighed *The Grim Reaper*, disgusted by Claudius, flattered with Hamlet, pleased above all with occasion for scorn. 'Possibly impotent, certainly *insipid*. And yet—*and yet*—such a power of empathy—I might say—ha!—of *negative capability*—possesses even your common or garden villain, that he is able not only to tolerate, not only *identify*, but—in his heart of hearts—to *champion* this—this—*wretch*. Which is why, of course, the hero always wins.'

'Then Claudius it is,' said *The Veil*.

The Invisible Worm insisted that *The Grim Reaper* was Horatio.

'*Exactly*. And who could be more villainous?' *The Grim Reaper* declared that, while pious childhood would always champion a Hamlet, studied manhood would always rate a Horatio. 'As for Polonius.' He looked witheringly at *The Veil*. 'Disguise yourself as an arras and you get what you deserve.'

'—TALKING about, man?' said *The Crocodile* indignantly. 'The arras is one of the all-time great disguises! Inferior only, if may presume to say so, to Claudine's *The Gate*, and—I think we may say already—to Harper's frigging "INVISIBLE WORM That Flies In The Night In The HOWLING FUCKING STORM". An ALL TIME GREAT if ever there WAS one!' Claudine was *The Crocodile*'s some-time girlfriend.

'My-my mother was in a state of shock—and I'd have to say "awe"—over that "Invisible Worm,"' said Drake, whose mother was staying with the Kroners. 'She'd never seen anything like it.'

'I see you modestly decline, Magnus, to mention the incredible Crocodile,' said *The Invisible Worm*, deflecting attention.

'Maaah, the Croc is rather fine, I own,' said *The Crocodile*. 'But the "Invisible Worm"! This motherfucker crawls on his belly on a frigging SKATEBOARD all the way to my house, holding—get this!—a BATTERY-OPERATED ELECTRIC FAN!'—he separated out the words—'in front of his BALACLAVAD FACE! I use the word 'face', of course, with the utmost LIBERTY! What are we talking? Sunglasses and a nose of CARDBOARD ROLL!'

'And the—eh-heh-heh—' said Drake, 'what's this, the rucksack-hunchback?'

'Wasn't there, like, a weird rose of some kind?' snivelled *The Goat*. 'With, like, love and joy and shit?' Harper reached into his rucksack, pulled out a dry red chrysanthemum. It dipped upon the moon, as if to drink.

'Don't forget the god-damn SLEEPING-BAG!' yelled Magnus. 'A stroke of creeping genius!'

The Invisible Worm felt like a lamb to the slaughter. '*The Lord of Death* wasn't bad last time,' he said tenuously. He stowed his pathetic chrysanthemum. 'What about Kepperly-Lie's *The Thing*?'

'Like, didn't he just turn up in a football shirt?'

'Precisely.' *The Grim Reaper* eyed *The Goat* as if he were dog-turd. 'The Lie intuitively realised that if *The Thing* were to turn up to a fancy-dress party, he would probably come as Benjamin McCormack Kepperly-Lie, grinning goofily in a Juventus shirt. The similitude, therefore the *disguise*, was *absolute*.'

'Just like your *Sorceress*,' said *The Invisible Worm*.

'Screw you, Hotspur. I was dealt the card. And for one who sports eyeliner at the first opportunity—'

'For the stage, you appreciate,' said *The Invisible Worm* to the assemblers. Drake drew back into his chins. He looked like fraternity and rivalry antithetically mixed.

'As I said, the first opportunity.'

The Grim Reaper omitted to mention his own minor excursions upon the stage, and *The Invisible Worm* declined to expose them. Omitted but not forgotten. Deep in his square heart, *The Grim*

111

Reaper cursed the day he was come to this stage of fools. Passing the faceless, shapeless house unworthy of Ruth Murphy and her true Toreagh ancestry, they reached the lane's end and took a grass track leading through trees.

'It was all Heather Baker's idea.'

'And that is the worst of all.'

'You don't get off Scot-free, you, The Veil over there!' barked *The Crocodile*. '*The Enchantress* indeed! A pretty duo you made of it too, the two of you!'

They stopped and congregated. The track was long and straight, gated at the end. To the right was a ditch in the verge. Beyond that was a small hedge, and over the hedge, the woods. 'But now is a different dance, gentlemen!' *The Crocodile* raised a bony forefinger. 'Daniel Drake and I will guide you from here—rustling forth through the copsewood, wary of patrols.' He bent in and zig-zagged with his hand. 'Collecting again at the waterside.'

They stepped the ditch and blent among the trees. They ambled blackly through undergrowth, until a van prowled near and they clung longly to the boles. A stillness of religion took them. They felt humans at the hide—or the van was the hide, spotlight on the hole, and they the feeding dewed antelope. For a minute, there were flashes on branches, breath and leafage interfering. Then the van drove off and they broke from cover, emerging opposite the island. But it was island no more. A pockmarked muddy isthmus rolled between the waters.

'Like a red bloody carpet!' chortled *The Crocodile*. 'But you won't find any royal sluts rolling from this one!' He screwed his head-torch and beamed round, malevolent. 'Kepperly Lie was RIGHT!' he said, managing to shout at a whisper. 'Who needs a God-damn PERMIT?' With a crabbed hand, he implored the isthmus. 'Permission IMPEDES. Nature, gentlemen, FACILITATES!'

The Grim Reaper cast his eyes on the isthmus. 'Nothing more facile than that,' he said, but his was also an imploring.

The Goat was sceptical. 'Are you sure we won't, er, sink?' he said. He prodded the isthmus with his hoof. *The Veil* followed suit, with a thick black trainer.

The Crocodile ignored them, crouching to the mud with his torch cocked. He was examining tyre tracks. 'Apparently NOT!' he concluded. He sounded disappointed. 'If a frigging FOUR-BY-FOUR can cross it, I don't think we'll have any TROUBLE.'

They bent down, but the conclusions were already drawn. 'Er,' continued *The Goat*, 'surely that's exactly why we might have trouble.' But *The Crocodile* was already stalking the clay. There was nothing to do but slop across. They followed the

113

tracks, hit certain solid veins in the mud, leapt to rocks and stumps, and in five minutes had reached the island trees. 'Of course, we'll have to keep it down,' continued *The Crocodile*, hand on the trunk of a pine. He shrugged. 'But, judging from these tracks, I suspect the Island's seen enough traffic for the night. I don't think we'll be bothered. After all, you don't revisit the scene of a crime, do you?' And with a cryptic gleam he slipped sidelong into the trees, following the tracks.

The Goat wouldn't give it up. 'Er, isn't that exactly what you do?' he said thinly. 'Isn't that well-documented?' He too slipped sidelong.

'I think, ahem, The-The-The Goat may be right on this occasion,' said Drake, revealing a deftness of foot.

'Which crime?' said *The Veil*. 'The Pump House?' He crunched over whatever lay before him, leaving destruction, and *The Grim Reaper*, in his wake. *The Grim Reaper* was morose. He had a sinking feeling that he was on Crocodile-time.

'A *metaphorical* sinking feeling,' he explained to *The Invisible Worm*.

'I'm glad you qualified that for me. I am.'

'Gah, you see what I'm reduced to. This is what comes of hanging about with a bunch of computer programmers and lab-technicians, whose idea of metaphor is trespassing around a lightly-patrolled reservoir station in the middle of the night, in their

114

pyjamas.' He frowned. 'Which is of course *profoundly* metaphoric. But not in the way they *think*. They *think* it's a statement, a *feat,* something to place on record. They're all tenor and no vehicle. Whereas in fact, if a self-aggrandising *quest* such as this has any value it is in the desolate, disappointing, anticlimactic vehicle.' He examined his *all-stars*. 'The tenor, if such there were, lies at the discretion of *posterity*.'

'And a more discreet entity one could not wish to find.'

They climbed theatrically into the woods, muttering mutual agreements. *The Crocodile* and Drake were some way ahead, where the torchlight was. Interposing on the light—sporadically or constantly, as was their wont—were *The Goat* and *The Veil*, who had entered into a conversation on martial arts. *The Grim Reaper* and *The Invisible Worm* held their breath, hung back, mindful of commitments. The lake was low but the moisture high, seeping through holly. Hyde Island was a flattish tract, flocked with alder, with a fence of evergreen. Shrubs and stunted trees filled the gaps, and the Ossly side was drowsy with willow. On the wood floor were nettles, brambles, bracken, and many a branch cracked under them. One such branch *The Goat* was swinging, as if to illustrate a point. *The Veil* was watching closely, leaning in, almost interfering. But they had to keep trotting to keep up with the torchlight, which made for poor demonstration. *The Veil* would have liked to stop a while and interfere some more, perhaps wrest that interesting branch from *The Goat*'s feeble hoof. But, unbeknownst to him, he had an equal interest in getting off the island, which could best be achieved by means of *The Crocodile*; so while his appetite dallied, his conscience pricked him on.

All of this *The Grim Reaper* no sooner saw as characterised precisely. 'A conscience we can *liken*, rather too easily,' he was saying, 'to a *leash*. Forever tugging at Quentin when he stops to touch at *trifles*.' *The Grim Reaper* clenched his jaw. It *was* too easy; he felt this as a weakness. His eye wanted whetting. Fairly soon he would need something new to observe. *The Goat* made heavy weather of a swing, thwacking a stump and *The Crocodile* called hoarsely through the trees.

'Take a look at this, gentlemen-rankers! That's what I call building your house upon a rock.'

He was leaning on the fence of a station, hand clamped on the wire. The station was a small brick shed, twelve foot by five, with ivy climbing the wall. The fence formed a square around it, topped with barbs, with a gate on the Ossly side. It was on that side they gathered, where a sign said *Trespassers Would Be Prosecuted*. 'Ha!' cried *The Grim Reaper*. *The Crocodile* frowned, scuffed a padlock on the ground, pushed open the gate. Drake followed, and an enthused *The Goat*. But *The Veil* remained, sceptical, until the prospect of being the last one forced his hand, leaving that sorry trophy to *The Invisible Worm*.

At the shed door *The Crocodile* was respiring noisily. Producing a credit-card, he placed it between door and frame and worked back a slide-lock. With a single finger he bade the door open, which it did, uncomplaining. He stepped inside, weight on a stretched front leg, and ran the torch around the room. It looked smaller on the inside. A narrow desk ran along the right hand wall, under long metal shelves of files, file-containers, papers, face up or stuffed into gaps. There were log-books, account-books, a few books on ornithology, calligraphy, cartography, also actual maps of the area. There was a brick, a bracket, a wood stand, with a pole stuck in it as if for ring-tossing. An old Polaroid, too, and the obligatory flower-pot (empty). The desk was of the same beige metal that filing cabinets were made from, in that mechanical, industrial age, before petroleum seeped into everything. It was cluttered with papers, paper-weights, paper-clips, ring stickers, staples, a stapler, a hacksaw, a pair of binoculars, a walkie-talkie. Its centrepiece was a radio, with four red knobs and a couple of dials. In the corner was another radio, portable, with the swing-pivot bottom and the FM, AM, MW dials. On the left wall were noticeboards,

117

strewn with memos, procedures, press-cuttings, ancient and modern. There were two calendars, one celebrating landscapes, the other, nudity.

'Ha!' cried *The Grim Reaper*. 'Ex-*actly!*'

He leafed through them. One was last year's, and the other a decade old. Under the notices were small shelving stands with plastic trays, jammed with paper. One contained floppy disks, erasers, nails, elastic bands, chessmen and breath-mints. There were empty bottles on the floor, more brackets, a tube, a box, a rag. A thick pipe ran up the corner, with a gas-heater beneath and two butane tanks. It was like Henry Reveley's study in there. There was an overpowering atmosphere of objects, 'disentangle them who may'. Pieces of fishing-rod, a spade, and a burst ball completed the collection, and at the end of the room a door gave onto a privy, just large enough to turn in.

'My God!' said *The Crocodile*, stroking the larger of the radios. 'That's frigging WARTIME!'

Drake picked up the walkie-talkie. 'Straight from the labs of Magnuski!' he puffed. 'That's-that's what I said. Magnuski. Our man *The Crocodile* has ancestry.'

'Explanation,' said *The Goat*.

'Y-you need to ask Colin Kroner. I wouldn't spoil his joke. God-heh, God knows,' and Drake's laughter said it all.

The Crocodile swept a hand over papers. 'All this motherfucking paperwork!' he breathed. 'What a price we put on RECORDS! On STATISTICS.' He examined a random log. 'It's not memory, quite the opposite.'

'Yes!' said *The Grim Reaper*, flicking through months of women. 'Pure statistics!'

'You wouldn't think it CREDIBLE,' continued *The Crocodile*.

'You wouldn't!'

'Check out the Polaroid,' said *The Goat*, pulling drawing-pins on top of him. 'Ouch. It's a minefield.'

'It is!'

'No lens-cap. No film.' He shook it. 'No battery.'

'I wouldn't touch that dial,' said *The Crocodile*. *The Veil*, who was considering touching the radio, was content to leave it alone, the moreso for that consideration. Instead he dragged the flat football from the corner and fell to taking on *The Invisible Worm*—repeatedly—in the closest of confines. The latter, attempting to fulfil the duty of tackling with that of ogling found that both were possible until *The Veil* shoved him into the heater and brought down a fishing rod on him.

'Crumbs. Autumnal women, wintry women,' *The Grim Reaper* was saying. 'That's what I'm talking about. Keep your summer wantons, your birds of spring. Let a bleak paleness chalk the door.' He

119

eyed *The Invisible Worm*, simultaneously unfolding a pale Pre-Raphaelite into *The Crocodile*'s beam. She was overlooking an icy shoulder, breast like floe with a chasm of waistlong hair. Her hips crowned a natural pool and, underneath, the word *December*.

'Crumbs. There's a landscape for you.'

'An Arc-Arctic one, I'd say.'

'It's all about global warming.'

'She can melt my pole any time she likes.'

The Crocodile withdrew, like summer itself, casting the Arctic into darkness. The torch-beam hit the closet door, and he pushed it wide, inspecting the space. There was a mop, a bucket and a brush. Above the toilet was a window, half-ajar.

'Hmm,' he mused. 'No window for the desk, but we've one above the toilet.'

'Quite right.' *The Goat* had a dry line in toilet-humour. 'They knew where the business end was.'

'I should say.' *The Crocodile* pulled the chain but the tank was empty. 'Isn't it funny,' he said. 'Of all the places to lack water.' He lowered the lid and removed his head.

'Hold on, I thought we weren't supposed to remove our masks.'

As if he had not done so, Magnus showed a spectrum of teeth and stepped up on the seat. 'What kind of nightwatchman,' he wondered, setting the torch on the sill, 'would lock the door from the inside and crawl out through the window?'

'A thin one?'

'Hmmf! Ex-ACTly.' He withdrew the head. 'Not many of those around.'

'Al-alright,' said Drake, always pleased to wrestle with a problem. 'What makes you think anyone's crawled out the window, let-let alone a nightwatchman?'

'That,' said Magnus climbing down. He swung the torch on the cistern and lid. Both bore a print which, as if to debunk Hazlitt's abstractions, spoke emphatically of the foot.

'Magnus? Are you sure that's not yours?'

The Goat was witheringly refuted.

'Looks-looks fresh enough. But could be from this morning. Or-or yesterday for that matter.'

Magnus guffawed. 'Hah, lift the lid! That should convince you!' They did so, and found the evidence incontrovertible. While *The Goat* clanked uselessly at the chain, Magnus inspected the lock on the main door. Whatever he was looking for, he did not seem to find, nor wished to relate. 'I don't think we'll get anything further from this,' he hupped. They slouched out and through the gate, while *The Crocodile* slid both mask and lock into place.

'Easily done!' he barked. He peered his way toward the fence, checking ground and gate. 'Easier than climbing out that window.' He stopped to examine the ground, the gate, the open padlock on the ground. Then he brushed himself down.

'What now?'

'Just follow the tracks!' *The Crocodile* seemed resigned. He led them through the woods toward a winking light until they emerged on the Ossly side, and stared from a willow over the sheet of water. The moon had made peace with the world, had settled on field, road and reservoir, with equanimity. *The Veil* was filled with apprehension. *The Invisible Worm* looked sober. *The Grim Reaper* was wizened, confiding in his friend a trite comparison, certain of sympathy. The water was, he said, an *emblem of the mind*. In the distance, at the Boat House, it was *all ambition*—making great strides! But close at their feet, it sullenly manoeuvred—black, brackish, unbearing of scrutiny.

'Hmf,' said *The Invisible Worm*. 'I know what you mean.'

'No, I don't get it,' said *The Veil*. 'Explain.'

But *The Grim Reaper* was spared. *The Crocodile*, with Drake beside him, had been frowning on the water, looking to left and right. All at once he said: 'gentlemen! I have to leave you— for the present.' He adjusted the angle of his jaw. 'Albeit in the capable hands of Daniel Drake.' He was already skirting the water, under the trees.

'Er. Where are we going?'

'Let's just say,' came a rasp, 'the reservoir and we have UNFINISHED BUSINESS. When we least expect each other, we should EXPECT EACH OTHER.' And he was gone under the fronds.

Faraway, headlights ran along the dam. Coal Hill was dark on the sky. 'Drake?' said *The Goat*, toeing at the ground. 'Like, what's Magnus cooking up?' *The Crocodile* had stolen his catchphrase, and he felt its loss. 'Like, maybe we should all just disappear,' he ventured, 'go back to the house or something. And when he most expects us—he shouldn't expect us—because we wouldn't be there at all.' This wasn't an entirely satisfying variation, but it was at least his own again. 'We'd be, like, quaffing martini and getting off with his sister.'

An owl hooted.

'You'd have to wear that crocodile-mask.'

'Unless,' said *The Grim Reaper*, 'she actually thought you *were* a crocodile. Ha! Disguising himself as a log! Yes, I can see it! Positively Egyptian! No, your crocodile is erotic, no doubt about it.'

'Hah-hah-hah-hah-hah' said *The Goat*, shaking with laughter. He was thinking too intently about getting off with Magnus' sister with the aid of a crocodile-mask.

'"The barge she sat in,"' said Drake. He stretched an arm over the water. '"Like a burnished throne, burned on the water; the poop was beaten gold;

purple the sails, and so perfumed that the winds were love-sick with them; the oars were silver, which to the tune of flutes kept stroke, and make the water which they beat to follow faster,'—and he beat the air with his hands—'as amorous of their strokes. For her own person, it beggared all description: she did lie in her pavilion, cloth-of-gold of tissue, o'erpicturing that Venus where we see the fancy outwork nature.'"

All but *The Grim Reaper* stood like smiling Cupids, picturing Cleopatra. *The Invisible Worm* clicked a button, fanning the incensed *Grim Reaper*, who, standing alone, had very happily made a gap in nature, which he disdained to whistle through.

'Fortunately we have Harper to do that for us,' he said, touching his front teeth.

'Seriously,' said *The Goat* to Drake. 'Where do we go from here?'

'Ah, this-this would appear to be it gentlemen,' said Drake, flaring his nostrils, drawing up spine and lip. 'For the time being. I'm not-not sure I should say any more than that. I'm-I'm not sure I can. Let's just say we-we came here at dawn to scope it out, so if you're footsore, spare a thought for yours-truly who has come this way twice today.' He frowned, clucking in the manner of *The Veil*. 'And wh-who knows but that I may have to walk home and back again before the night's out.'

He looked in the direction of Dimly where the soft fire burned through foliage. *The Veil* was feeling the damp. He stamped his feet, flapped his arms. This seemed to encourage him, however, and led directly to him flapping his arms at *The Invisible Worm*, then *The Grim Reaper*, practising various punches and pushes, which the former dealt with like a brother, but the latter like a woman scorned. At first he ducked and dived, but then, raising his fist, as he had once to a dancing clown in Moscow, said 'Fuck off!' and stood stock still with his teeth still resting on his lip. *The Veil* smacked his own big lips with a laugh. *The Goat* licked his with a quick tongue, as if he had not drank a week. The only person whose lips were not prominent in any way was *The Invisible Worm*, whose lips were so thin they tapered into night.

They waited for ten minutes, looking around them. The owl seemed to have gone, but birds called from the sedge and cars flashed faintly. Then all they would hear was the flap of wind. At length, Drake began a discourse upon acting. 'Saw not the air thus and thus' he protested, sawing the air very much thus and thus, 'but let all be—smoothness which begets temperance, etc.' He stopped sawing and his hand began to flow. *The Goat* was animated by the persistence of the fire. *The Grim Reaper* began mutterings of discontent. He was beginning to think Byron was right: Shakespeare would *go*

125

down—or would be *taken down* if necessary. Finally feeling the cold, he hunched into his t-shirts and fixed an eye on Drake, whose theatrics had mercifully ceased. Drake was one of those people who looked like many: a mould of some kind. Big bones, big jaw, a little fleshy; a gentleman-boxer type. He was grunting about something with *The Goat*. It could have been computers, tikwondu, *Magic: The Gathering*; *The Grim Reaper* couldn't care less. But Drake was curving down his mouth, expressing his lip, in such a way that he was coming up a dead-ringer—for somebody.

The Grim Reaper intimated this to *The Invisible Worm* quietly. Drake was usually compared with Val Kilmer, but he wasn't sure that was it. *The Invisible Worm* thought he looked like Jeff Bridges.

'Yes,' said *The Grim Reaper*, who, since Drake's theatrics, had been willing a more ignominious comparison. 'But then again, *no*.'

Drake bit his lips and folded his arms, staring on the water. For a moment, he resembled his seafaring namesake. An interesting instance of a throwback, no doubt. *Sic parvis magna*. Or was that the other way round?

He was still staring on the water when *The Crocodile* rowed into his eyeline.

'Here he comes now—Apollo bloody dorus!' said Drake, relieved. 'Thought you'd never find the fucker!'

126

'An odd thing,' said *The Crocodile*.

'Where the hell was she?'

The Crocodile shrugged. 'Oh, under a willow. Only not the willow we LEFT her under. Not this willow here.' He pointed up beside them. 'With the bike-spoke reflector nailed to the motherfucking trunk!'

'So that's what that winking eye was.' *The Invisible Worm* had been wondering. Now he felt up the trunk and established the fact.

'Amazing how useful a BIKE-SPOKE REFLECTOR can be,' said *The Crocodile*, drily, yet sullenly. 'When you want to find something in the benighted woods. Unless someone moves your boat.'

The Goat climbed unstably in. 'Who would move your boat?'

Drake raised eyebrows at *The Crocodile*. 'The same person who would climb out of a toilet window?'

'Hff. Or NOT.'

'You're sure it's not sabotaged?' *The Veil* touched an oar-lock.

'Hm! Actually not such a stupid question! I checked it out first. And I rowed it here didn't I?' *The Crocodile* shrugged again. 'Come on, we won't sink!'

The Grim Reaper strode in, as if it were a saloon. *The Veil* followed Drake, and pushing from the shore attempted to make *The Invisible Worm*'s entry a problematic one. He made it, however, with only a soggy tail for his pains, and away they pulled, like the *barque de Don Juan*, Drake and *The Crocodile* rowing, through bars of moon, to the reservoir middle, and the battlemented manor tower. *The Crocodile* made efficient, skimming strokes. Drake's made big satisfying *whumps* in the water, following through with a *swash* of power.

'Er,' said quizzical *The Goat*, leaning double-elbowed on the edge. 'You steal a boat this morning, row it to the aptly-named Hyde Island, only to row it back at night? Isn't that a bit—elaborate?'

The Grim Reaper propped his chin on his palm. 'Yes, mystique loves nothing more than *contrivance.*'

'On the CONTRARY,' said *The Crocodile*, flatly, 'the Boat House, at least of late, is watched closely by night, but carelessly at dawn, as I myself have observed—hence our ELABORATE CONTRIVANCE.' And he rowed in silence like one undervalued.

But *The Goat* was not convinced. 'So carelessly,' he continued, 'that someone found your boat and moved it?'

The Crocodile tilted an acknowledging head.

'The qu-question is, why would someone steal a boat we had already stolen, and move it a hundred yards away.' Drake looked like a man drawing lots.

'Practical joke?'

'Not one of the all-time how-howlers, is it.'

Lured back by Drake into the conversation, *The Crocodile* managed both to shrug and row. 'My guess is, he thought he was putting it back where it was. He's sweaty, he's nervous, he's in a hurry—he gets it wrong.'

'Nervous?'

'Did you see the CRAP he left in the TOILET? That stuff wasn't just fresh, it was LIQUID.'

'It was—' *The Goat* was lost for words. 'Putrescent.'

'Besides, unless I'm sorely mistaken, he couldn't see properly. It was nighttime after all.'

'How do you know?'

'Because we SAW the fucker!'

The Veil clucked as if it all made sense. He was hunched into himself like Napoleon Bonaparte, in the greatcoat of Glum. They had got quite far out by now. The road-lights muzzled the dam. Nearby, wavelets broke on a dark hulk: the tower of Folly Hall.

'It doesn't clear up how he found the boat in the first place.'

129

'Hmf. I'll admit, there's more than CARELESSNESS in that. But you know what they say. The best-laid PLANS.'

'Why is the Boat House carelessly observed?' asked *The Veil*.

'Our nightwatchmen have been a little SLACK, lately. After the night-shift, Moore picks Nemmins up from the Boat House around six-thirty a.m., drives him off, home presumably—Nemmins, we TAKE IT, does not drive—then returns by seven for the day shift. Same kind of time the Pump House burns down, incidentally. Or should that be ACCIDENTALLY? Either way, in that half-hour the Boat House, Pump House, Outlet Tower, all the northwestern part of the reservoir, is unguarded.'

'Hold-hold on. Nemmins, fat, Moore, quiet?'

The Crocodile nodded assent.

'The Croc has done his homework!'

The Crocodile nodded assent.

The Goat marvelled. 'So. Like. Someone *is* guarding the guards.'

'Maah, let's put it this way. Someone's watching the watchers. ME, actually.' And *The Crocodile* coldly sniggered.

'Yes,' weighed in *The Grim Reaper*. 'Nothing is so gratifying to the ego as an atmosphere of near-total *espionage*.'

'Of c-c-course, there are cameras, but the Croc here reckons there's a blind spot, for a ten metre stretch of shore, on the dam side of the Boat House.' Drake grunted over the splash of oars. 'Which is where we stole the boat from. Embarking from there, they can't see you till you're—what was it?—twenty metres out, by which time you're getting blurry. In any case, they wouldn't have recognised us.'

'Only, like, some Crocodile-man?'

'L-look under your seat, Saint. You should find a couple of sn-snorkel masks.'

'A pretty damn USEFUL DISGUISE! On water anyway.'

'How do we know we're not observed now?'

'The simple answer is, we DON'T. Actually, that's what niggles. It's as if we've been SANCTIONED.'

'Ha!' scoffed *The Grim Reaper*. 'You can't get away from *sanction*. But that should have been obvious from the start.'

'Just ask the Ossly anchor,' said *The Invisible Worm*, as they bumped against battlements and moored hold. He had been slumped at the boat end, like one whose time is up. Now he touched the tower and stepped easily onto the roofstones, followed by *The Goat*, Drake, *The Crocodile*, *The Grim Reaper* and *The Veil*.

'Look at that, would you!' roared *The Crocodile*. 'One small step for men. One giant retrograde leap for us audacious mummers! Bet your life, no one's trod this roof in fifty years, if not a bloody lot longer!' They looked down, then up, at the dark lake about them, feeling for a moment the rebirth of the shipwrecked. Theirs was the dry oasis, close eyrie, precarious calm, and they slapped the mossed medieval stones, laughing at superb permanence.

In the Outlet Tower on the dam, Nemmins turned a tight eye to a monitor. Underneath date and time, it showed a black and white reservoir landscape, from the Boat House perspective. In the stain of Boat House lights, to the right of centre, six figures were cavorting on the Folly Hall tower. Three more monitors made up a square, but the other screens were still-life affairs: boats, gates and fences were their only story, on a dark backdrop of fields. 'Tells I to watch for sommat funny,' Nemmins said slowly. '"Like what?" "Jus' funny." Alright—all well!—but what counts for funny?' He banged on the box, as if to ask the picture. ''Cause—at what time of night fug knows.' He glanced at his wristwatch, confirming: 'one in the mornin', 'ere's that bunch of clowns rain-dancin' on the lake! What's fuggin' funny if that int?'

Unexpectedly he belched, looked askew, and, in a luxuriant guttural, roared, 'TUSKER! MUZZEYE! ONION FUGGIN' BHAJ!' to nothing and no one. For an undetermined time the words collided, fractured into sound, shuddered down the tower in dark cacophony.

He resumed the monitor. 'Keep dancin', boys!' he chuckled, watching the Skeleton sweep his scythe over the battlements, while the Russian and Worm threw up shards of arms. ''Ole's gon' hear of this— mark a break-in on Hyde Island, an incriminatin' window—them snorkelin' oarsmen this mornin' an' all. Poor luck for them I forgot my keys—no 'countin' fer forgettin', tough shit for these hipsters. 'Ole won't forget, for sure. Hee hee, gon' put two and two together, innee?' Nemmins almost burst. 'An' make fuggin' NINE! Hee hee! NINER!'

He squinted again at the screen. The figures were hunched over, shaking their arms at intervals. 'Course, 'ee won't take it well,' he demurred. 'Problems for a watchman, when sundry freaks go bouncin' 'bout his waters. Best think before I snitch: too much gamin' goin' here—an' on all fuggin' sides. Hole int one to dance with—to double-fuggin'-deal when 'is blood's up.'

The blood came to Nemmins' face, darkening freckles, yellowing his hair. 'Hole,' he said quietly, and then for no apparent reason, 'HOLE!' in the same guttural roar as before. The word wound round the chamber. This seemed to relax him a little. He burst into wrinkled giggles, thwacked the monitor and peered at the circle of mummers. The Alligator wound his limbs, Medallion-Man puffed

133

himself up, and the Worm lifted the finger of vision. The Russian shuddered in his frame and the Skeleton was doing press-ups on the battlements. Most prominent of all was the Big Man, cross-legged, unmoving. Nemmins took out a magnifying glass, and moved it over the screen. There was something in the Big Man's repose more disturbing than in all the movement about him. Occasionally Nemmins saw his raised black hand. Sometimes, under a moon-bathed face, he discerned the stir of veil.

Slowly the circle would fragment. One by one the mummers would drop off, fall to Cruyff-turns, experiments with fire, theatrical gesticulation. Was Nemmins seeing things, or did one or two of them don *further* masks, and drop into the water? Time and again only the Alligator and the Big Man would be left, the one alternately hunched and rising, the other stonefaced, sunglassed, like Achilles at the ships. The thing was more ritual than game. The Alligator rose, as if invoking. The Big Man blocked. The Alligator bent, stretched, invoked again. The Big Man sat. Was that a veil, or just moon on skin? Either way, the issue seems decided. Skeleton and Worm go flashing on the battlements. The Russian laughs for joy. The circle gathers again, as if chronology were nothing.

The moon was on Meal-side by the time they were gone, making little footlights by the boat.

'Cheers, chums, for the show,' said Nemmins. 'Take a fuckin' bow—burp! BHAJ-I! IN THE FUCKIN' EYE!' And he hissed like a pressure-cooker. 'Oh friends,' he said, wiping an eye, 'if you could see yourselves, jumpin' like monkeys at the hole. MONKEY 'UN!' he bellowed and subsided into wheezes. For some while he gazed on space, at the round room's sweep of wall. It was an unusual room for an Outlet Tower, filling the building, ringed with a metal staircase. Aloft, a circular balcony formed a whispering gallery. This was where the monitors were stowed, and beside them, as if hedging bets, a telescope pointed on the water. Above were two skylights in the roof, which Magnus knew well, who had already scoped it out. Below was a clutter of machinery, piped and armed and handled. Nemmins had not the first idea how it operated. He was merely the watchman, tight-eyed, big fisted. He closed that fist again, flicked looks from screen to screen. The mummers drew close to the Boat House, steered into shadow, went off camera for a while, then strayed back into surveillance. In the fourth monitor, he watched them climb a side-gate, gain fields, tiptoe like fairies in daisies. '*Such* a bunch of homos,' he was still saying, and *homos, homos, homos* the gallery replied, as he leaned to the screen to trace their movements. But at the same moment, the field like one vast canvas uplifted, as a blizzard of geese

135

rocked the air, and, in their very frenzy, seemed to freeze, wiping the mummers from sight.

3. Country Matters

Harper rested his eyes, compassed with luxury. A mass of chrysanthemums moved in the breeze: languid regiments of reds, yellows, pinks, snows and ambers, sometime meeting halfway down a file. Lately, blues were the rage, but they wouldn't wash here. Little pinks grew separately at the field bottom, for selling at the gate. On the near side a ditch ran with streamwater, forming the field's border; on the far side weeds ran riot. Sometimes Harper would be called to mow them with a long-swung saw. It was wheat from chaff stuff. He was the real Reaper, to Jude's impostor. Then again, it was hard to tell. One man's Death was another man's flaming angel; one man's sword was another man's scythe. In the earth's imagined corner, Harper raised his secateurs. They say you reap what you sow, but sometimes you reap what someone else sows.

Harper was doing that now, plunging and cutting with cold morning hands. He had not been around for the seed planting. The flower-man had done that alone. Harper had helped with staking and meshing, swinging a hammer in the heat. He had swung himself into stasis, become an archetype, lauded by enormous monuments. A banner above him announced *WOMEN AND REVOLUTION* and the *Potemkin* fired shots across the cows. But he had been abandoned by the revolutionaries, unable to mix it in the country. Left alone, the archetype had come over conscious, uncased his limbs, turned individual again. Independent even. In no time at all, he was John Henry, mythological piledriver, real American Vulcan, slung round with rainbows, shine like gold.

Everything was wet with dew. It had been a glorious August, dry as dice. Now, as the month waned, days were hot but the nights dewy. Passing up the aisles, flower and leaf soaked you in loads. It was erotic, but not like Lawrence wants it; not defiantly, studiedly so. Lawrence: as abstract a man as ever loathed abstractions. Harper turned from Lawrence, thought of Alicia Long, imagined her screwed face, sullen lips, blonde crown bobbing on the harvest. Here it came, spoiled in sunlight. She was rapping, backchatting, catching him out. Spots on her face and a toothy smile. Harper definitely wanted to get mythological with her, maybe start a little communism of their own.

Something wet pushed its way into his fist, touching the centre of his palm. It was the dog, bearing gifts of stick. 'OY!' cried the flower-man. 'STOP DAYDREAMING THERE AND BRING

'EM IN!' He held up a cup of tea and turned a couple of buckets. Harper put the secateurs in his cagoule, pushed down the aisle, gathering all the stems he could hold. The flowers bounced on his shoulder like a swagbag.

'I said to myself, I bet he's forgotten what day it is. If I didn't call him in for tea he'd probably be out there till sunset, holding up his secateurs as if he was about to cut some flowers.' The flower-man sat down on a bucket. 'You know what, you remind me of James Horne. Did you know him? He was forever standing around daydreaming, talking some bloody philosophy or other.' This was disingenuous of the flower-man who liked nothing more than talking bloody philosophy. He shook his head, but he was smiling.

The dog was crouched before them, a gold-coloured collie with intelligent leer. She was looking intently at the stick, then up at Harper encouragingly. Harper moved his wellington and the dog growled. The stick was too far away though. Picking up a big detached flower-head, Harper threw that instead. It was a frumpy overblown one, and it wafted a pathetic five yards.

'You see!' cried the flower-man. 'Can't throw a bloody flower further than five yards! You must be weak as wee-wee.'

'Well throwing a flower-head is a difficult thing.'

139

The flower-man picked out another overblow and tossed it spinning to the stream. 'Look at that—at least, ooh, thirty, forty yards.'

'Yours wasn't as overblown as mine. Mine was all flower and no form.'

'Sounds like you, all flower and no form. What are you doing anyway, picking all these mangy overgones? You should be chopping those off in the aisles. I bet half your bloody stock are big duffers.'

'It's a strange feeling snipping those heads. The way they roll—crashing through the stems—dumping groundward. Kind of thing you associate with dream.'

'Ah, well, you see, that's because you're a dream-er. Behold, the dreamer!'

'The corrupt core turned outward.' Harper gestured inadequately. 'All leaf and no kernel if you like.'

'Come to think of it, they look like you an' all.'

'An airy heaviness. Hard to describe.'

The flower-man sipped his tea. 'Are you sure you're not a little of bit of a weird-o?'

'If it were ordinary healthy heads I wouldn't mind. Cut down in their prime to feed the new order. But the old, gone heads are sinister. Life begets life. It falls and fertilizes. Death on the stem—how can that be good?' Harper gripped the mug, warming his hands. 'It's that public show of

140

rottenness. Miss Havisham in her wedding weeds. Dead in the day. Nor laid low nor raised up. Waiting for a touch to tip the scales, then the edifice crumbles. Doesn't seem nature's way.'

This was more like it for the flower-man. 'On the contrary! Isn't that exactly nature's way?' he said. 'We all get old and overblown don't we? Hanging round for the nick of the blade. Nothing strange about it. Your problem is you're too much of a perfectionist.'

'But you would think it would happen sooner. There's a time to dance and a time to fall over, and some of those lovelies are past both: five past kissing time, as my grandma might have said.'

'Your grandma say that? No wonder you turned out like you did.'

'But a kiss of death in this case.'

'You mix your metaphors like your chrysanths. All pinks and yellows, and most of 'em dead.'

Harper laughed through his nose. The flower man was looking at him side on, seeing the nub through the guff. 'Incorrect' he said at length, as if in response. 'It's quite simple, you see.' He smacked his lips, showing his hands as if he were holding a ball. 'The old flower gets a bit past it—fails to replenish itself, hmmm?—grows weaker—until—ah—*precisely* ready to fall—exactly at the right and appointed time, you see.' His fingers shimmered, descending. 'Then it grows, you know, mouldy,

141

rubbish (a bit like you)—fills the soil with nutrients—and, in the upshot, raises a clean new crop in its place.' He held up a firm high flower. 'There it is, you see, life out of death.'

To the flower-man mystery itself was familiar. He had had experiences in India. Someone fed him a mind-altering plant which persuaded him of universal munificence. Death was right under your feet, and life was there too. And the best of it was, you didn't have to go to India to discover it.

'But the things I'm talking about' protested Harper, 'are not part of the cycle. They're exaggerated, parodic, catastrophic. Less dead than *un*dead.'

'That's a bit gothicky, isn't it? Not quite in their time, that sort of thing?'

'Correct,' said Harper, appropriating the flower-man's vocabulary. The flower-man had been to public school and retained some funny phrases. 'Not like a ghost, though' he said disdainfully, 'more like a wraith.' Harper's *Horror Top Trump* pack had enabled him to distinguish these things at an early age.

'What's wrong with a ghost?'

'Haven't they had their day? Some time in the 19th century.'

'Only if you haven't seen one,' said the flower-man, leaning back on his bucket with a knowing air. Harper could see a story coming on. The sun warmed his hair and the left half of his face. Keeping his face where the sun could hit it, he watched the flower-man from the side of his eyes. The flower-man had seen his grandmother a year after her death. 'In that house!' he said, pointing next door. 'You knew I grew up there, didn't you?' Harper peered through the branches. It was the oldest house in the village; fourteenth century, whitewashed stone.

'Any other haunted houses round here? According to Pat, Holdstone church is rife. Personally, I always fancied the Old Vicarage.'

The flower-man assumed a whimsical, mock-superior air, as of a doctor about to give prescription. 'Not to my knowledge,' he sighed. '*However*—' and he pursed his lips. '—I do have it on old Jenny's word—you know old Jenny up the road? Mows the churchyard—silver hair—very friendly? Says the old Freely-Lowe house on the hill back there is a dead cert for—ah—restless spirits. You know, that kind of thing.' He sniffed, raised his face to the sun. Then he closed his eyes. 'Jenny has—you know—a nose for these things—a little bit like myself—and she says—ah—when she, oh, passes—the house in question—she *feels* I think would be the right word—a disturbance—' He ran a hand through thick greyish hair. 'Account of old Rebecca Freely-Lowe.'

A blue eye glinted. The flower-man was in his forties, looked young and old at the same time. He had a sharp nose. He could have been thirty or a hundred and three.

'You know the story of old Rebecca?' he was saying.

'No.'

'Before your time you see.' He shook his head. 'I don't know, these youngsters.'

Harper reflected. It was true: youth was a weakness.

'Rebecca lived up in the old Freely-Lowe's farmhouse—up there on the hill-brow, middle of the fields?' Harper had passed it. 'Very strict household—you know—wartime—strict—ah—Victorian-style upbringing. Church-goers, hmm?' His voice got higher, more theatrical. He had a lingering narrative style, making a question out of everything. 'Methodist, Wesleyean, something of that sort.' He wafted his hand. By now he was a non-stop staccato. 'Anyway—wartime?—lot of Americans coming over? Hmm?—She was seduced by an American soldier, like many other—ah—women of the *period*—and—discovered—in her *amour*. Big blow to the family, you see?—very close, farming family—intimate—lonely house?' He began to wrap up. 'Father locked her in the house for years. Not allowed out. Not even to church. And rumour has it—allegedly—to the, you know—*supposition*—of the general community (of whom I am, of course, a stalwart member)—that she—ah—went a little off the rails. Very sad. In the end, became quite mad, you see.' He smacked his lips again. 'Come to think of it, she was a little bit like you.'

Harper threw the stick for the dog. She was back like a gunshot, chuntering through wood. 'Such a cliché,' he said smiling.

'Cliché? Cliché?' said the narrator, mock-offended. 'Do you doubt the *veracity* of my tale?' As if throwing pearls to swine, he continued. 'Ah— some years later she was allowed to go to church on Sundays again and many people—testified—to her—distracted—state of mind. Whole family—oh moved out eventually, you see. And that was that really.' He was squinting at Harper. 'Don't believe me do you?'

'No, I believe you.'

'Grab up these piles and take 'em down.' The flower-man threw a festival of flowers about his shoulders and ducked the bough which concealed the field entrance. Harper followed, severing some heads accidentally on the bough.

'There's a caravan next to the house now' said the flower-man neutrally. 'Put 'em down, we'll sort 'em later. She lived there with her sister, but now it's just the sister there.'

145

'It's interesting though. I definitely know the house you mean. The decrepit pile at the slope top—looking to the lake?'

'Correct. Except the lake wasn't there then of course. You just stop old Jenny when she's mowing the graves. She'll tell you, plain as day.'

'No no, I will.'

The flower-man wasn't wholly serious about Harper's slacking, but he was half-serious. He had a living to make after all. The rest of the morning till the mid-afternoon, Harper spent lost in abstractions, taking extra care snipping the old flower-heads. No sooner had they dried than a squall of rain wet everything again. Then the sun burst out and the wind whipped them in the mesh. They had about re-dried by the time he collected them into the barn for bunching and chased the dog round the yard. Harper sorted while the flower-man wrapped and bucketed. They were quiet. Harper was thinking variously about Russia, America and the Freely-Lowe farm. The flowers were spread over newspaper, stacked in latticed piles. Every now and again a headline caught his eye. *WWII Explosives Found In Tunnel* said one. *Broody Sheep Fair Cancelled* said another, and it was subtitled: *Foot and mouth strikes again.* Here was a pertinent one: *Glum Arson Attacks Continue*, it advised. *Coot Bridge water station destroyed in latest atrocity.* Unfortunately, a stray stem had ripped through the article. And on the facing page, one headline stood out from the others: *Thieves Steal Eanswythe's Anchor: precious relic said to be gift from Elizabeth I.* It was last month's article, on the theft at St Swithen's. Apparently the anchor was associated with rain, though it was hard to tell as the paper was wet. Whatever the case, there was cricket on the radio. It was the close of the season, close of a tense day's play. It wasn't sure, though, if the match would be decided. The forecast was variable.

'They'll finish it,' said the flower-man, snuffing the air. He was an optimist for two reasons. He thought the world was alright at bottom, and, in any case, it wasn't worth worrying about.

'You can feel it in your leg?'

'Well, you know, when you've worked the land as long as I have—you *acquire*—you know—a certain—call it an intuition—concernin' the operation of the seasons, weather-cycles, the warp and woof, hmm?'

'That's what she told me,' said Harper, indicating the dog.

'Good grief, that is appallin' isn't it?' The flower-man chuckled despite himself. He had a lopsided grin, bottom-heavy like Boycott's. 'Sometimes I don't know why I bother. Clearly my words are wasted on the likes of you.'

'I suppose you too subscribe to the Eanswythe theory.'

'My,' said the flower-man sadly, 'yours is a sceptical generation. Come along with your new ideas, riding roughshod over centuries of rustic lore. Oh no, mind you, I couldn't accuse you of bein' modern and up-to-date. You're still stuck in the nineteenth century, you are. I'm much more bloody modern than you. If you had your way we'd all probably still be listenin' to gramophones, drivin' a—bloody—coach and four.'

There was a late flurry of fours at the Test Match. The crowd sounded demob-happy.

'I can't deny it.'

'What I want to know is—another big bloody duffer here!' The flower-man exhibited the bunch in question with its frowsy pink chrysanthemum. 'How do I know that's one of yours? Why do I get the feeling you spent half your time cutting finished flowers? I've got a whole pile of 'em at my feet here, which I have to deselect from your mangy old bunches. Cor, dear, you know you don't know what work is, you lot.'

'I don't know how that got in there, I—it—I think you're keeping a stock of them over there just to frame me with. It's all elaborately staged.'

'You're elaborately staged.' A tail-ender was in, swinging away. There were big hits, play-and-misses, last orders for all. 'You know I worked for

148

a while in Essex when I was your age, on a big farm, picking potatoes. They used to get gypsies coming in to work for the season. You know, they'd come along, pitch their caravans and turn up looking for work. I can honestly say I've never seen harder workers in my life. They were paid for what they collected, see, and they'd be there, dawn till dusk, up and down, up and down, untiring. You lot don't know you're born.'

'What about you? Were you up and down, dawn till dusk?'

'Ah! well, you see, I was—learning the trade, you see—going into the more technical aspects, ah—from a theoretical perspective. I didn't really have time to mingle with the ordinary workers. I was—too important. Stick another one in there, it's a bit thin.' Another bunch was tossed over.

'What were you doing in Essex?'

'Ah, that would have been work experience.' He was taking flight again. 'Yes, you know, agricultural college—mmm—acquiring first-hand, er practical skills, in the administration,'—he swept a hand—'development, day-to-day running of a large, arable farm, that sort of thing.' His eyebrows climbed as high as they could go. It was like watching the serene ascent of an air-balloon. 'Course, it couldn't hold me—in the end. I had to get on—you know—bigger and better things? You've got a pink in with the amber.'

'What did you do after?' Harper was taking a couple of whites, a couple of yellows, a couple of ambers for the white bunches. Generally, for the red ones, he would mix reds, pinks and whites, partly because there were more pinks than yellows. You didn't mix amber and pink. You didn't mix yellow and pink, although you could make a few red, yellow and whites—even throw an amber in there. The important thing was to do it quickly, so as to get bunches into buckets as fast as possible for the evening run. The flower-man had a man in town, who sold them at next day's market. This was what made the radio convenient. Harper was incapable of speaking and bunching simultaneously. Worse than slowness even, was miscalculation of colour. A pink could end up in with the amber, have to be tossed back and remade. Harper was concentrating now, which was why he said little.

'I rented a little caravan on Dartmoor, actually. Yes. I lived there with Annie. Very nice girl was Annie—a bit mad, you know—more your sort than mine—liked to paint. But we lived there for a year. I was cleaning windows for a living, and in my spare time I'd walk all over. I hung a grass-chart on the wall and collected samples from the moor. Great time.'

'Sounds fantastic.'

'Well it was and it wasn't. Life never is wholly one thing or another is it? Things didn't quite work out with Annie in the end, and I was a bit stuck in a way. I knew I didn't want to join the rat-race—all the people chargin' about, tramplin' on one another, all for what?—for money. That's it, you see, just for money. No thank you. Wasn't interested in that. But what was I interested in? I was askin' myself that question—you know, a bit like you, wonderin' who I was and where I was goin'. In other words, a bit of a hopeless waster really.' They chuckled. Harper had a large U-shaped work-surface, chipboard supported on heaped plastic trays, originally used for cuttings. He had his reds and pinks on one leg of the U, his ambers and yellows on the other. A huge pile of whites occupied the U-bottom, capable of playing both ways. He would turn first to one side, then the other, select his six, seven if thin, and place them on one of two stacks, beyond the ambers and yellows. The stacks were square-shaped, the stalks of one side underlying the heads of the next. Like this, you could get stacks three feet high on the surface, which the flower-man, who had his own U-shape on the other side—so that the whole formed a double-U—would work through apace, rolling them into his wrapper, tearing it off and piling them up, also in that middle leg, next to the ambers and yellows. Somewhere in the middle of these stacks

151

and piles was the radio, wet with chrysanthemum leaves. It was crackling now, and through the crackles were squeaks of mirth.

'So I took off, you see, and resumed my travelling. India, Australia. I got a job on a cruise-ship, believe it or not. I met this chap—in a bar it was—nice bar, lots of lovely Australian girls, you know, havin' a pint or two. I was a young man remember. And we got talking, and it turned out he needed staff for his cruise-ship, which was sailing all the way to America—right across the Pacific Ocean, to San Francisco. So my friend and I, there, we didn't need askin' twice, and I would just do odd jobs on the ship—cleaning, bar-work, you know—and it was great. Lots of beautiful girls— you know. We shared a cabin, as crew, so if we— you know, got lucky—the other one would have to wait outside. And like that we crossed the Pacific, to San Francisco, then worked our way down South America, right round Cape Horn, and up again, through the Caribbean to New York. And we'd stop at places on the way, and get a day here and there— and it was great. A couple of times we got off, hired motorcycles and drove up the coast to the next port of call. Finally we got to New York and myself and a couple of friends, we said, "sod this" and called it a day. We said goodbye, hired some bikes and buggered off down to Virginia, North, South Carolina, Georgia, all that. Great stuff, see.'

Harper took the new-wrapped bunches, in bundles of ten to fifteen, and flipped them into buckets, which stood in serried ranks outside the barn, part-filled with water. 'Great stuff,' he agreed.

'Now perhaps that's the kind of thing you ought to do—just bugger off and see the world for a bit, find out what you want from life. At least that's one way to get rid of you.'

'I think I probably should.'

'You don't want to be working here all your life. At least I hope you bloody don't.'

'It looks idyllic to me.' The flipping was a delicate procedure, like spinning a rugby-ball. Get it wrong and the bunches would spread. Some would not touch the water. Some might fall out altogether; you'd have to stuff them in separately.

'It's a good life. I'm my own boss, and you can't underestimate that. I never was the kind of person who wanted to take orders—you know, do this, do that, cut your hair, wear a suit. That wasn't for me.' The bowlers took the inevitable wicket and it was stumps. A lot of excited chatter superseded. 'It's a good life—but you're romanticising it, which is probably why you work so bleeding slowly. In the end, it's about a balance. Like when I was travelling. At a certain point, I said to myself, 'that's enough of that' and got a plane back to England. And I tell you, I was happy to see England again. Life goes on, and I had to get on with *my* bloody life. In the end, I got tired of travelling, see—seeing the world. 'Cause, in the end, people are the same the world over, aren't they? Different customs, languages, hairstyles—you've certainly got a unique hairstyle—but in the end, they're the same the world over. They're the same the world over.'

They began loading the van. 'See that!' said the flower-man. He was crouched in the van, at the slide-door, pointing to a birch beside the barn. 'Look there!—over the tree.' A couple of swallows were riding the air. 'The flies are high. Fine weather tomorrow.' Harper handed over his buckets. He didn't know how seriously to take this. The flower-man looked quizzical. 'You don't believe me, do you?' he said. 'I bet you ten pounds it will be fine tomorrow.'

'I bet you a day's pay.'

It was the flower-man's turn to balk. 'You're offering me a day's free work?'

'If it's fine.'

'Mind you, it's not much of a bet, as you don't do any bleeding work anyway. 'I'd get going if I were you, before I take you up on it.' The flower-man slammed the door. 'They'd have gone already if bad weather was coming,' he said about the swallows.

'A day's pay!'

'Bugger off!'

*

Magnus called by just as Harper was getting his jacket: lean, geometric, busy as a compass-needle. His King Charles was whining at the collie. He leashed her in, cracked a joke, crackled with energy, sensing exploration. He conversed five minutes with the flower-man, then turned to Harper, inclined a head and bounded off down the drive to Meal Lane. Jude was there, loitering in the shade, by buckets of chrysanthemums. Above him on a telegraph pole, a sign showed a man being struck full in the breast by a bolt of lightning. Underneath it read *Danger of Death*. Magnus stared at it, hands wrangling at the leash. He gurgled, flared nostrils, broke into a cackle. 'Ha!' said Jude, throwing back his head. Jude had been mowing the Kroner's lawn in the shirtless afternoon. It wasn't an arrangement; he had just breezed in out of the afternoon and begun mowing. No one could do anything about it—least of all the Kroners. Mrs Kroner would feel obliged to pay, and would do so smilingly. Jude would smile too. It was a good way to make money. Money he would then spend on medication. At first this would disgruntle him; he would grow resigned; then, all of a sudden, *enraged*; then disgruntled again. But ever and anon, *enraged*. The mower, with Jude at the helm, was

155

circling despairingly the Kroner's birdbath when
Magnus woke up and signalled from the door. Jude
collected his cash and they plunged down Sandal
Road, between cluttered cottages, to the ford. Here
the Meal and Leaze collided, never far from
indistinguishable at the best of times. Both fell
from Higher Marching, origins lost amidst fields
and copses. And moreso in summer. The Leaze
sometimes lost the name of stream. You picked
your way among its ditches, lucky with puddles.
One such ditch rode like a maverick ladder, to
Magnus' house. They called it *The Gulley*. You
could plot your way along *The Gulley*, hanging
from roots, and hit the Leaze on its way by St.
Swithen's. Thereafter it wound through gardens,
trickled under a footbridge going nowhere, formed
the artificial border of Sandal Road, like the central
heating in a Roman baths. Here, at the bottom, it
crawled, commando-like, under a cottage. This was
the old post-office in The Road: a miniature street
from an era of detail. No chance of not seeing what
was in front of you then. They must have been born
myopic. The old post-office had an arch in its
underbelly. They couldn't divert the Leaze, so they
had built right over it. Why be Herculean? You
could just build things over, round, next to, jammed
between other things. It was a cluttered world.
Everyone died. Just look at the fields and copses.
The old post-office grew over the stream, arched its

156

back and put roots down. Here came the Leaze, in its paved course, straight as an arrow to the ford, commingling with the Meal. The Meal washed in under a double-arched bridge. Arm in arm, they turned through small tunnels, or leapt lightly to the road above them. It was a potholed road, lumpen, crepuscular. It sifted the Meal like a gold-prospector, leaving sick lathers on the bridge-side, gleaming auburn waters on the other. Magnus, Jude and the King Charles traipsed over it, turned right down Meal Lane, hugging the river, right to the flower-farm gate.

Jude looked slyly at Harper. 'Earning a little of that country money,' he said, 'eh, Blind Willie?'

'That's about it.'

They struck again up the lane, in the cool of the hedgerows, beyond Oak Grove—a mock-up cul-de-sac; no oaks, no groves there now—outlasting the houses, exiting the village. The lane was long and almost straight. Only a couple of s-bends slowed its progress. It ran through orchards and sheep-fields, keeping close to the Meal, never more than a field away. At its long end, it dipped down, before the big push up Shingle Hill. Here another stream gathered, channelled beneath the lane, before feeding the Meal.

'Alright,' said Magnus as they dipped down with it. A footpath pottered off to the left, between hedgerows. 'The Cleave Chimney, the pillboxes, that abandoned hospital we SCOPED OUT, are things close to my heart as you know—and everyone should value landmarks like these, map every vein that knits 'em, know 'em like the back of his hand.' He looked accusingly round, displaying the back of his hand, its network of veins. 'Keeping his quiet vigil, like some god-damn unacknowledged legislator!' A rhythmic banging could be heard downstream. '—In fact, I've been thinking, I could run some sort of walking weekend, pointing out local anomalies. Seriously, can you imagine it!' He wagged his hands. *'Tired by life's monotony? Longing for spice, variety, variegation? Join the Glum Valley walking tour! Discover the meaning of anomaly!'*

'Yes. You could collaborate with The Man Who Would Be King.'

Magnus shrugged. 'It's fantastic therapy. If nothing else.'

What disturbed Jude was the possibility that Magnus was serious. Psychology did strange things to people, made them swear by the origins they invented, get analytical on their smallers and betters. He turned aside, determining to take Magnus at face value. 'Why not write a book as well?' he said, setting out a foot. 'With little fold-out maps? You could get—ooh—a good five years from it before they ceased to be anomalies. By which time you'll have made enough money to live on a larger scale.'

Magnus ignored him, returning to his lead. 'Though, I confess, this particular anomaly troubles me.' He put a hand to his chin, looking down the path. 'This is the one bangs away in my mind and won't let it sleep.'

'Apart from this afternoon.'

'Even then, it was "a trouble to my dreams".' He fixed his eyes on Harper. 'Yes, you know the one! I've shown you the beauty before.'

'That tank contraption?'

'Bet your life the bloody tank-contraption! The pounding, interminable tank-contraption, and all its mechanical appurtenances:—that pump and pipe you remember, buried in the briars of the gulley. And in that same familiar gulley, of all ghast, unmentionable things—a closet! No arras in this one, either'—prodding Harper—'no incestuous suggestion. Just some anachronistic pump, and hingeless swinging door.'

'Sounds as incestuous as it gets.'

Caught in a craggy laugh, Magnus ploughed on. 'Just standing there by the stream, with its own pump and coughing little mouth. And the aforementioned tank, in the field's middle, centring—CONTROLLING!—the valley and its rhythms! No blooming but booming for this frigging TECHNIC! No dying for my machine. Just the hammer-blow, ongoing, till the hills crumble in the streams.' Magnus was loud in the quiet of evening. But, as they tottered down the track, turning ankles, the banging grew louder and the voice was pitched just right. Over another stile, they cut through a tree-line, and there was a brick tank, in a narrow field, close to the stream. It was livid, stained, organic-looking, ten feet tall on a stilted base. When they came close, the sound changed. A new one emerged, like hammer on metal, about the pace of a human heart at rest. Leaning against the tank was a wood-ladder that looked as if it had been there as long as the tank itself.

'WHICH IS TO SAY A GOOD SIXTY YEARS, IF A DAY!' shouted Magnus, roaring above the beat, shaking the ladder approvingly. 'THEY DON'T MAKE APPARATUS LIKE THIS ANY MORE! THIS IS THE OLD BARN-AND-HAYLOFT VARIETY'—and he winked exaggeratedly, tugging at the rungs. 'YOU DESERVE OUR CONGRATULATIONS, ENDURING AS YOU HAVE. FEW INVENTIONS SO INGENIOUS, FEW SO *APPROPRIATE* AS THIS OUR LASTING LADDER!'

It was the kind of hyperbole Jude might easily puncture—but, for that reason, decline to. He considered the tank. It was certainly variegated:

bruised a hundred shades, flaking, strained, as if soon to leak. But it was monotonous too, with its crass interminability. A violent, bullet-headed jabbering in the void. If this was Magnus' anomaly, he'd hate to see his sameness. Sun gleamed on the trees. Jude dug in, imagined himself in a pale Dimly room—a black cat happening by—maybe kissing Fran Peters, who was herself tall and willowy, but would hardly serve to climb a tank by, to gaze at your reflection in the water. Horrid misapplication! Jude rejected the image. No, not kissing Fran Peters. Eating a bowl of *Fruit and Fibre*, which it so happened was central to his relationship with Fran Peters for a plethora of reasons. How many times had a bowl of *Fruit and Fibre* intervened to moderate their relationship? Just like the pivot of a see-saw, a bowl of cereal was the crux on which they swivelled and stared, across what Jude termed *a certain distance*. Which was no doubt the reason why both Fran and Jude's mother had conspired—whether separately or together, a conspiracy it remained—to keep at all times a packet of *Fruit and Fibre* in the cupboard, and, for dire circumstances, another of *Special K*. And this—like all conspiracies—Jude was not prepared to countenance. So he chewed his *Fruit and Fibre* and calmly, metaphorically, put a pencil through her name.

Magnus gripped the ladder like a long-standing friend, set it aright, then scrambled up quicker than squirrels. 'IT'S AS YOU WERE,' he said, stood against the sky with trouser-bottoms bristling. 'THE PUMP AT THE BOTTOM (THAT THING LOOKS VICTORIAN), AND WATER TO THE BRIM. JUST AS BEFORE! DON'T TAKE MY WORD FOR IT! SEE FOR YOURSELVES!'

There was no reason why they shouldn't take his word for it—but no advantage in saying so. Magnus locked his arms on the tank's edge and inched over, vacating the ladder. Harper ascended in his place, pulling into blue, nothing if not an accomplice. Jude remained below, hung out to dry.

Inside the tank, the water held the light. Winged things skated on its surface. Tangled in the ivy crown was a wire, reaching down to what looked like a garlic-crusher. Some kind of pump. Here the beat was denser, but the water only stirred, as if sound were out of step with movement. If you leaned your head out far enough, you could catch a metallic register, and beyond that, a duller thud. He leant toward the water and looked. Nothing but his own wild hair on his face, insects skating on his eyes.

'EVERYTHING JUST AS WAS, AM I RIGHT?' barked Magnus. 'IN THIS BEATING BLOODY HEART!'

162

'FULL OF WATER!' said Harper, as if he didn't know. Magnus made no affirmative, gazing muscularly into the tank. 'I DON'T THINK MUCH CHANGES AROUND HERE! I SUPPOSE THIS SET-UP HAS BEEN WORKING FOR AN AGE!'

'CHANGE! THIS THING IS FRIGGING SELF-PERPETUATING! THINK ABOUT IT! HOW MANY PULSES, MONTH AFTER MONTH? WHAT KEEPS IT IN STEP, YEAR AFTER YEAR, *DECADE* AFTER *DECADE*? WHERE'S THE PRESSURE COMING FROM TO DRIVE THAT PUMP?'

Harper lowered his head until his nose touched the water. 'SHOULD WE GO UNDER?' he shouted.

'—THINKING THE SAME MYSELF. MOVE ALONG THERE.' It was Harper's turn to move over, scraping his trainers on the sides. Magnus stepped back to the ladder, shook his veiny hands beside his head, gurned, grimaced, and exhorted himself. 'RRRRRGH!' he snorted, Teutonic ancestry writ large across his face. Then he dunked that ancestry for a long two minutes, and, with an 'ARGHHHH!' and a 'WAEGHH!', emerged in dripping triumph.

'HELL, THERE'S SOMETHING TO TELL YOUR GRANDCHILDREN ABOUT!' he hooted. 'NO ONE CAN SAY WE DIDN'T DO IT! PUT OUR OWN NECKS ON THE LINE! HAH-HAH-

HAH, WOOOH!' And he shook drops all over the surface of the water. Of course, Harper had not done it yet, and could tell his grandchildren nothing; but no doubt Magnus had factored this in. And now it was too late. Whatever Harper's next move was, it would be anticlimactic. He dunked his head to the neck.

Very far away he could hear Magnus cackling and protesting. Inside, the beat of the pump moved and surrounded him. It was as if the water were gulping. In a short time he grew accustomed to it. His head was suspended in the water. He didn't care about the insects. Years of lying down in woods, puddles and pigsties had accustomed Harper to insects too. He could have grown gills and stayed a lifetime. He was remembering the night he had gone swimming in the reservoir with Rebecca Folkes. How she had stood tiptoe in the water, holding out her glasses, asking him to take them. How she had wanted to touch hands, unbalance a little, go tumbling underwater. How precisely he had taken her glasses, by a single arm, shunning that touch, that slovenly tumble—carried them like relics to the shore. It seemed a shame. Where was the milk of his human kindness? Where else but an awkward, ugly coupling in the lake? He had waded back in, but the frisson had gone. Water was no longer their element. They had swum half an hour, between Hyde Island and the shore, in ever-widening circles.

'TOO MUCH ACCUSTOMISATION, METHINKS!' roared Magnus, jerking Harper out by the collar. 'ANY MORE AND YOU'D HAVE COME OUT LOOKING LIKE *THE CREATURE FROM THE BLACK LAGOON.*' Harper's hair was plastered to his nose, and he flashed a gappy grin. Streams from his hair streaked his jumper. No matter though, because the jumper had been found soaked on a stile, by the Glum. Elbow and shoulder patches, ridges top-to-bottom: a farmer jumper, a jumper used to elements. Harper surveyed his jumper with pride. His neck was longer than it might have been, body more bone than flesh. 'But under that cloak of bone and skin,' maintained Jude, one afternoon, in the reservoir woods: 'thighs of *coiled wire*, calves of *beaten brass*, loins—yea, *loins!* dost think we go veiled through the changing-rooms?—loins, I say, of *iron and steel!*' And they pulled down their trousers in front of plump Ruth Murphy, fat Lizzie Tate. Ruth Murphy and Lizzie Tate turned away, then turned back despite themselves, standing, murmuring.

He was about to murmur himself when Magnus thumped his back, barking, 'DON'T GET ANY IDEAS ABOUT GOING TO ALICIA LONG'S LOOKING LIKE THAT!' Harper fell down the ladder to grass clumps. 'SHE WON'T HAVE IT YOU KNOW! YOU'LL HAVE TO SHOWER OFF AND BRUSH UP, AND GET THROUGH A

165

WHOLE BUNCH OF PREPOSITIONS BEFORE
YOU GET THROUGH THE FRIGGING DOOR!'
Magnus sounded as if he had been spending too
long with his grandmother. The intervention was
timely though, because in the green eye of Harper's
self-conceit, already a plan had hatched to traipse
six miles to Alicia Long's, like, if not dressed as,
The Creature From The Black Lagoon, stand on
her very stepstone—still dripping—claiming
nothing less than love. 'On the other hand, he
muttered through the hammering, 'can one ever
claim such a thing?'

Jude loitered near the tank, cast a level look
roadward. 'It doesn't have a context until you give
it one,' he commented, in the milk and ease of
genius.

Magnus was of a different mind. 'YOU WERE
THINKING IT! YOU WERE THINKING IT YOU
BASTARD!' he roared from the tank. 'IT WAS
PASSING   THROUGH   YOUR
MONOMANIACAL   BRAIN!'   'Monoman*i*acal'
was a word Jude used. To hear him use it was to
think life depended on that single *i*. Jude had heard
it from his father. Harper remembered them
disputing a point as they unloaded the dishwasher.
Like most disputations in the Harlow house, it
came down to semantics. 'N-*no*,' had said Jude's
father. 'I, I chose my words *very carefully*.' And,
bending down for a fork, he stopped what he was

166

doing and stared Jude in the eye, a full five seconds. Jude said nothing. There could be only one winner.

'NOW!' continued Magnus, oblivious. 'APART FROM ALICIA FRIGGING LONG, TELL US WHAT YOU SAW! VISIONS? OMENS? SCEPTRES PASSING THROUGH TEN GENERATIONS?

'Not exactly.'

'OF COURSE NOT! AND WHY? WHAT NEED PROPHECY? WHAT NEED FUTURITY? TOO CLEVER FOR THAT, BY HALF IS HARPER! YOURS WAS THE REAL CLAIRVOYANCE, RIGHT THROUGH DIRTY WATER, TO THAT POSTWAR PUMP! AM I RIGHT? WHAT ELSE IS THERE TO SEE? NOT A FRIGGING THING! HAH! BECAUSE IT'S THE GOD-DAMN SAME AS BEFORE!'

He slid down the ladder, cocked his head, spoke sharp and not so loud. 'Only *not* the same!' he leered. Jude huffed. 'Why not?' rattled Magnus, ignoring. 'Because everything else is different. Let's take a look at that gulley there, and its loquacious stream, making obeisance to our customary Meal!'

Magnus and Harper picked their way through nettles, Jude coolly following. All the while the beat grew moister and hammer knocked only on wood. Half-way between tank and bank, the sound

167

swung and seemed to come from a different direction altogether—from somewhere in the gulley. Half-sliding down the bank in the shade, they broached a kind of brick closet, nestled in mud. Through the unlocked door was another pump, hooped hat at a Keaton akimbo. In synchrony with the beat, thin spurts of water shot from its side. Decades of such spurting had worn a shallow bowl in the floor. About the bowl, littering the cement, were five different-sized spanners and bolts, and something curvaceous in the corner. Whatever it was had once been a defined thing, with a particular use. Years of attrition on the closet floor had made it solidified slime. The pump vibrated. At its front were two tongues, coughing incongruous drops. The drops hit a worn channel, and ran to feed the stream. Upon the tongues, someone had placed two polished stones and a block of wood.

Harper stepped inside, through trailing grass. The roof was plankwood, stuck with cement; walls were two-bricks thick but crumbling. Moss in the joins, green or ashen. Some slurred together, like film on the eye. Two or three littered the rust-colour floor, with plastic scraps and plate-metal. He touched the planks, slapped the pump, toed its legacy of water. High and central was a ventilation brick, plastic cap and bottle on the sill. He knocked out the bottle, looked around the walls. Stains made stripes. Two nails had caught a thread of sunlight. Hung on one was a small plastic spool; round the rim: *P. T. F. E. Thread Seal T—*. 'T what?' Harper wondered. Leaning round the nail, he read off: *ape. Conforms to B. S. 43. 12 m × 22 mm × 0.075 mm.* Thread seal tape. What was thread seal tape? Thread *seal* tape, or *thread* seal tape? Surely not thread seal *tape*? Jude would have an opinion, of course. Not on pronunciation. On *emphasis*. If pronunciation was a mincing pedantry, emphasis was Jude's magnificent *stance*. If pronunciation was a cowardly law, emphasis was axe and execution. The fate of nations, sir, the fate of *nations*. Harper spied Jude in the doorway, deciding to forego his opinion. In fact, he already knew it. Because if opinion was of *any use at all*, Jude would have pondered, it was only as a completely transparent euphemism for *scorn*.

Magnus pointed to the gulley. 'OBSERVE THE STREAM!' he yelled. 'THAT FLOCK-DRUNK PLEASANT WINDER, WHICH A COUPLE MONTHS BACK DOWNROLLED MEAL FIELDS! WHAT DO YOU SEE NOW?'

'A SLUGGISH THING, SIR. A CHOKED, BEMUDDIED THING.' Jude was warming to the task, seizing the opportunity to belittle.

'YOU SAID IT! WHERE'S THE GOD-DAMN WATER?' Magnus thumped the side of the closet. 'NOWHERE IS WHERE! NOT THAT THAT

169

TANK WOULD KNOW IT! I JUST DON'T GET IT! THE TANK BRIMS AND STREAM SHRINKS AWAY! SO MUCH EFFECT FOR SO LITTLE CAUSE.' He gazed on the closet pump, its coughed drops. 'OR SHOULD THAT BE THE OTHER WAY ROUND?'

'I *MAINTAIN*. AS INCESTUOUS AS IT GETS.'

'HAH! PROOF, IF PROOF WERE NEEDED, THAT RHYME MAY EXIST WITHOUT REASON! THOUGH THERE'S REASONS BEHIND THOSE UNREASONS, I'M WILLING TO BET!' He cackled gleefully. 'BUT THAT'S ANOTHER DAY'S SCOPE! WE LOSE OUR TIME, AND THAT OLD SUN AIN'T WAITING! HAH! COME ON, WE'LL CLOCK SOME ANACHRONISMS YET!'

*

They pursued their course through the field to the pair of pipes—the same you could see from Shingle Hill—which shot out of the hillside and over the stream. Ascending an artificial mound, heaped for the pipes' re-entry, Magnus and Harper tiptoed a hundred feet along, twenty feet over the abyss, carrying the spaniel. Jude went below, wading ankle-high through the stream. They met on the other side. The fields were flung with sheep, standing on the brow, ears like horns in the sun.

Something else horned on the sun, which the sheep had left alone. Harper saw it first, silhouetted leftward: a tall, thin origami figure, all oblongs and triangles, halfway up the field. It had what appeared to be arms, armour, a goat's head, about eight foot high, in white paper, grubby now and dented, two rods in its hand. It might have been a skier: Bjørn Bjørnsen perhaps, sticks at the ready; or the ski-jumpers Bjørn had watched on a winter afternoon at Holmenkollen, falling like angels from the light. There was that Japanese daredevil whose skis were a perfect parallel, barring his begoggled face. Bjørn saw him fall, direct from the sun: a thing of stillness, wind-assisted. A fraught hieroglyph, between meanings; he dropped into a *Telemark* and was gone.

Harper approached with caution, almost nausea. For all they knew, this was Japanese as well. A faint wind was up, attempting to tug the figure from the field; but it was weighted at the base with cardboard. On the cardboard was written:

A POOR PLAYER

'Yes, yes, *A Poor Player*,' said Jude wearily. He kicked some origami shins. '*A Red Herring*, if ever I saw one, strutting and fretting its hour upon the field.'

171

Magnus confronted it, hands on hips, one leg resting before the other. 'Yet signifying SOMETHING,' he said. 'NECESSARILY.' Magnus' favourite writer was Machiavelli. He read *The Prince* at school; he always read around his subjects. *Das Kapital*, and the *Ninety Five Theses*, and *Ten Days That Shook The World*, he read them all, and still failed history. Tortured and gnashing, he hung over his desk. Around him flew the zigzagging multicoloured lines of scattered *brain-diagrams* containing nodes like *Colloquy of Augsberg*, *Five Year Plan* and *Influence of Copernicus*.

Jude drew on his saliva. 'Yes. If only because nothing is so *passé*. The floating, self-cancelling signifier: a tedious riddle of years ago.' Jude turned his back on *A POOR PLAYER*.

'An art exhibit?' pursued Magnus. He sounded as if he were taking notes. 'Maybe one of the Helsen Monger girls'. Huh, landowners will have daughters, and arty ones at that.' He stared it in the face. Something told him it was too good to be any of the Helsen-Mongers'. But the significance of the figure could not be probed. Magnus' thin lips pressed and leaned; then he stalked away, feet outpointed, legs crooking and straightening, fearlessly precise. He was like an expatriate big-game hunter; incongruous but competent. 'Nothing comes of nothing,' he barked at the origami. 'SPEAK AGAIN!'

Climbing up, they crossed the Shingle Hill road, and looked on the Meal, travelling in trees. Then they looked east, the other way. The opposite ridge was topped by a tall, thin obelisk. The Cleave Chimney.

'Hell is that?' grumbled Magnus. He had circled, never solved it. There was a small barred outlet at the bottom; at the top, a sort of bird-box with numbers. Near the outlet, a plaque read: *Low 42*.

'Depth?' suggested Harper.

Magnus mused. 'Pressure?'

Jude thought a *4* was missing. It was an oblique, yet *embossed*, comment on the parlous state of English football and its traditional system. He was about to enlarge on the outlet, but Magnus intervened.

'There she stands!' he hailed. 'For all to see! But try to find her in the RECORDS!' He grunted. 'Talk about hid in plain sight! No, if you want info round here, ask the farmers. Or flower men.'

They frowned on the sky. It looked like Cleopatra's Needle.

'It is, of course, a folly,' Jude concluded, sweeping a hand at obelisk, origami and the rest. 'Aren't they all? Regardless of *utility*. The countryside is littered with them, as any cursory ramble evinces. Stonehenge, the New Forest, the

Long Man of Wilmington; toys and baubles of the rural majority, grafted on the land, in urgent effort to supply the lack of *marks*.'

'Didn't that one have his genitals removed?'

'Like I said.'

They dove on down the meadow to copsewood and waterfall, sheep bleating in the evening. They waded the meadow, hurdled barb-wire, slipped through hollies to a green dome. Here fell the twelve-foot fall and the water whitened in their eyes. Then they scrambled up through briars, over another fence, and stood in an evening field, whose lower reaches, having trapped the sun, were crowded with cows.

'Look on that, sirs,' said Jude, encouraged. They walked on through the cows. 'Think on the city, its *seed* and feebleness, its *halfway measures*.' The cows parted, closing ranks behind. 'Where anything may mingle with anything else.' Now they got curious. 'The easy, smooth, new-shaven city,' continued Jude. 'Then behold!—on a *sudden!*—the *country!*' The cows moved sullenly, in pyramid formation. Magnus picked up the dog. 'Radical, far-fetched,' said Jude, glancing backwards. 'Its nooky deviances, *crannying* virtues. Unnatural fears and hate at its height.' He moved more quickly up the hill. 'None of your metropolitan *conscience*, urban *awareness*, charitable *concern*. It's all life and death in the country. Mercy and

174

curses. Usually the latter. Sticking the knife in, just like one of its insane killer farmers, slitting pigs, strangling geese, burying the bodies in the wall. It's all the same to the country. The country! A retarded Cyclops, shagging sheep, sisters, tractors. The cows all dressed like Pasiphae. No, pile avarice on envy, envy on ire, ire on gluttony, any vice you choose— they don't touch the hem of lust, however encouraged.'

'It's raised too high.'

'Love—not philanthropy—I mean soiled, *contextual* love—painted intensest in its blind backdrops.' The cows stepped up the pace. 'See imbeciles, gossips, all the sleepy *hearsayers*, of which the country is replete.' They fell into a trot. 'Ask eclogues and pastorals, idylls and roundelays.' Trot became frolic. 'Witness Arcadian shepherds; their loves and buggery.' The chase began in earnest. No one had wanted to draw attention to it; not Jude, not Magnus, not the spaniel, not even the cows. But now it seemed appropriate. 'It's all about rite of passage!' puffed Jude. 'Take it how you like!' They ran laughing up the hill, brilliantly inevitable. Cows broke round like Harper's comets until, crammed into a corner, they found egress through the prickly thorn.

'Ha!' panted Jude, on the other side of the hedge. 'You don't *know space* until you've been crammed into a corner by a *herd of cows*.' They continued down a lane, half a mile, on the edge of Higher Marching, before a cottage appeared on the left, on whose stone wall somnolent sunflowers rested their heads. There were stepping stones, a vegetable garden, a green door. Something in them did not love that wall, that door, those vegetables. Death was in those sunflowers, mean, breathless, absorbing the sun.

Shouts came from a nearby farm. They took a right, over a gate where a pump coughed water. A stream slept in a delta of mud. A short hop, a climbed stile and they emerged in fields, sun intersected by the lines of trees. They crossed the broken lines, a first, a second, third, until, under the sun, they saw the Freely-Lowe house staring across the fields. It looked like the wake of an avalanche: a greystone pile of no particular line, as if a small hill had crumbled to the Meal, leaving a house-shaped core. Porch roofs, rambling walls, slant-buttresses lent to the effect. An orchard grew wild one side, and ivy doubled the thickness of the walls. They drew near, to leeward, where stones strewed the hill. Behind the house was a long outbuilding, a stables perhaps, broken into barns. Further still was a girdered hayhouse, with corrugated roof. It belonged to another farm now.

The house was well situated, great views across the valley, perfect for a family. A green haven, out of the swing of the sea. And yet, you only had to

176

look at that shaggy outcrop, browbent, hollowed, held together by accident. It needed just a match. What horrors, what shutters, what awnings it had seen. Whole lives cramped into pianos, pantries, boxrooms. The gulps and gasps which fenced the silence. It was beyond endurance, didn't bear thinking about. 'No seriously,' thought Jude. 'You'd be mad to think about it.'

Under some holly bushes on the right was a caravan almost as decrepit as the house, and what seemed a woman's figure in the window. It was hard to tell. The window had not been washed for years. Magnus paid it no attention. 'I've been meaning to scope this place out for a while now,' he declared. 'Good thing this flower-man of yours reminded me. Seems an interesting man. "There is no ancient gentlemen," after all, "but gardeners, ditchers, and grave-makers". "Adam's profession"—isn't that right?'

'Like something from a horror-film' said Harper, pointing to a wrought-iron gate, overgrown with weeds.

'Doesn't it just!' cackled Magnus, over-confidently. 'Hold the *Foul One*.' They approached the gate, slipped through the adjacent wire, exchanging the King Charles. Jude hung back, looked around. 'No,' he said. 'I think I'll just go and fall asleep, *under that oak*.' He pointed downslope to the sententious tree, clenching and

177

unclenching his jaw. It was a lonely oak in the midst of the field.

'What's this? A GENERAL UNWILLINGNESS?'

'Yes,' said Jude. 'I'm not convinced by your *scoping out*, an amateur dalliance if ever I saw one. A lacklustre substitute for a dead *discovery*.'

'There never WAS,' retorted Magnus, 'such thing as discovery. Only REDISCOVERY—by those who had forgotten. And if we have lost the art of surprise, it is because we have lost the art of forgetting, which is of course BEYOND ENDURANCE! The human mind cannot fucking take it all in! HAH! BRAIN-DEATH! BRAIN-DEATH! Fortunately, the more macrocosmic, we get, the more detail we lose. Like I say. Rediscovery will be local, hidden, anomalous.'

'Sounds marvellously *bourgeois*,' grumbled Jude. 'If not verging on *fetishism*. Local histories, hidden sins, anomalous closets. A man's closet, of course, is his ego. And if there's a skeleton in it, *well*—the ultimate product of capitalism.'

Magnus frowned. 'Talking about individualism. Talking byways, bridleways, tracks and trails. Talking Johnson's kicked stone, the idiosyncratic fact. What choice do we have? We ate from the tree of knowledge.'

Once again, Jude pointed to the oak. It was a useful reference; but, more than that, a token of

178

solidarity. 'Consider *that* tree. Consider the field, the patch of grass.' He pointed at the long grass round the house. 'Nothing bourgeois a*bout* them.' He pointed into the orchard. 'See the branches thrashing. Hard. See the roots. *Radical*. It's your human being's bourgeois. I don't care where he comes from. Could be the son of a whore, raised in an open sewer. Man is *born* bourgeois. It's in his nature. I'd go so far as to say it *is* the Original Sin. What was Eve, what Adam, if not the first of the lascivious bourgeoisie, tucking into a *treat*.' He swayed toward the orchard. 'You see, you forget, Kroner, what you of all people should remember: that there is no better way of knowing a place than *falling asleep* in it.'

Magnus shrugged, began investigating the barns. Everything looked just as it might have sixty years since, except crumbled to pieces. There were fragments of jars everywhere, a wooden ladder, bits of machinery. Doors were hanging off hinges. Hay littered the ground. In one was a plough. It looked constructed of rust, as if rust were mineable. They pranged the plough, knocked the wood, scuffed the hay, squatted by boxes, or hung from beams. There wasn't much to be said; it was good to get outside.

The orchard was wild. Blackberries grew up to the windows and the air was heavy with jasmine. Harper saw a snake beside a pane in the grass. Before yesterday, he had never seen a snake in the

179

wild; now he'd seen a second. It was the wetness of the spring, meshed with summer heat. Yesterday, he had been walking in a cornfield near the reservoir. The rustling stalks had reminded him of snakes. His eyes were on the dirt path, but he almost stepped on her, before she uncoiled and looped off through the field's side. This time he saw her sooner. He was passing by the hedge and there she was—perhaps two feet in length: an adder. She wound into the hedge. He poked in his head, but she lay still and invisible.

They shifted round the house, to a low, broken wall. In the distance, through the screen of trees, they could see Jude, under the oak, stretched at his pleasure. Climbing through a broken window, they found themselves in a narrow room, much like Magnus' utility. It was dark. A flowery sofa had half-fallen through the floor. 'Watch your step!' said Magnus. He gleamed like his hourglass. 'It's like fucking Indiana Jones! Got to spell Jehovah the right way or you fall through the floor!'

They stepped carefully to a hallway. On the right was what looked like a workshop, but turned out to be a brewery. The floor was rugged cement. Big jars stood round the room, and a press was in the middle. 'Christ!' said Magnus, setting down the spaniel, 'Puritans they may have been, but they knew how to brew bloody cider!' He picked up a clay jug, chuckling. Down the hall was the living room. They entered into a big dimness, low-ceilinged but wide. Some time elapsed before its objects arose, and they were many and slovenly, all just as in life, but collapsed inside. There was a dining table at one end, candlestick at its middle. Chairs fell about round it, as if their last occupants had been serious carousers. A rug rotted in the centre of the room, indistinguishable from the floorboards. In one corner, a piano beside a short door. Near the window, an upright, scrolled-armed armchair with a cover once of flowers. In front was a small table and, on top of that, a plate and pewter mug.

Magnus' voice was hollow. 'It's God damn Pompeii!' he croaked, peering at the cracks in the ceiling. 'Whoever got shot of here was in a hurry. And they weren't about to stop to do the dishes.'

'Or they left by degrees. Week on week, month on month, even year on year, a book, a plate, an heirloom at a time. Eventually they slunk from the place, with a sick look back. They couldn't bear to touch it.'

'YOURS is the sick look back!' Magnus tried the small door. It was a cupboard, still stocked with crockery. 'Just don't believe this place,' he was wondering. 'Looks like the plague came and scattered 'em away. LOVE was that plague which scattered them away!' he rejoined immediately. 'Swept in like a broom, turned everybody MAD!'

181

He cackled again. Magnus didn't appear afraid of anything. Everything in the world was explicable to him, and those things not-yet explained merely awaited their opportunity.

Harper wasn't so happy. He had half-expected to find a corpse in the cupboard, or sitting in a chair at a window. Hollow-cheeked and ambiguous, Harper threatened any minute to go plunging into self-parody. He had a line in hyperbolic self-deprecation, by which he provoked the world into judgement. He would emerge in the social fields, attempt to fight strength with prowess, and retreat to the bitter stormlit crags, where he might roll only one die. If he could have ridden a cold stallion a pristine mile and straightened out the coastline with his flying, he would have done so—then, thrown from his steed, from some imaginary terror, plunged to his death on the congratulatory rocks.

The spaniel wasn't happy either, circling and whinging. A dead domicile was an inauspicious place for a dog. Magnus approached the piano and raised the lid. He had dabbled in jazz once upon a time. He paused, held a finger to a key. It was a dud. Another key—also a dud. One key struck a second's worth of *d*. The dog didn't like it one bit. It yapped, then fell silent, staring at the window as if it saw its fate reflected.

They explored the house. Magnus spread spider's limbs and leapt about upstairs. Harper followed suit. In one room the floor had caved in. You had to inch around the edges, shuffling your hands on the wall. Through the hole they could see the spaniel whining up at them. 'Silence, *Foul One*,' said Magnus. He began poking his head into the loft, but Harper drew the line there. One thing interested him in an upstairs bookcase—*The Imitation of Christ*. He stole it from the shelves, saying 'no one in need of this'.

Coming to the top of the main stairs he was surprised to find the King Charles sitting on the middle step. The stairs were darker above than below, so the dog was almost a silhouette. 'Oh!' he said, putting his hand to his heart. 'You again, old stauncher! With your wheezy death-rattle! Magnus, look at this. She scared the life out of me.'

'Dogs!' barked Magnus, clambering downstairs. He picked up the spaniel and patted its head vigorously. 'Man's best friend, eh, what's that *Foul One?*'

'Ridiculous creature, yees, ridiculous creature!' said Harper. 'Could've tripped right over you and broken my neck.'

They were about to leave when Harper noticed an open envelope on the window sill, beside the armchair. It was cramped and brittle, a dead fist time is prising. Inside was a letter. It wasn't clear if the letter had been composed here, or received here, but a pen beside the envelope suggested the former.

183

Harper snaffled it from the envelope and Magnus rotated. 'What you got?'

'A letter by the look of it.'

'Read the fucker.'

Harper unfolded it, bits falling off in his palms.

'Sticking to me.'

'Sweaty palms, eh? I'm HARDLY surprised.' Magnus adjusted his stance. 'Read!'

Harper turned it to the window, decyphering the handwriting. He read, reacted, stopped, read again, and Magnus interjected in his turn.

> *Dear Geraldine. Do we know a Geraldine? Not so far as I know. How lovely it was to receive your letter. La, la, la. I am glad to hear that you are feeling well again. How have you settled in? Etc, etc. What? It's always hard at first, but matters will right themselves in time. Oh, get this. There is a time to laugh and a time to weep, as the proverb has it, a time to cast away stones, a time to gather stones together. I am sure laughter is just around the corner for you. HAH-HAH-HAH! What about the stones? Where have they gone? All over the freaking hillside! Gather those together if you can! I am glad to hear that you are*

*feeling well again. I was greatly
concerned to read of your tribulations.
La, la, la. What? Hold on. Listen to
this. Remember, it is the duty of a
Christian to defeat the Tempter, though
He comes in many shapes and guises.
He must have the Horror Top Trump
Pack! The Foul One is cunning. NAO! I
can't believe THAT! Hear that Foul
One, you're a cunning, cunning thing.
You're SHITTING me! Seriously. We
are most vulnerable to Him when at our
ease. We must always keep our wits
about us, crying in our hearts, pleading
for mercy to bring us nearer our Lord,
to guide and guard us safe and free.
Extraordinary! I urge you to stay to the
narrows. Fantastic! Myself, I know, I
cannot eat, read, walk in these dear
fields, without feeling Him behind me.
Even the river takes up His refrain.
NAO, dear God! Not the
somnambulant, melancholy MEAL! La
la la. It is a sore distraction, Geraldine,
and a constant watch, but we watch in
good faith, praying Jesus and Mary
may shield us well. La, la, la. Do write
soon. Trust to the Gospel and beware*

the Enemy. Fuck ME! You are in my
prayers always. Ever yours, Rebecca.

Magnus was widemouthed. 'Crazy frigging story!'
he said. A chill was coming on. Harper replaced the
letter and clambered through the utility window. A
lot of starlings were going crazy in the orchard.
They wheeled around and flocked among the
apples. 'Big fucking song and dance.' Magnus
followed through the window, still carrying the
spaniel.

There was Jude, leaning on a trunk, munching a
nonchalant apple.

'A striking image,' said Harper.

'I've often said it' said Jude. 'Eating apples is all
about image. Look at Adam. It was all about
convincing the unborn generations. The Tree of
Knowledge was a set-up. The serpent: spin. The
whole Fall was a front, a publicity stunt, and the
Devil a particularly charismatic impresario-cum-PR
man, with an eye for a deal.'

Magnus flicked at the apple. 'How's it taste?'

'*Tart.*'

'And the apple?'

Jude took this in his stride. 'The *apple*,' he
demurred, 'is a mere *flirt*—all banter and *chit-
chat*—feigning all manner of richness and sin,
delivering only good clean fun. No, your apple is
the English girl of the orchard world. A rude

186

complexion, a cheerful smack and, at best, a sense of crisp competence.'

'Sin or no,' said a voice, 'them's int yer apples.'

A fattish figure stood on bandy legs in the long shadows at the orchard end. He had greasy swart hair, a pale complexion, a wrinkly priggish nose, and his eyes, could they have seen them, were blue. As it was they were nothing at all, swiped, as if by a robber's band. It was his mouth which impressed: a low, flat one, with plump lips protruding. It could pucker like Jude's, but it had width too; a frog's mouth, with the lope and sneer you'd expect. The mouth of Hole.

'*Weeell*,' said Jude, slow as he liked. 'You know what they say about *possession*.'

'An' what are you? Possessin', or possessed?'

'Yes.' Jude picked the peel from his teeth. 'We were speaking *specifically* of the Devil's aptitude for specious *brag*. You see, the *Devil*,' he said, settling in, munching his provocative apple, which he was pleased to see growing more provocative by the mouthful, 'is like *house-prices*: artificially inflated to create a credit-economy, encourage a favourable *business-climate*.'

'Opiate o' the masses?'

'No. No one actually believes in the Devil—or in house-prices. They just play along.'

'But people do credit it, dunt they—or the whole thing'd collapse. Market confidence, innit?'

187

'A euphemism, of course, for greed.' Jude bit neatly near the core.

'You're munchin' my apple a mite confidently there.' Hole took a step closer. One hand held an air-rifle. Transparent plastic gloves were stretched to his forearms.

'No, gallingly enough, I have to agree with Quentin: there is no such thing as confidence—only *skill.* Although of course, Quentin says that extremely unconfidently. You see, Quentin's is a complex credit-economy, based on over-confident assertions that there is no such thing as confidence. And then *bang!*—a wild cacophony, the wheels fly, money blindingly changes hands, trading on ludicrous assertions. It's all about keeping one step ahead.'

'You'd better keep a step ahead, friend: this Water Board land, now. See, I've 'eard tell of your prankin' about, strange hours, round the Pump House, over Hyde Island. You wouldn't want to earn a repertation for loit'rin' where you aren't wanted. I mean, we fergive those that trespass— once—but three strikes an' yer out, as they say in baseball.'

Hole stopped before them. 'Jude 'Arlow.'

'*Hole.*'

No smiles, nor shaken hands, but a wrinkled eye went between them, speaking respect of kinds—the mutual-respect of the prop-forward and the number-eight, near enough to lean on, far enough they don't have you by the balls.

'We know each other of old, dun' we. In the days when you's a mite bigger an' I a mite bulkier. What's 'appened to us, eh 'Arle?'

'*Ooh*, training-schemes, I'd hazard—management courses—a welter of *careers-advice*.'

'An' look where it got me—top of the fuggin' chain of command. No one wets their whistle round 'ere without my say-so, leastwise with water. Where are you, 'Arle?'

Jude squinted at the sun. 'Oh, on other people's property. Yes, it's becoming something of a *theme*. Breaking and entering, trespass with intent, the unwanted mowing of lawns. You name it. *Ha!* There's no knowing where it might end.'

Magnus broke a branch from a tree. He gazed downslope—to the struggling Meal. Harper was at the fence, facing the dialogue. He was watchful, approving Jude, keen not to join him.

Hole observed: 'Yer jest weren't appreciated, 'Arle.' He took out a lighter, flicking at the wheel.

'I wasn't wholly jesting. Which is not to say I was serious either. You see, what people don't realise is that there is a *vast* no-man's land, between seriousness and jest, in which virtually all conversation takes place. Hence the *penury* of *advice.*'

189

Magnus tossed his head. He looked cryptic, theatrical, pushing out the envelope. 'Of COURSE, there are truthful jests, aren't there? And a good many SERIOUS LIES.'

Hole considered him briefly, turning back to Jude. 'I got some advice for ya. Of the career kind too. Take a runnin' jump over that fence there an' try not to get stampeded. Them cows're fuggin' frisky at the moment—specially if I sets 'em rollin'.'

'We were just GOING,' said Magnus, half-turned, steel in the face. He prowled mechanically to the fence.

'See, we dunt take kindly to trespassers, truants, interlopers, an' the like. 'Specially ones wiv scythes an' hourglasses. An' fuckin' flamethrowers like these.' He wafted the lit lighter. It was Saint's lighter, the same flip-lid, same ornate scrollings. 'We're over-careful, p'raps,' leered Hole, 'account of the "incidents". Arson, break-ins, boat-stealin' snorkellers. You dunt know what's next.'

'YES, it's an ODD THING.' Magnus looked distracted. He gazed to the middle-distance, where a deer browsed in the copse. 'It rains all April, and May too, yet the water-levels fell. Then the Pump-House burns down. Then Coot Bridge. You'd almost think someone had it in for the reservoir.' He looked modestly at Hole like a belle coming out in society. For a moment he was all eyelashes. Then

190

he shrugged like the Barbarian his ancestors had been.

Hole stepped into the sun, but it didn't warm him. He looked like a mortuary. 'Crow, isn't it?—Ahah!' He slopped grins over Jude, like pails of milk. Jude smiled formally. 'Na, general wear-an'-tear,' he said casually. 'Course o' time. Nothin's built to last nowadays—in't that right, 'Arle? We're none o' us what we was. Cracked an' broke's the old lake. Progress o' time. A change's as good as a rest—in't that what they say?' He gazed on the flame.

'MUST BE.'

'You look like you need a change, Crow. Change o' scene. Time enough to rest when the night o' death cometh.'

'You're not WRONG.'

There was an impasse, while Hole examined the face of the lighter. The sun winked from the chrome. 'You know,' he said at last. 'Figures an' symbols, an' the like. They's a dangerous thing. Leaves things open to interpretation, dunnit? Walkin' round with hourglasses, strings o' time fallin' like it don't mean shit. A fuckin' hourglass. I mean, what's 'at about? Someone could take that the wrong way.' He prodded the flame with his finger.

Magnus shrugged. 'Then turn it round.'

'Yeh? I'd turn round self, 'f'I were you.' Hole clapped shut the lighter. With liquid hands, he tucked it in Jude's trouser pocket, tapped him on the chest. 'Funny in't it,' he gleamed, keeping eyes on Jude. 'How soon the 'ccused 'comes accuser.'

They clambered over the stones. The sun was sinking low. Emerging into the field Magnus saw the woman was gone from the caravan window. Harper was watching a deer springing along the downward slope, and the dog was watching it too. They spent a while by the river, where the sun had not touched the grasses. They were still dewy, even in evening. The bank was low, screened by trees, and the sunlight came through in patches, playing on the water. It was all very alluring but one thing held Harper. Was it the same snake? They were all generic after all.

They climbed through meadows to a ridge, on Helsen-Monger land, all too aware of the beauties of nature. The valley moved lusciously under their gazes. It looked like the Acherousian one Harper had crossed, in a bus one evening, toward a lonely village. Light fading: a green-metal strip on the ridges, lower levels swallowed in wet. He had looked at the guide book: *not what you would expect from the valley of the dead.* How wrong they were. Just what you'd expect and more. Mournful. The very fronds drooped with water. The road wound through the passes. Witness struggled with sleep. Harper propped up his eyes, watched patches of mist loiter on the hillsides, collect in smooth troughs. He stood out on the village road, as if mentioned by night. He was still, looking round at mountains, while the bus drove on to the coast. He spent two days there, roaming, under suspicion of the police. He came to the same conclusion as the guidebook: the Acheron was a warm green river; the Acherousian lake was a frog-infested pond, drying in the sun. He crossed a cracked football pitch, baptised himself in the river of Lamentation, got the hell out of there. The sky was a guillotine. A red parabola bent upward, carrying a head in its lap. The sun went down, borne in its own arms.

4. Mime

It was still early. Magnus was a speck at the remote end of the long dam wall. Behind, the sun climbed from earth, pinning him to camera, as if camera were King. Or perhaps it was the reverse: the camera pinned Magnus to the sun—a solar King. This was easily done: the two were confused. Magnus did not mind being the sun's pin. He set his life at exactly that fee.

Behind the camera, Harper made just this observation. Jude was silent. He merely smelled tar and mingled water, measuring the time. At some unspecified, yet *given*, moment, Harper would give him the cue—an imposition, but one Jude was prepared to countenance—and he would take precarious position on the wall. To be precise, on the third pedestal from the Outlet Tower, thirty feet above the amphitheatre. Above the amphitheatre, the wall was punctuated by railings jammed between pedestals. There were four pedestals, and three railings ran between them. Each pedestal was three feet wide. Harper's grand plan was to cram both himself and Jude onto one of these outcrops, kibe-to-toe—where a tilt to the left would mean a scuffle with the road, while a tilt to the right, certain disjointure of spine. Then Magnus would join them, kibe-to-toe-to-toe.

'Toe be or not toe be?' Jude wondered. He flapped his cloak.

'You best toe the line.'

'That's what I call toe-faced.'

Harper put his eye to the lens. 'It's toe late for all this.'

There was a mournful silence, marked by Harper's lowered arm. Barely perceptibly, the pin began to walk. To look at its upright line you'd not have known it. It looked more like the sun was pushing it aside, inviting defeat. It was one of those rare acts of self-negation; powerful, demonstrative, like a martyr's. The sun dared the lens to mate. The lens was nonplussed. All it saw was sixty-four checks.

With breathless slowness, as if by conveyor-belt, Magnus moved to right of shot. The camera willed his progress, reluctant to finish it. It inched to open spaces so that Magnus collided with the left-frame. Again he drifted. The pulse of the sun departed him, and lank limbs made their appearance like gophers from the holes. The camera framed it, double-slow. It was enjoying the torture.

Harper took a breather, watched with the naked eye. He wouldn't hit the right-hand frame for a while yet; maybe he never would. Somehow the ropes had slipped through Harper's hands. The pin was a law unto itself.

'Who's directing whom?' he asked.

'Doomed for a *certain term*,' said Jude, 'and enjoying every second.'

'Too fast in fires.'

They laughed, but there was no doubting it: Magnus was president. He could outwait all of them, even Benjamin McCormack Kepperly-Lie, casting his line from a peninsula. The Lie was used to long-waiting, but Magnus' intensity baffled him, causing him to change the angle of tackle. The Lie was a master in changing angles—of attack and tackle both, as it suited him. He had strolled out over an isthmus, unassuming as you like. 'No wardens today,' he said. '—They've got bigger fish to fry.' He made a casting gesture. 'Get a spot of anglin'' in. Haff-haff-ohono.' He looked at Jude and Harper in turn.

Like a crow gaining the nest, Harper resumed the eyepiece. The King had hardly moved. He seemed to have been coming down that wall all morning. He was still just a lash, on the pencil-line of the wall. At length Harper discerned a blur about the head, escaping into radiance. The air round it was smokey. The sun, balanced on the hill to Backward Mass, beat the sheeted stone, summoned dust, like fowl from the bushes. The head was the bush, burning and bewigged, exemplifying vagueness.

Who's there? murmured Harper, rehearsing his line. With it, like a silver fish, came the course of the day so far. *Who's there?* He spoke it in the spillway, in the blue dark dawn. The words rang on the stanchions. *Who?* They clambered up metal, pattered on amphitheatre steps, to the mouth of the arch. *Who, who,* spoke the concrete, all crack-throated. Looking into the gloom, for a moment Harper suffered the swoop of the void. He closed his eyes, opened them on blanks. It was waking up, not knowing where. The spillway drove through to the Pump House. Little by little he saw substance, lines, gradations. Weeds in the clefts caught his eye.

Turning about, he was amazed by the dawn, ranged like a posse round the gods. It blazed in ambush, barrels primed and trembling. Until he saw darkness, Harper had thought it dark. Plainly it was light though, bright like sepia. Like a man with two faces he looked both ways. He didn't know if he was coming or going.

A shot came up the spillway. It had two tones: a high quick *crack* and a dull boom. Over the lake, geese flew from the fields, formed a *V*, migrated all at once. Harper turned full circle, shocked by the shot, upborne by the birds. If they had drawn a great bell to sound the dawn, he could not have been more stunned. He stared skyward till the flock dissociated. Dark knocked at the door; shades from

197

steps fed in. He tripped up those shades, through a dead audience, and taped a cross to the top step. Here they would film the play-within-the-play. Here he would catch the King. Here, when the lake came back and tumbled through the theatre, he would cease to saw the air and lie in Ophelia's overflowing lap.

Not for a while though. The steps terminated in the hard mud of the reservoir bed. Twenty yards away the water held position: unconscious castaway. Harper peered, as if to see beneath. The lake was mercurial, reconciling poles of dark and light, optimum medium for the dawn. But it didn't do to look too long. Bjørn Bjørnsen had a theory about the senses: each person had a dominant one, like a zodiacal sign. Bjørn thought Harper was ruled by taste, but Harper knew it was sight. To smash the glass of the eye was his great task. He needed to become a toucher like Magnus; a listener, like the Lie; a taster—like Jude.

'In the broadest sense.'

Jude cogitated. He was standing in the Gods, a solitary God, benighted, outnumbered by devils. Feet were wet and spread; cloak was stuck to him. Between thumb and forefinger was a single scythe. 'Yes. Form is temporary; taste—is *permanent*.'

'Fran Peters' anyway.'

'All I remember is the fruit and fibre.'

'One judges by the fruits.'

198

'No, not judgement—just *deserts*. This is what Magnus, for all his crampons, fails to grasp—what the *world* fails to grasp, plummeting through the orchards of *experience*, snatching twigs and wands of intellect: that, like a *fortuitous current of air*, simple taste might save. *Ironically*,' stressed Jude, as if irony undid itself, 'this is what your *connoisseur* can't swallow. He cannot conceive that taste confounds *profession*—confusing taste with power, cannot deal with indifference, has the gall to call it *abstinence*.'

'When any real abstinence turns disgusted from itself.'

Jude scuffed precisely at a weed. 'Well this is what we've long been—*silently*—expounding,' he said. 'I don't think people realise—don't think they could *fathom*—our disgust.' He chewed awhile. '—Which is not to say it is *unfathomable*. On the contrary, it is wholly superficial. There *is* no grand extrapolation of—juvenile exploration *into*—such relentlessly *aesthetic* premises.'

Harper looked at the lake. 'Just a bitter bottom—flat and ashen.'

'Crumbs. Fran Peters again.'

'An aesthetic premise if ever I saw one.'

'Because,' insisted Jude, 'they will insist on *scoping it out*. Presuming—and it is a *vast* presumption, sir—that *behind* such premises lurks a desperate instability. Whereas the desperation is

199

entirely tenable. You see, this is what they fail to grasp about despair. It is by its nature *entirely tenable*. It is behind nothing at all, threatening nothing. Anything else is not despair.'

He executed a slide rule pass.

'*Presuming,*' he continued, 'that behind such premises, something as paltry as *motive* is lurking. When, fools! we just couldn't find the food we liked!'

Sideways-on he half-closed eyes. It was dark in the kitchen of *The Yew-Lawn*. Windows looked west into night, where the wan moon was a face at the feast. East of the windows was a more distinct supervision: bowls, cookbooks, cutlery—all looked to the clock. Taps, spoons, scales and their bronze weights, steady under its aegis. There was a contentment to the room.

The hand touched the hour. Four o' clock. Perched on a stool, Jude munched rhythmic with the strokes. Perched in his hand was a cereal-bowl. On the next stool was a blue cat, with combustible purr. Otherwise was a stone silence.

On the surface: *The Evening Chronicle*: *Water Board Win Weapons Appeal* it read. *Watchmen granted powers of arrest*. It was about the protection of national resources. Following recent cases of reservoir sabotage, in Toxteth, Liverpool, and here in the Glum Valley, more stringent measures were ensuring security, cracking down on crime. And more measures were suggested. There was even a call for an inquiry. All national resources should be subject to a security review. Power stations, mines, railways, arable land, all were easy targets, it was claimed—for terrorists, anarchists, masochists, you name it—and the more defunct, the easier the target. Some said this was paranoia. It was hard to say where national resources stopped and started. Terror was a national resource too. Others said the critics were complacent. They were refusing to accept the seriousness of the situation.

Jude shifted on his stool, refusing to accept the seriousness of the situation, on the condition that this was the most serious situation of all. A snore came from the floors above. Jude scorned the snore, last resort of the defeated. A defeat one felt one's own presence occasioned. Jude spooned in an agglomerate of corn and rice. His lips formed a *phalanx* and the cheeks withdrew.

'Crumbs. Sarah Kent,' said Harper.

'She can form a *phalanx* any time she likes.'

He replaced the bowl, squeezed the cat's neck-folds, pattered over stones to the front hall, pausing on his way to consider two wall-hangings. A framed door-frame and a photograph of Piers. He eyed them with a kind of sentimental certitude. In the hall, he took two socks from his *all-stars*. He put them on. He put on the *all-stars*. Hanging on hooks was a cloak and he slung that round. He dug the old skull mask from the cupboard, took the scythe from the corner. No one had questioned its presence there. Questioning, as a rule, was not done at the Harlow's—not unless entirely apposite. He gripped it, tested it in palms, touched the door-handle.

The doorway was small. Jude fitted perfectly. He looked from the stepstone, as if shoreward, then waded from the confused generations. The air was a curtain, drawn by cords of sweat. On the eastern sky was a hard line, blue as a playing card.

Now he hit the road, placing one foot before the other. The rubber gave just enough. A tester—a taster—he was, testing steps, tar, the swing of scythe, as if his touch were returning. The road fell away, and visibility with it. Things hung on the borders. Stonewalls hung from gardens, snails from stonewalls. The flowers hung too, ideal and intelligent, looking like candle-extinguishers. Earth needed night, and her minions conspired to keep it. If lights hit the scene, the ground damped them, road drew them in. Jude was drawn in, from auburn in the moon to grey in the shade. It was just the beginning—slowest, most ordinary, of stages. Nothing actually happened, but everything had potential. Blades, bushes, boulders, were passed and noted. Grass trimmed the gaze. Soon he hit the bottom, spurned the church, the cross, the house of

Harriet Morris. He lit a right, hung a left, slipped over fields like a star. The moon was like the lake, pulling and letting go.

'Harriet Morris.'

He took a stile, had a gap, did a hedge like you'd do a defender. Then he was on the Bullish path and the lake lapped closely. Bullish reservoir was not suffering like Glum. There was the Glum sinking shameful to the ground; here was Bullish lathering the banks. Jude had business by Glum though: Harper and his theatre *sans* audience, which Jude would believe when he saw. Notwithstanding, Horatio could not be taken lightly. Jude had determined Horatio would be dressed as *The Grim Reaper*, not because he was *The Grim Reaper*, or even thought he was, but because he was attending the Elsinore fancy-dress party. Which would explain why Gertrude was annoyed by Hamlet's gear. If Harper didn't like it, that was unfortunate, but what could be done? Horatio had a life to live. He couldn't consider Harper's feelings every time he did anything. Jude swelled at the thought of it. Sweat stood out, nerves weighed heavy; nothing moved but the birds. Here a cluck; there a chatter. Warblers woke in the reeds. Sand-martins scattered like arrows. Ducks slept on the banks and eyed him. 'Funny,' thought Jude, 'they do two things.' The air pressed feathers, warm as tongues. Sleep seamed the eyes. What was Jude? Nothing. An addendum in the minutes of night.

He rounded the bends, skirting south and east, intent on the fields and backroads. The main road to the Glum, over *so-called* Coot Bridge, would be watched, which Jude took as strong affront. Besides, that road was a barren waste—with that worst of hills, the imperceptible incline—and Jude took this as a strong affront too. Jude distrusted an incline. Inclining this way, inclining that: inclines needed to make up their mind—and so did slight gradients. No no, it was Bullish to Sack, Sack to Meal, preferable by far. Give him the peaks and troughs of the Stubblow roads. The highs and lows as well.

Laughing low, he reached the lake's extremity, turned north, near the Stubblow road. It was a fisherman's path, permit-only, pedestrians banned by order of the Board, whose threats and expansion signs dotted the fences. West was all gaping: willows in wetlands; and the moon, a pale chrysanthemum. But east was different. East was hemmed with hedges, and a blue line burned. Proud-borne, high-handed, the scythe reflected both. Here the moon, there the line. Jude looked up, as to a scutcheon. A scythe, a moon, a line: he liked it. It represented him well. He clacked its handle on the tar. Over his dead body would they prise it. From his cold, dead hands.

A beat hit the water. It was geese, pulling like electrons from the nucleus, gone for good. The scythe blessed their flight. It was on permanent loan from Farmer Chile. Permanent, that was, because they would forget all about it. Even if they didn't, Jude could just deny all knowledge of it, and that would be good enough for them. Even if they took it back, there was nothing to stop Jude just walking into their house and requisitioning it, not even Mrs Chile in her nightgown. She would positively encourage it. That, after all, is what he had done yesterday. Chile and family were not to be found. Jude had walked straight through the back-door, reclaimed the instrument from the parlour, sallied through the same back-door, prepared for anything. He had been quiet that evening. He had stayed up all night, reading silent biographies. Chaplin, Rasputin, Mata Hari. One of these was the odd one out; Jude had been wondering who. Certainly the latter two had points in common. Both advocated liberal sexual relations, both exploited the bug-eyed orientalism of fin-de-siecle Europe, and both fell foul of British Intelligence. It was hard to think the three were not connected, especially as British Intelligence consisted chiefly of one-legged curb-crawling anti-Semites. Chaplin, on the other hand, fell foul of American Intelligence: an altogether harder thing to do. Interestingly, his star ascended at the same time the other two stars went out. That

205

couldn't be a coincidence either. It turned out Chaplin's birthday was four days before Hitler's— although four days was a long time in the calendar year: Jude's, after all, was the same day exactly. But in many ways their careers followed similar trajectories. Both were masters of slapstick, both benefited from a vast propaganda apparatus, and both fell into a slough of everlasting pathos, which they unerringly translated into glittering political vision. One sensed Rasputin and Mata Hari would have been a little embarrassed by taking things to such a logical extreme; would have skulked off into expensive furs, exotic dances, and other occultist trickery. Jude gazed on the blade. No, no, there was something vile about Chaplin; something soft and rotten. He could keep his four days' distance. As for Harper, he was born the day Rasputin's daughter died. He'd just have to run with it. You play with the hand you're dealt.

Suddenly on the blue line a blue pulse started, seeming to touch his heart. *From his cold, dead hands.* Bluecoats welled in the dark. It was a watch-party at a gate, commanding both path and road. Three men were smoking in the warmth. The bigger leant on the gate, looking lakeward. The others stood by a van, blue light rotating on the roof. You could see the fireflies of butts, hear the hum of voices.

It was the Water Board.

The options were few and Jude was between them. They would stop him. They wouldn't like his gear. Even if he stowed the gear, they would send him back, perhaps charge him with trespass. He could walk back and take the main road to Meal, but it might be the same story there. And going back was not only defeatist, it was tedious. There was nothing for it but to pass unnoticed.

To one of less logical extremes, this might have been tricky. Jude hardly broke stride, wading through reedbeds, illegally disturbing grebes. He chuckled as the mud sank beneath him. He was still chuckling—he was chuckling even more—when the water closed above his five feet and eight, leaving only a blade. The patrolman peered, thought he saw a scythe. No, it was a silver fish. It bounced through the gloom and was hid by willows.

But behind the willows it rose again, emblem of survival; and beneath it came Jude, slapping his way from weed. An entirely successful venture. If the water chilled, the walk would warm him. He crossed to the lake's north side, sheltered by trees, and headed where the path hit the road. Jude hit it too, with a quiet gusto. The men were out of sight. It would be safe enough to Stubblow. There was nothing really to guard—just a pile of farms.

Not that Nemmins knew that. *Fourpoints* was the first farm on the left, and the hatches were battened.

SAY NO TO BULLISH EXPANSION said a sign. Jude took out a permanent marker he happened to have in his cloak-pocket, turned the *B* to an *F*, added two horizontal lines to the second *L*, crossed out the *EX*, wrested the second *A* to an *E* and added an *S*. He chuckled, with reservations. Jude had no idea why the farm was called *Fourpoints*; it could only see south and west, across the lakeland. Eastwards was a slope, with copse and hedges. Northward was Stubblow Hill, suddenly ascending. As hemmed a farm as you'd find. Perhaps it was because it could be *seen* from four points, which was almost as good. In any case, Nemmins' old man had holed up, seemed to be preparing for the worst. A law unto himself, they said, and ratified by dogs. Three dogs, to be exact. They chewed Grant Hatchard's foot so badly he took to wearing steelcaps; same steelcaps that kicked a man to pulp in a public toilet on the suspicion of being queer. Grant Hatchard was tried for *GBH*, but got off on a technicality. Not that it mattered; soon after he stuck his head from a stolen car, the car entered a tunnel and Hatchard was decapitated. That was the end of Grant Hatchard. It turned out the man wasn't queer anyway. Not that it mattered.

Jude ploughed up the ruts, pivoting scythe in potholes. *Slip-slap* went the *all-stars*; hems dripped continuous; sweats made tribute to the flapping deltas. It was an unpleasant confluence. Jude

sought his body amidst the fluid. There it was: real
wheels under the bells and whistles. A man could
get tired of his body—the gut in particular—but a
man could turn to it too, as to a rock in a chaos of
waters. A body was stupidly consistent, never more
so than when it failed. You knew where you stood
with a body. He knocked his chest as if petitioning
entry. But he didn't want entry; he just liked the
sound. It was a dull thud, pointlessly repeating the
work of heart, but it woke Jude to his whereabouts:
short of the drive to *Fourpoints*. Just in time too,
for only then he heard the van a bend behind. No
time to run. No time even for ambivalence. Either
side—high hedges. Cursing the Enclosures Act,
Jude jumped to his right, hit a ditch and scudded to
the bottom where a hundred skinny stems closed
round him.

The van came to a halt up the road. There was a
slam of doors, a whine of dog. Two voices spoke
over the engine.

'Cheers then, drive,' said one. He sounded quiet.

'No problem. You should get yerself a licence,'
said the other. It was a deep voice, sonorous.

'Drivin' or fishin'?'

'Fuck me. Both, if you're for more of these tricks.
Trust me, I don't need the bother. Fuckin' creepin'
round churches. 'Ckin' coverin' your arse while
you're larkin' on the lake. I swear, I'm coverin'
nothing if 'Ole 'ears of it.'

209

''Ow's 'Ole gon' hear of it, Mo?'

'Hark at Nems, gettin' interrogatory.' There was a softness in the voice. Even the grass was calmed. 'I'm jus' sayin'.'

'We jus' tell 'im it was a quiet night, Nems was doin' a spot of fishin'.'

'Nems who can't swim. Who hates the water. Lawfearin' Nems. With a stolen boat. When he should be guardin' our national resources.'

'Tell 'im I got hungry.'

'Yeah, that's plausible. What about Meal Common church? Got a rush of penitence?'

In the next field cows were browsing. You could hear them brush the bushes. Jude was hoping they wouldn't brush right through them. That was the thing about cows. Approximation. Whenever you looked at them, they were a step or two nearer than they were before.

'Maybe. But he int gon' ask, is 'ee, Mo? An' if 'ee does, hee, Alligator an' 'is cronies only gone given us the perfect alibi. Best thing I did, ferget my fuggin' keys. Hee! We come back, and there's them Snorkel-Faces, stealing that boat! What I call perfect fuggin' timin'.'

'That's two months ago now.'

'Crime's a crime, int it.'

'Why didn't you report it then? What have you got on them anyway? Prancin' on the tower? "Messin' about in boats"? Big fuckin' wow.'

210

'Break-in, an't we, Moore? Breakin' and fuggin' ent'rin'. Fuggin' Hyde Island. Couldn't been me, could it? Only a thin man's climbin' through that window!'

'So you keep sayin'.'

'Evidence stacks up, dunnit.'

'If you say so.'

'Aaah. Fuggin' stitched 'em up there. Fuggin' pinned 'em to that one! Hee. What I call two birds wiv one fuggin' stone!'

'What's the other bird then? Forget it, I don't wanna know.' There was the repeated chafing of a lighter. 'Sure you switched off them cameras?'

'Told ya. Changed the time on 'em, an' all.'

'Yeh, I didn't understand that bit.'

'I jus' rewound the clock half an hour, so's if they was never off.'

'Int someone gonna notice they're half an hour behind?'

'Wound 'em forward at the end of the night, see. You'd 'ave to watch the tape ta the end of the night ta find the error. What trig's gon' do that?'

'What if they fast-forward it?'

'Won't notice, then, will they, 'cos they'll skip an hour jus' fastin'-forward.'

'Don't get that, Nems. Work that out in the Shippey Shed, did you?' There was something like a sigh. Then Moore continued. 'I dunno, Nems.

211

Sounds fuckin' remedial to me. What about the church?'

'What about it?'

'Cameras?'

'No. Not yet anyway. 'Sides, I dunt break in. Got a key an't I? Inside information.'

'I don't want to know, Nems. Seriously, I don't want to know. Get yerself all the fuckin' licences you please, and leave me out of it.'

'Reckon I won't need either fer a while. Other kind o' licence we'se gettin' now.' There was a slap on palm, then a *whang* and a laugh. 'Fuggin' toolin' up!'

'Watch that bonnet, mate.'

There was a pause. The jollity ceased. 'Serious now,' said the first. 'Got priviges, an't we? Got rights. Rights to bear weapons. Rights ta fuggin' use 'em an' all.'

'Sound like your Dad.'

'Fuggin' mandates.'

'How's 'Ole likin' you, with your Dad opposin' 'im?'

'Can't blame me, can 'ee! Int my fault Pa's stubborn as fug.'

Another pause. ''Ee'll need to be. 'Cause this place is marked down. 'Ole's got its number.'

The first said nothing. When he spoke it was sullen. 'Int gonna happen.'

'If the Glum has flaws, it's a root and branch job.'

'Them's rumours, Mo.'

Three feet from Jude's head, a badger emerged from a hole. It was a large hole, larger than your average badger. Unperturbed, your average badger shuffled over the narrow acreage, into the line of trees.

'Ev'rythings rumours, Nems. Either way, you've got a bit of time yet. It'll take more t' expand Bullish than a tractor an' a stick o' dynamite. Lot of obstacles still to negotiate.'

'A three hundred an' fuggin' fifty year deed, fer one. Services rendered—to the kingly fuggin' crown.'

'Got a lot of faith in that, 'aven't you? Not that it's kept yer old man from riggin' a fuckin' barracks here—'ckin' barb-wire everywhere—or's that fer cuttin' cheese?' The voice quickened. 'Don't you fuckin' dare.'

A fart broke like a flock of geese. Barking started in the house.

'Hee-hee, ask a fuckin' question.'

'Grim.'

'Been waitin' all night fer that. *Beans* waitin' all night, hah-hah.'

'That's my cue, Orson. Best get in, 'fore you touch that alarm off.'

'Can't stop a fella on a roll,' said Nems, growing in bravado. Then for no apparent reason, 'Aaaahh! 'Ole!'

213

'Shut it, Orse, you'll bring up the patrol.'

'*Bloater*,' said Nemmins, becalmed.

'You're the fuckin' bloater.'

'*Moby Dick!*'

'Fuckin' right.' A door opened and shut. 'Bigger 'an you'll ever be.' The engine revved and was gone up the road.

Jude lay quiet as hay. All this was interesting. Nemmins and Moore. One of the innumerable advantages he had over such as these—certainly Nemmins—was a serviceable memory. He remembered them well. Nemmins would know him dimly or not at all. The intervention of a few trumped-up *years* had sanctioned the shuffle of his mortal remembrance. Jude could see it now. Nemmins would blink at him, piggily, forgetting to remember to forget. 'Harpo,' he would start, and 'Jully'. He would sweat, he would suffer. He would become enraged. All this was to Jude's advantage. Moore he couldn't be sure of. But Moore was gone.

He waited a minute, listening. Barking grew clear then occasional. A door was shut. He watched a rabbit hop blithely from the nearby hole. 'Such a thoroughfare,' he thought. At the risk of granting Magnus and his methods a credit they scarcely warranted, that hole seemed worth a scope. Not now though. When all was still Jude extrapolated himself from the hedge, like a crab backing out of a transaction. Again he stood in the road. A light

214

came on in the house, and the gate was open. Absent-minded, he wandered to the threshold.

'Scoping, eh?' Harper spoke from the side of his mouth.

'I forgot more than you'll ever know about *scoping*. I just don't turn it to a *rite of passage*.' Jude hated a rite of passage. *Right* of passage, on the other hand, was an entirely different thing, and he exercised it now, stepping smack on the middle of the drive. It was a ribbed-cement drive, sand-coloured. Barbed-wire was heaped in the yard. Butane canisters stood under corrugated iron—two hundred or more. Makeshift stables housed compost-packets, piled to the roofs. To the left was a grey breeze-block barn, like a gas-chamber. Jude's perfect nose smelled chemicals. It flared and turned away, to the middle of the yard. He had seen enough. Old man Nemmins was entrenching himself—that was evident. That he was a sociopath was neither here nor there.

Turning east Jude retraced his steps. The horizon line was running. The cement pressed his soles and they ceased squeaking. Even the dogs were quiet.

Suddenly headlights hit him. For a moment he stood there, examining himself: cloak, scythe and *all-stars*, all of them either clinging or clung. A van door opened and the words *Water Board* swung into view. A man swaggered like a Bridge to the bonnet, nauseated but confident.

'Well well,' he menaced. 'The Grim fuckin'
Reaper.' He was a pig of a man: chop-faced, pug-
nosed, fat at the gut with slits. A big red package,
splitting a headlight.

Jude pressed the scythe in his womanly palms. He
slipped on the mask, as one might a pair of glasses.
A voice broke from it, reedy and pleading.

'*A piece of him.*'

'Too late fer that. I seen ya.' Walsh eased onto the
bonnet. 'Seen ya a couple of months ago an' all,
trespassin' by the lake. I mean, you don't ferget a
face like that.'

'*Tis but your fantasy.*'

'Your worst nightmare, mate, which's wet
yerself, by the look of it.'

'*IT HAAAARRRROOOWS ME WITH FEAR!*'
screeched *The Grim Reaper*. A tongue juddered in
the mouthhole.

'—the fuck—.' Walsh had seen a lot, but this
disgusted him. He went round the door and
sounded the horn. 'NEMS!' he roared. 'YOU'LL
WANT TO SEE THIS! CARNIVAL'S IN
TOWN!' Barking started in the house, and another
light went on. 'You got 'bout thirty seconds, I'd
say, 'fore the dogs arrive. You'll be a piece of
somethin' then.'

But *The Grim Reaper* was too far gone to
backtrack. As far as he was concerned, the point at
which one had gone *far too far* was *exactly* the

point at which one should go *much, much further*. Success lay in self-conviction. Fortunately for *The Grim Reaper*, he was very self-convincing. He cramped himself up, protruded his jaw, shimmered masked eyes. '*So frowned he once—*' he began, slow-building. *The Grim Reaper* had perfect teeth, and he flashed them now. '*When in an aaangry paaarle—*' he menaced, '*HE SMOTE THE SLEDDED POLACKS ON THE ICE!*' He swung the frightening scythe.

'Freak,' said Walsh softly, unbuttoning his baton. He really wanted to attack *The Grim Reaper*. Nevertheless, he respected a scythe. He eased toward the bonnet, hands upturned as if playing a party trick. One held the baton. 'Fuck do you think this is?'

'*Some strange—eruption!*'

'Will be when Nems gets 'ere. Huh, fuckin' sure o' that.'

'*A most emmmulate pride.*'

Walsh cocked his tongue, nodded, weighing mask, eyes, scythe. Was this madness or strategy? Did it matter? At a certain point emulation became so self-convincing it had to be dealt with purely in its effects. He smiled at the baton, let it dangle.

'Nems don't take to intruders, see. Bit jitt'ry they are 'ere, 'bout their property rights.'

'*A seeeealed compact—law and herrraldry,*'

217

'You know about that? Wildfire, innit!' More barking. Then a shout, a hush. A rattle in a door. Walsh smacked the baton absently on his thigh. He seemed in two minds. 'Yeah, well, seal's the word. This'll be sealed all over, twelve months from now. Sealed as the sea. Mark it. Gon' fuck Fourpoints good an proper.'

'*If it will not stand.*'

'Nothin' stands on the sea, mate.'

The Grim Reaper inhaled. '*Sea—fire—earth—air—*' he savoured.

'Elementary, eh? NEMS! TAKE A LOOK AT THIS! REAL FUCKIN' FANCY DRESS AFFAIR!' And there was Nemmins, blotting into view, at the crux of a forked leash.

The Grim Reaper looked to the east, he looked to the west. The blue line was a red blur. Birds shook the lake, as if the night itself. Then, '*LOOK, THE MORN!*' he shrilled, and he pointed wildly. '*IN RUSSET MANTLE CLAD!*'

''OO'S THERE?'

East was streaming sun but the west was thundery. The Pump House hedge was metal-fenced. Jude leant on it, stared at Magnus. He was still miles away, moving at his leisure. However much he moved, he remained there: a melancholy burden. Who could understand him? Some grand scaffold he was building, some mock martyrdom: appropriating Harper's play, isolating himself for

218

the good of all. Way out on that wall he was girding loins, walking to oblivion. What was Jude supposed to feel—grateful?

'A Man of Sorrows,' he murmured in answer.

Harper, whose eye was squashed to the eyepiece, released the pressure, turned to look at his friend. This was devout, he was thinking. He put his mouth to the microphone for the voiceover:

Marcellus [*sotto*]:
Why does this strict and observant watch
So nightly toil the subject of the land?
And why such daily cast of brazen cannon
And foreign mart for implements of war?
What might be toward that this sweaty haste
Does make the night joint-labourer with the
day?

It was humid. Brows were glistening. They were still watching Magnus, one through camera lens, one through contacts. He was a world away, raising a camel-leg. He didn't look like a man snatching at straws. The wall was a swung switch, lithe and punitive. It buzzed, as if merging with the air. Above were warped rays, like the lines of motion. Magnus was extreme. He went to lengths. But Jude was right; it was all extension of intellect. Magnus was couched power, a sprung threat. Taste had little

219

to do with it. Sooner or later, he would compel you to act.

'LOOK WHAT I SEEN SNOOPIN' IN THE DRIVE.'

'THEN 'E'S SNOOPED 'IS LAST. *Girls!*' The dogs growled low. 'FETCH 'IM IN!'

The Grim Reaper jerked this way and that, looking furiously from eyeholes. As usual, his options were few. A house was an intolerable burden, butane a bad influence, and compost would only slow him down. The dogs were halfway down the drive. They looked like inchoate worlds. *The Grim Reaper* ran for a doorway in the barn-corner, with their morbid clicking at his heels. He gained the barn, pressed to the wall and readied. The barn was dark. All he saw was doorway, all he heard was throats. He thought of earthy tunnels, rock and drip-ridden. The tunnels expanded, leapt ravenous from the light. And as they froze, half through the uprights, their hearts were exposed by a flourish of scythe.

Mouths closed, whimpers left on lips—'as if they wanted the shame to outlive them,' said Jude. He stared down. All he could see was the sheen of eyes. He had never killed anything, never fried spiders, torn the wings off insects. He left that to Saint and his geeks. *The Grim Reaper* admired the spider, the hard red ant, their industry, their single-minds. He admired a certain scuttle. Like an ant

220

now, he scuttled for the middle, where the grey doorway light was almost lost.

The middle was cold and dry. Bags of gravel, by the seeming. Pipe and hose, and rows of insulation. The floor was square-paved, part-sheeted in plastic. There were ranks of metal shelves, tanks on bricks, the smell of disinfectant. Slung along the middle ranks of shelving were a handful of light-bulbs, which the scythe soon brought to the ground. Big freezers stood oddly at intervals, hooked hold of with wires. They shuddered like they were the cold ones. It was a storage facility, dead as stars.

Voices from without: '—Thought I saw a 'loper,' Walsh was saying. 'At the lake.'

'Too right's a fuggin' 'loper.'

'Your gate's open. Thought you were jitt'ry 'bout that.'

'Had ta check the kine 'fore breakfast. We've a calf's been poorly. 'Loper's fuggin' lucky 'Ole's got my rifle. Still—' There was a *whang*. 'This should pique 'ee.'

Two figures hove in the doorway. The rounder spoke. 'Where's them dogs?' it said. 'Moll! Nell! Get 'ere!' Its head turned against the light, quieter now. 'Heh, feastin' I reckon.' Some moments passed. There was the futile, repeated clicking of a light switch. Suddenly the figure jigged like a balloon.

'—WHAT YOU DONE WITH MY DOGS?' It blew and cried and knelt in the dark. 'WHAT THE CRUD YOU DONE? FUGGIN' MOLL!' It was working with its mouth, feeling for pulses, wrinkling eyes like oysters.

'YOU'LL PAY FOR THAT, FRIEND,' said the other, with the voice of instruction. There was a silence. 'NEMS GOT FRIENDS TO 'VENGE 'IM.' The words were echoless. 'WON'T WEAR YOUR SHOES FOR RANSOMS.'

The Grim Reaper watched them in the aisles— two rolling silhouettes. A barricade of light-bulb boxes was his refuge. He hardly dared breathe. When he did, he did as through a straw, narrowly. Broad breaths made the mask a furnace.

'Nems, let's listen. Let's jus' listen.'

They stood between freezers. With a heave of chest, Nemmins stopped wheezing. Eyes blinked left and right. There was a far lowing from the fields.

'Only one way out, int there? We'll flush 'im. We'll *listen*.'

'Fuggin' flush 'im right.'

Walsh took the door and Nemmins stayed. His eyes were sand in hourglasses. *The Grim Reaper* was watching too, but the mask contained him: he could only see in straight lines. Right were cans and planks; left, tanks and shelving, full of polystyrene boxes. Beneath were the bulbs and electrical tape

222

and you couldn't move for squeaks. Above was his only refuge.

He tilted his chin, looked straight up. From the top of a barn hung hams and carcasses: packed pigs, trussed cows stared from the girders. Fish loomed on him. Trout and pike in rows. Beady eyes reflected his face.

'I didn't know Sarah Kent was around.'

'She can hang her hams any time she likes.'

Circling his head he saw lumpen masses, hooves and heads gleaming on the outlines. The roof was full of them, low like thunder: five hundred square feet or more of meat. Someone had been having fun in the fields. Was that smell formaldehyde? Maybe the old man was an artist. Jude tilted the mask till it cupped his crown. He stared in cold anger.

Nemmins was staring too, all around, up and down, and back at the dogs as well. He was frightened. He wasn't like Hole, a *listener*. He was a *watcher*. He had been watching all night, on the reservoir paths, in the forests, at the shores; from the Outlet Tower, Boat House, top of Coal Hill. Nemmins was a watcher—and good at it too. They don't invest you with posts like those unless you're up to it. But he didn't fancy this listening lark. Not that you heard them much at all, nowadays, what with the rise of the magpie. Then again, what would Nems know? he was a night-owl now. Ten till seven, that's a long shift. Just one little task to do, while his time was unaccounted for. But that was between him and Moore. Then it was lifts home, sleep to catch up on. The sails had gone right out of him.

Walsh's voice lilted on the plastics. 'Easy Nems. Stay on the case.'

'Kill my dogs—'

'An' he'll pay for 'un.'

'Can't 'ear fer 'ummin'.'

'Easy.' Walsh leant in the frame. Nothing moved except eyes.

It was an old trick. Jude tossed a lightbulb three aisles down and the *smash* lit touch papers. Walsh jumped up. Nemmins shook. 'KILL MY FUGGIN' DOGS!' he bellowed and came barging through freezers, between shelving, jabbing at boxes with a pitchfork. Light as antelope, Jude stepped between tanks. Another bulb made a perfect parabola and hit the next aisle's pavings. Nemmins made a sharp left and right, crying 'CREEP IN THE GRASS!' He shoved a hosepipe, elbowed a box of screws. They shimmered on the floor. The fork turned left and right. 'HOLD IT NEMS, WE'LL SMOKE 'IM!' yelled Walsh, but it was too late. Poised on the pedestal, tank at his chest, Jude smote exactly a fat sow's strings. She fell like an omen on Nemmins' forehead. Another swing and a gallant calf came down in a pile of legs. A couple of pike slapped against the pile, adding insult to injury.

224

Jude stood down, breathing and sweating, resenting the beast he'd become. The mask fell over his face. Before he could remove it, Walsh came pounding down the aisle, baton poised, lips gripped and seeping: 'know what they say, though. No smoke is there? No fuckin' smoke is there? NONE WITHOUT FIRE!' And he rushed on *The Grim Reaper* with the tight limbs of a man whose bulk overcomes the neuroses it creates.

But *The Grim Reaper* was cold as killing could make him. Walsh ducked the scythe, but hit a fast one-two from the reaping fists. Staggering like a man who realises he has been on the wrong track for his entire life, Walsh fell under a rain of blows. 'Remember yer face,' he croaked, but *The Grim Reaper* did not stop pounding till his own was a lump of blood. And there he left him, the mute claim of the carcasses.

Removing the mask, Jude stepped over the dogs and emerged as an alarm began looping through the yard. Nemmins had left the house open. If he didn't shut it off he would have the patrol on him; and he was indisposed to disfigure more faces. The alarm came and came again, cycling its sound, waking the farm and adjacent lake. Between east and west moved a delicate light, and Jude moved as if its representative, entering Nemmins' house like Jacob, through the open door. He shut off the alarm and the sky was gone. In its place: plastered ceiling,

225

artistically whorled. A brass chandelier hung from the centre; under it, a broad oak table and settle, all skilfully done. Nemmins senior had taste. On the table, ham, eggs and toast, quiet-steaming. A pot of coffee puffed perfect genies through the spout. Jude rifled through the cupboards, picked out the peanut-butter. He had already had a first breakfast. Since then he had whipped two dogs and a couple of curs, and a gut could tax it.

He sat in a teak chair, helped himself to a second breakfast of toast and coffee, exploiting without scruple the peanut butter. The ham, of course, he disdained to touch; but if, perchance, some morsel of egg found way to his fork, all slipped among the slices, it was impossible for a vegan, already making considerable concessions to peanut butter, to maintain total control. That would have been absurd. It was a post-lapsarian world.

Jude wiped the last finger of toast over the plate, empty but for a tranche of ham. Draining a second mug of coffee, he leant back and looked about. Through the window were washlines, plants, vegetable-plots. The window had been opened and through it came a paradoxical clack of beak at water. Jude leaned further and spied fat, regal creatures with large, twisted feet. They were stepping about, with flabby appendages, dabbles of water on their beaks. A crumb of gravel and they plucked it down. They sat, and behold—the egg!

'The chicken,' mused Jude. 'God moves in mysterious ways.'

Through the other window were picks and shovels, wire and beaten iron. You could accuse Nemmins' father of many things—and Jude would, in time, he would—but *philanthropy*, culpable as it most certainly was, wasn't one of them.

Harper did a sparrow-hop. 'There's a word for you.'

'Stick that in your books, boys.'

Nevertheless, that the old goat had some congress with the outside world was evinced by a large pile of *Gazettes*, *Heralds* and *Mercuries*, that spilled off the settle round an open fireplace. Jude sifted through them, picked up three recent copies of the *Chronicle*. *Water Board Gets Bullish*, said the earliest. *Council lobbied for reservoir expansion*, and there was a picture of a young man in an ill-fitting suit. He was smiling, rubber-lipped, under a curve of swart hair; one hand sporting an umbrella, the other a glass of champagne. The caption read: *Hole: expansion*.

Jude gave a 'Ha!' and, borrowing a biro, inserted an *h* after the *W*, crossed out the *er*, added an exclamation mark, changed the *B* to an *R*, crossed out the *d*, added another exclamation mark, crossed out the *s*, turned the *i* into another exclamation mark and crossed out the *sh*. Addressing himself then to the subtitle, he prefaced the second word with an *s*, with a long slash after the first *b* cut the word in two, changed the second *b* to a *d*, threw an exclamation mark after the next *d*, crossed out the *f* and *r*, turned the next *r* to a *d*, crossed out the *ser*, turned the *r* to a *d* again, and swept another exclamation mark to the end of *expansion*. Relatively satisfied, he passed to the middle paper. *Exotic Birds Breed In Glum*, it teased: *Birds of paradise spotted in Broody*. There was a caption here as well: *Bird of paradise: exotic*, and there was said bird, looking exotic, spying from the side of its eye. 'Ha!' cried Jude. It was all too easy. With a few light strokes, he made the *x* an *r*, the second *i* to an *a*, the second *r* to an *l* and, the *Gl* to an *R*. Then he added an exclamation mark, like insult to injury. 'Salt in the wound!' he triumphed, flurrying the latest paper. He spread it wide, held it to a lamp. *Ancient Anchor Cut Adrift* said the headline. *Police admit defeat in search for Ossly relic*. Jude looked to one side, breathed sharply through his nose. It was the much-fetishised anchor of St. Swithen's, Meal Common, about which had twined a delusional local legend and its boon companion, the idiotic ditty. To wit:

> *When Eanswida anchor weighs*
> *Shall she many waters raise*
> *When Eanswida anchors low*
> *Shall the water evenso.*

This Jude had been made to recite in a primary-school play, much against his will. Some said the rhyme was coined when the anchor came to Ossly, which put it at over four-hundred. Some said it was coined by Benjamin McCormack Kepperly-Lie's uncle for his barndance band, *The Turnips* (appointment only, also available for weddings and funerals), which put it at about forty. Since almost everyone who cherished the anchor and its legend—councillors, schoolteachers, book-club members—were gladhanders, boomchasers, new-wavers of one sort or other, it was all the same to them. They clung to any contrivance, new or old; you could tell it was bona fide by the squeeze-marks. Still, Jude had felt the humiliation: a Dimly boy, casting Meal Common's anchor. He let fall the paper, looking thoughtful. It didn't matter, it was gone now—adrift like Southey's boat their little ditty. Another blow to Harper and his ilk. 'Anchors.

He chuckled, rocked in the wood, balls to the floor but the soles bent. He cast an eye instead, around the kitchen, hand in the sink like a light anchor. There were the usual appliances: kettle, toaster, cheese-grater. There were personal things too: a magazine rack, a knitted quotation from the Psalms. Then there was some junk on the surface: keys, clothes-pegs, socket-covers, plastic knives, the head of a clarinet. Nemmins senior was into

229

self-sufficiency. Cupboards were stocked, windows stuffed with herbs, and they all had frame-locks. Looking about, he realised all the doors had bars: kitchen, utility and the door he had entered by. This same side-door faced a metal gate: blue-glossed, hedge-jammed, barbed-wire the length of it. The gate gave to a track, more grass than rut, which left the road beyond the main entrance and ran weedy between fields, threatening fields of its own. Of course, from where it was sitting Jude's eye could see nor track, nor weeds, nor fields, though it *felt* them in all their seedy morbidity. What it *could* see was the hedge that screened them, and it ran along that hedge, probing for gaps in its fuzzy logic. After all, you never knew when you might need a gap in a hedge. Twice already today that same eye had been grateful for a hedge's permeability. Next time it would not be grateful; it would be lenient. Thinking this, thinking how it was going to have to get hard on fallacies and flaws of all kinds, the eye reached the limit of the hedge, as defined by the window frame, and was for seeking out trifles new, when, all at once, it was forced to travel back the way it had come, with the gleaming black head of Moore for its *ignis fatuus*.

Jude knew Moore. Moore knew Jude. They went back a long way—all the way to Upper Dovecombe Junior Judo. They gave each other respect. Moore was the only tutelary Jude could not dispatch with a stealth sweep, swift half-nelson and illegal roundhouse lifted from karate. Moore was the only full-back Jude could not palm off, break through and barge on his way to the line. Moore the only suitor against whose brawn Jude's wit ne'er won fair maid.

For his part, Moore had witnessed Jude's legendary demolition of Nathan House, who, spoiling for a fight to enhance his credibility, had fallen so soundly, under a series of Harlovian blows, that he went to pieces, lost all his friends, and—like the lightning-riven trunk—'never more a leaf revealed'. Moore did not seek combat, but combat sometimes sought him, and, when it found him, the hood came over his eyes; Moore was another man. Often as not, so was his assailant. But Moore had been there, the day House's blood spotted the daisy-spread lawn. Jude was the one combatant Moore feared to tangle with. He had admitted as much to Harper, in a cloakroom one time.

Now, though, was no time for recollection. Moore must be faced or fled. Yet why flee? It was only Moore. The whole incident was explicable. Unless, of course, he had been to the barn. Perhaps Walsh, or Nemmins, had called him in. Perhaps Jude had not beaten them sufficiently. Moore might not wait for explanations. He was already at the door. It would look bad if Jude were discovered eating

Nemmins' breakfast at Nemmins' table, in Nemmins' battened kitchen. A kitchen, after all, was a *doom*. The birthplace of tragedy. All that happened happened there. And not only this. Jude had been caught unawares, at *breakfast*, in a place where he thought himself *unobserved*, and by a *familiar figure, bobbing* under the window. It was horrible. *Horrible*. He touched the scythe, he turned aside. He wiped his hand, he smiled. Jude was slow to surprise. He had, as he repeatedly asserted, anticipated *everything*. But, in skipping such a banal evolutionary stage as *surprise,* his ego had allowed, by way of compensation, for heightened states of rage and panic, pronouncing them wholly reasonable reactions to boorish circumstances. Accordingly, in the midst of indecision, he played the latter of these trump cards and went pounding from the kitchen, through the hall, up the narrow farmhouse stairs.

Moore paused on the threshold, like Esau, come to claim birthright. Faintest of lights moved on the window frame, shimmered on the draining-board. Then the wash-line cut through it, and light was a hung sheet, contained. Moore frowned and it buried in his eyebrow. Moore had black eyes. He could snuff sparks, but he could light them too. Most of his time was spent putting out fires.

He cracked a knuckle, knocked it on the wall, dislodged gravel. He waited, leaning on the frame.

The kitchen was a quarry. It had a swept-through look, like hair after wind. Without those movements of air even windless summer arranges, it contained the cold of grave. Looking on it now, the air at his back felt warmer. Even that ray strengthened in his brow. Moore shivered, crossed threshold and self simultaneously, stood as one in sin. There are unwritten laws. Who knows whether to stay out or step in?

But he was in now—steeped so far, to go back were as weary. He moved round the table, saw papers on the floor, unlit logs in the fireplace, smelt ash, pine, print. Something else he smelt, obvious, predominant, which for that reason had not troubled him. Now it broke surface. It was toast, ham, coffee. On the table, a toast-rack, coffee-pot, and in a circle of plate, a knife and fork, like stopped clock-hands. The plate was white, with painted yellow rim. In the off-centre, a slice of ham.

Moore was not unreasonable. He reasoned with the best of men: wisely, not too well. Someone had been breakfasting here. Either someone called urgently away, or someone without appetite. Nemmins was none of the last. What would have called him so urgently?

Horatio [*sotto*]:
Some enterprise

That has a stomach in it, which is no other
But to recover of us by strong hand
And terms compulsatory those foresaid lands
So by his father lost—lo, it comes again.

Jude stood up from the microphone, watched Magnus hog the wall. He seemed to have gone backwards, like some cinematic train bearing down on a heroine. Cords would turn sand, rails to ragged cords, before that train hit home. What immovable object could withstand that?

'Couldn't say,' said Moore. An urgent call was likely to come either from where you least expected it or where you most expected it. There were no in-betweens. Moore's call, however, was not urgent. It was resonant. It touched the house.

'Nems?' he said. And again: 'Nems!'

The house was quiet.

'What was that alarm about? Tryin' to wake up the whole valley?' Moore leant on the table. 'Nems, you there? I 'ave to get to work.' He placed a fish-hook beside the toast-rack. 'You forgot this, look. In the van. Not a great idea.' His voice declined among the flagstones.

Moore was hungry but he didn't want that ham. It was blanching by the second. He took a turn round the kitchen, stooped to the sink to wash. He stopped. There was blood in the basin. A little: a streak come off like a comet. It stuck to his eaten

234

nail. Moore didn't like blood, couldn't have been a doctor. He washed it from his finger, not his imagination. It stayed there all day, like sunspots, eating eventually to the heart, as the long influence of water exposes fissures in the earth beneath.

'Though they're not common, honestly,' said the Lie. He was just passing, en route to 'angle'. 'It's easier above ground, when all's said and done.'

Still, that was Moore's analogy, which, once thought, was powerful as fact. And like any fact, he fought it. Mountains from molehills. It was innocuous blood, after all. A healer of holes. Nemmins probably pricked himself on those barbs about. Any cat, canine, carving-knife had done it. No need to cry blue murder.

The light sank in the water. Like that, Moore could look at it. Held there, it wouldn't wield the migraine. An enemy must be kept under, till it wouldn't fight more—even then, weighed down, kept from floating up. Of course, it would always come up in the end—there were no permanent solutions—but sometimes you just took the short-term option. What was the world anyway, but short-term lease, least of evils and bad job's best? Moore took the short term option. He reached for a tea-towel on a string over the window, wiped his hands, spread it, greyly, on the clay sill-tiles. He saw himself in the tap, turned and was gone, foreseeing no good things.

Upstairs Jude was foreseeing no good things from his choice of the bathtub as hiding-place in a besieged house. Why pin himself here, scythe leaning on the curtain-rail? The whole thing was absurd—he hadn't met Moore for years. He wasn't even an enemy. True, he wasn't a friend either, but he was an old-time ally, and was not this worth more than either? Not if Moore took the inevitable stairs, wandered the warped corridor, moved amid the door-frame and opened the slow shower-curtain. Jude's very presence would mean fear, shame, violence—out of nothing—and write them over the spotless tiles.

It was out of hand. Jude felt a strong desire to call out, come down, slap comradely backs. What did Moore mean by working for the Water Board, anyway? He was no pawn, to wear that boyish blue. What power could wield a man like Moore? Not for Moore the corporate-ethos and team-collective. He was a full-back. He stayed behind, where the field was dark, sky was clear, shouts were distant cannon. He saw it all before him, uninvolved, unimpressed; his only charge, defend with life the *line*. Jude liked the idea. It offended him someone had to forgo it. Moore had always been there. If a sortie, a sally, a set-piece broke down; if ruck became maul, became melee; if a chance slip, drop, or interception, revealed horrid gaps in the great coherence, there was always Moore, eternal Moore, *solid* Moore, *made—before—*the *foundation—of—* the *world!* Picking up the pieces, delivering goods and groceries, of particular kinds, to peculiar ends, saying nothing to no-one—this was Moore's role in the universe.

He put his fingers to the curtain, slid it a little. 'M—' he started. It stopped in his throat. A creak broke from the stair. Someone was coming up: Moore of course. Who else? Walsh? Impossible. No no, it was Moore, but he wouldn't enter the bathroom; a strong male code would forbid him. A man's bathroom was his castle. On the other hand, a bathroom was exactly the kind of place a man might meet with accidents. Hadn't the young Moore once been dispatched through a bathroom window, to find a corpse blocking the door? Or was that the Lie? Either way, it was common knowledge, and Moore would be recalling it now, staring down the corridor, dreading to enter. Jude strained, as if hearing that stare. A bathroom was a doom: everything ended there. How to explain his presence, in the bath, in a black cloak, dressed as Death (though that of course was the easy part)? The scythe pointed a treacherous head over the curtain. With squirming larynx, Moore would finger the door. A gentle push, hardly enough to bear, and the room laid waste, all white and seamless. Sickened, repulsed in heart, he touches, parts the curtain, inch by easy inch—sees the apparition of a face, white as tiles. A gyre, a gurgle, a jet-black squeal, high as a woman's; and a low man's moan, drawn as by vortex.

Jude parted the curtain, silent as the grave. He stepped from bath to bath-mat. Taking up the scythe he fingered open the door. The corridor gaped, all green and flowered. Leaving the bathroom as a spirit leaves the world, he stood in the rare corridor air. Silence. He tiptoed fast, *all-stars* to the edges, aware as he was of the sonic geography of old floorboards. There was only one place left to go. The bedroom. But this was hopeless. A bedroom was a *doom:* last place you wished to go, first place you must. For the third time that morning, Jude panicked. He turned round and about, left-side, right-side, in my lady's chamber. Kitchen, bathroom, bedroom: a house was a mantrap! He felt like a *Cluedo* piece on a low die-roll.

Moore moved through kitchen, through doorway, turned corner. Was that a creak of ceiling? He stared up the stairwell and saw a silhouetted thing, hanging, bedraggled, skirt about its ankles. And for the remainder of his life, when fear required a form, Moore always saw that same slack silhouette, that rag embryo, waving, useless, at the end of that tunnel. 'Fuck me!' he murmured, and next second was gone, galumphing through garden like a man dragging thunder.

238

'Tunnel or well?' Harper looked from Jude to the lens and back. A rainbow fell on his eye.

'Not so fast, Harpo. Dock or nettle?'

'Alright, Dock.'

'Arnnn, really?'

'Tunnel or well?'

'You try me, sir.'

'What of it?'

'Well.'

'Make up your mind.'

'Ha ha ha.'

Back in the bath, Jude heard that 'Fuck me!' and galumphing. This was a nasty turn. If there was anything worse than Moore catching Jude utterly awares, it was Moore desisting from the same, for reasons known only to him. What could make large-hearted Moore run like the hounds were on him? After all, the hounds were lifeless in the barn. It boded ill. Jude stared intently at the tiles. With the drip of tap, as if something always known, the sense he was not alone came up from deep. With a finger he removed the curtain. With an arm he reached for scythe. The door swung. The corridor extended. Looking at him, down at the end, was the bedroom door, touching lightly its frame as if there were a draught. If there were, Jude felt it, right down his back on a sluice of sweat. The door grew and the bathroom shrank. The stairwell stood between, an ocean away. How to reach it—fast or quiet? It was a question which grew on the eyes, impossible yet unavoidable, encompassing vast moral and intellectual spheres.

'Fast—or *quiet?*'

'I'm going to surprise you, sir, and say *quiet.*'

'Crumbs.'

Flailing the scythe just as far as walls allowed, which was a tight, jerky flail all round, Jude opted for the first. Almost overshooting the stairwell he skidded to a halt. The door assumed full size, eased like a lion on the prey. He didn't wait. He bolted like laundry down the steps, tripped into the kitchen and fled the house. Not, however, before spying the Lie's bronze 4/0 double fish-hook, with the mermaid lure, agleam on the kitchen table, raising it to his eye, and extemporising in the following manner: 'Ahh. Our old friend, the *hook.* Tenaciously attached—co*located* even—with our old cliché, the *crook.* Indeed, *conferring* crookery upon its possessor. Pointless—gutless—to resist. What goes around,' he said, pocketing the item. 'Comes around.' And, with that, he burst through the side door, down the drive to the open gate, spurning the house, scorning to look back, shunning—positively *shunning*—an upper window, framing the shade of a behatted head: as florid, extravagant a head as you'd wish to see. Because— and this he must admit, hateful, *hateful* as was *admission*—he must have wished to see it.

240

'*Hook* or *crook?*'

Harper checked on the camera. The lake was a shimmering mantle on the wall. Magnus trod it down like so many reviving passions. On that long dam wall he held the balances: levity, gravity, both were in his hands. Here was a man who refused to bask in glory; who lived with his laurels upon him.

'How much time do we have?'

'Time for such a word.'

Jude rucked through a hedge, avoiding the roads. In the distance, Moore's speeding van. Cow-pats, mud-slides and ditches were his element, as he slithered and scampered up the hill. A stile he took as he found it. He tangled with a trough, but came off the better. On he ploughed, through abrupt banks, incidental gullies, up the sudden middle of fields, short legs fannying around, with that bedroom door before him and the alarm sounding a square country mile.

Harper leant on the fence, did some sounding of his own.

'Then the word is *hook.*'

The word fell to the ground and dropped under the arch. Jude let it. He merely watched Magnus in the middle-distance. He was like a clown coming down a corridor, in an enormous Russian hotel. Why expend his energy? Why this insistent conquest? Jude was not convinced. There was no competition. It was pure solitaire, the kind grandmothers played. Here was no martyr, giving up the ghost. Here was a man hammering it home. Magnus, the self-proclaimed man of tomorrows—this determined strut was a petty pace. He forced a man to the last resort—the tawdriest of alternatives.

'Speaking of which, where's Saint?'

'I don't know. He was making noises—snivelling whiny, almost emasculated ones, it must be said—about Ophelia, but I thought I'd placated him with Bernardo.'

'Could you not have told him he was Bernardo *playing* Ophelia, brilliantly neglecting to tell him that that is exactly the kind of thing a mad, spurned virgin would believe?'

'I did. He maintained that Bernardo was not that kind of man.'

'No, you see, the trouble is, I suspect Bernardo of being Saint *in disguise*. And I suspect both of them of being the kind of men who, contrary to instructions given, promises made, will take a titillant, pedantic pleasure in *lying in* of a morning, side by side, like two limp, anaemic, meagre slugs-a-bed.'

'Except,' said Harper from the stage, 'that Saint is brilliant. And, as we have said many times, in the last resort, completely trustworthy.'

'Well, Saint *is* brilliant,' said Jude as if he wasn't. He was standing in the Gods, a solitary God, benighted, outnumbered by devils. Feet were wet and spread, cloak was cast about him. Between thumb and forefinger was a single scythe. 'And in the last resort he *is* trustworthy,' he continued. 'The trouble is, if anything has ever been *too late* in this life, and it must be allowed that it has, it was, inexorably, this same last resort. Moreover, even if it is not yet *too late*, one can never be sure that the last resort is as ultimate as it seems, until it certainly has become too late, either to recognise it, or to trust in anything. To all intents and purposes, then, Saint is a complete waste of time.'

Harper thought about it. Jude was surely right. A waste of time. The last resort: a vast weedy waste, drying in the sun, detaching whole and appearing in the sky. What did it record?—it *was* the record. He sat down on a step to revise his notes. There were four camera stations in the script: *A*, *B*, *C and D*, corresponding to the four sides of Pedestal 3, which stood at their nominal centre. *A* was the other side of the road, by the Pump House fence, level with the wall. *B* was in the Gods of the amphitheatre, where Jude was now, looking up from low. *C* and *D* were on the wall itself, some distance behind, and some distance beyond, Pedestals 1 and 4. These stations were to be taken by the same camera, moved with its humble tripod. Saint was to have helped with the handling, freeing Harper to perform. Could Harper play Bernardo playing Marcellus? It seemed a bridge too far. He took a

hold of a pencil, put lines through lines. *Exit
Bernardo* he scribbled.

Looking to the Gods he was surprised to see two
of them. There maundered Jude, along the Gods,
to-ing and fro-ing, staring darkly at Harper. But
there, along the curve, exactly on the cross of
Station *B*, was another: a tall lithe other, hands in
pockets, hems arching over multi-purpose boots.
He stood like a gunslinger, hourglass at his hip.
Hair like flies encircled him. Round his shoulders,
a shawl, all holey. He pressed his lips and
swallowed.

'Gentlemen,' he said.

'Just on time,' said Harper, recovering.

'Precisely when I meant to,' said Magnus, waving
Harper's instructions. Here was a bitter sweet. He
squinted under the wig. A t-shirt read *Avoid
Extinction* and under the legend was a dodo, game
but thankless.

'Have any trouble?'

'Oh, I wouldn't say TROUBLE.'

*

Magnus touched the summit of Broody, wiped his
face, looked left, looked right, as if searching for
the dawn. He had left Claudine sleeping in Pale, a
pillow scattered with cards. The *Shanodin Dryad* in
her palm implied a night of it. That Magnus was a

244

toucher she could testify—and the reverse was also true. He had ridden hard, climbed the Sinfils to plateaus of heath and forest. Now he got off his bike, stood possessingly, in the middle of the road, wandered to a gate for a better view. The land fell away before him, in breathing heaps, to the far grey swathe of the Glum and Cooley Valleys. The natural world seemed prematurely wakeful, readying itself for the human alarm. Lights on the rim were Woorish. That cluster must be Glum Greater. Over here, a high dark surge suggested Dovecombe. Out there in front, though, that flat expanse, unwilling or unable to define itself—that was the Glum reservoir.

Magnus had leant a fraction forward, bent his thought that way, as if an advance party, to inform it of his arrival, when he heard the hum of a car coming. He tapped vaguely at the gate, willing it to pass. But it slowed down, stopping beside him with the engine running. *The Man Who Would Be King* wound down the window.

'Hullo! Can I offer you a lift?'

Magnus regarded the whole solemn world. 'No thank you. My bike's over there.'

'Mags, isn't it?'

Magnus nodded confirmation.

'Stretching the old legs, eh? Good on ya, son.'

'Sunrise is rather LOVELY from Broody.'

245

'Sunrise—bit optimistic aren't you? Heh! Forecast says storms.'

'I must have missed the FORECAST.'

'Oh, I never do. Up with the larks and the radio on for the news and weather. That's me. Anyway, can't chat—busy day ahead. Fancy seeing you here at this time of morning. "Night", I should say.'

'It's a SMALL WORLD.'

'Isn't it just. Sure you don't want that lift? I can put the bike—'

Magnus shook his head.

'Well, cheerio. Hope you get that sunrise! Nothing like a bit of optimism.' And with a wink, *The Man Who Would Be King* was closing the window and winding downhill, as if unaware he was watched.

'Unforgivable,' said Jude, as they gathered round the Gods, naturally spacing themselves three yards apart. He frowned at his *all-stars*. '*Really*. Even Jesus would never forgive what he do.'

'There's pathos for you.'

'As *functional* an aesthetic as you're like to find.'

'PATHOS!' roared Magnus. 'PATHOLOGY, more like.'

'What's that then?' said the Lie, appearing on the wall. The Water Board flag flapped about his head. 'The study of paths? Haff-haff-ohohohono. To be honest, I could have done with a bit more "pathology" on Coal Hill just now. Haff-a-haff.

Gets quite confusin' up there.' Stutteringly, Jude, Harper and the Lie began to laugh. The laugh picked up consistency if not momentum, fed on itself like any organism and, through a solemn minute, made up in length what it lacked in *line*.

Begrudging in length what it admired in line, unwilling to accommodate itself to a thirty-five degree gradient, a relentless pace brought Jude puffing to the crest and crossroads of Stubblow Hill, where, uprearing like an alien, his attention was arrested by a tall, white, freestanding sign. *Meale Cummon 2* declared the lowest arm, urging onward. *Cleave Hill 1* read the next, sweeping east as if to clothes-line his progress. Above that, two arms shot west, reading *Stubblow Sack 1* and *Stubblow Church ½*. Pointing behind him, a last arm said *Dimly 1 ¼*. This latter arm he reached out, on tiptoes, to touch, as a footballer touches a club scutcheon, feeling only then a stage completed. Then he eyed the other arms in descending order, appraising the signpost as he might any woman. *Stubblow Sack 1* and *Stubblow Church ½* were dismissed out of hand; that left a hand for *Cleave Hill 1* and he duly weighed it. In his mind's eye he stalked the long Cleave Road, between lonely, immaculate verges, in heavy silence, watched, oppressed, sweating a storm, to burst through sunless woods, come like the clap down long Cleave Hill. No no. Cleave, he concluded, would

247

not *do*. If ever there were a recipe for disaster, it was Cleave, plotting its dead trajectory like a man marks a grave. Much as he hated to say it, it must be *Meale Cummon 2*, as bereft an alternative as a crossroads can provide.

He was about to make good on this decision when a shout drew his attention to the west. Under the hedgerow, where all was shadowy, were the Goodhead twins, if Jude recalled correctly. Legend had it, that *one would always tell the truth and the other always lie,* and no one credited this legend more fervently than they, especially when drunk, which was almost always. They were lounging in a ditch, eighty if a day, enjoying the fruits of the morning.

'An' mornin' to you!' cried one, nuzzling blackberries.

This was aggressive in itself.

'Not quite,' said Jude, who hated an air of pragmatism as much as an air of mystery. He wiped his brow on an arm.

'One fer walkin' I reckon,' observed the other, ripping an apple. 'All the way away and never comin' back.'

'Beaudiful day o' it,' said the first. He was hugged in damp animal-skins, relieved at the arriver, though the arriver were Death.

'None but rain,' interposed the second.

'Blue's can be.'

'Like the suits o' them watchmen.' The second pointed down the *Meale Cummon* road. 'Like these here bruises—'. He exhibited the right side of his face. There was a large purple circle about the cheek and eye. 'Fer speakin' as I see it,' he said. 'An' there's more where they came from.'

'S'all synonymous.' said the first. 'Blue begets blue, when all's said an' done. After that, it's a question o' degree.'

'Is it,' said Jude, mechanically. 'Is it.' But he was in no mood for the Goodheads and their relentless obfuscation, preferring, on this occasion, the altogether more listless, positively foliaged, obfuscation of the *Meale Cummon* road. Leaving them there like a pair of wet sacks, Jude took that foliaged road. From the blue-black above, cloud formed and followed him.

Again the gradient upped the ante, and again the trees closed round, forming a profound arch over the hint of road. At the top of the tunnel he saw a van and a huddle of watchmen, like Caesar, all bald among the leaves. Avoiding them was simple. He bundled up bank, slipped in field, dove via ditch, haggled through hedge, clambered by wall, leapt (ten feet) to lawn, hotfooted over turf, dodged a dog, crossed a cross-barred gate and landed on the trusty road, dusting down cloak and scythe. 'I believe I'll dust my scythe,' he said. Fifty yards away, the watchmen watched him disbelieving—

and jiggered if he didn't watch right back. What were they going to do—gun him down on the byway? He turned his head, shrugged his shoulders, slopped off in the direction of Higher Marching, scythe slung like a knapsack.

Just before Saint's lonely homestead was a stream. Jude followed it through fields, pleased with the coincidence, and came out on Lower March Lane. He took an eastern lane, bending left where lane became track. A tiny junction arose, which he sensibly ignored. On he trod, past barn, stile, caravan, to the same quaint cottage he had passed last month with Magnus and Harper. Sprouts and cabbages were abundant in the garden. Sunflowers still nodded wealthy heads eastward, turning to Jude with rich disillusion. Jude bent an eye on all the silent exterior. He didn't stand on ceremony, cut a right over gate, past pump-shed and pylon, through sump and struggling stream, by hedgerow again and sudden via gap, before anyone could do anything about it.

It was a different world, east-side the hedge. The horizon was like Fran Peters' skin, all peach and dew. Fields opened up and rolled down, to feed at the miserable Meal. Jude kept to the hedge, as to a masculine code, unspoken but real. Real *because* unspoken. It wound happily upward and he wound with it, on hillock, hummock, tump and knoll, through bilberry, briar and rose. 'And the city is sought for *society!*' he breezed, changing handshakes with honeysuckle, pleasantries with elms, and the holly became his familiar. Grown lambs gambolled, deer danced in the distance and, rightwards, through the superb field, clumps kept a broken line.

Suddenly, in the midst of all this splendour, the Freely-Lowe house reared its head. 'Gah,' said Jude. '*Again. A house.* Everywhere you go—a *house*, standing there as if it owns the place, training the eye, uniting disparate entities. As if it had a monopoly! As if it were a free world!' He tackled a spurious knoll. He threw an implicated stick. 'I'll give you unity!' he thought. 'Have that for your private property!' Jude did not know the lie of Glum land like Magnus or Harper did—and for good reasons, as he thought. These lies were all the same, constantly uniting disparate entities. Down the clump-line he trotted, faster and faster, not for fear but momentum, till he reached the dolorous Meal, and there he hopped from rock to rock till he hit the southern bank. Here the world was still grey and somnolent. Here the cows browsed slow, anticipant of life. Here he moved among them, gained a stump, preached cogitation, common sense. There he was gone, among fieldlets, alleys, bridge-like stiles, to views, avenues, epiphanies. A ladder was nailed to a tree, with a seat at the top. Jude perched in the seat, saw

251

the land slope away before him, to brick-barns, stables, haystacks and their poking proverbial needle: the tall corner-spire of St. Swithen's tower. 'Meal Common!' he scoffed. 'Aye, madam, 'tis! Democratic as daisies! Promiscuous as primroses! See her flounce through the Glum, dangling her anchor, tinkling her little bell, wielding till the grave her self-created secrets. Which, like all secrets, come at the cost of her conversation.' Jude cursed Meal Common, and her precious little lore. Relentlessly bourgeois, relentlessly burgeoning; even now he could see scaffolding like ivy in the trees, hear the early hammer of the drill. He could see the day coming in Meal Common, when not having a home garden would be against the law. And precisely *because* democracy ruled the world.

Leaving to his right the rise, the grand ridge of beech, he wound gently down, somewhat tired in leg, by meadow, barn, *habitat-scheme*. Larks were nesting; dog must keep to leads. The larks patrolled the sky, appearing to enforce this law. The church tower neared, but it wasn't yet clear how to reach it. Indeed, the nearer it came, the more confused the picture, so that all that was certain was that, amidst a riot of branch, hedge and dwelling, was a tower, flag-topped and gilt with jigsaw-pieces. For all you knew, it might have no base; been lifted away, like Fellini's Jesus, perched on a wall for a souvenir.

252

One goes as crows fly. Jude had only to negotiate one more electric-fence, trespass a last pasture, skirt a final, obliging, all-foliaged gulley, hard to discern from the farmhouse windows, before, cutting an ultimate corner, he stepped to a low tiled roof, walked the length of a long shed's apex with the scythe for a balance, slashed thick ivy to the shed-door gable and dropped eight foot into graveyard grass.

He fell on his rump, sprawled hands with a 'Heigh!' and sat there, by a juniper, mighty pleased with circumstances. 'All in a morning's work,' he asserted, looking from hand to hand, and east over the graves: slab and pedestal, cross and knotgrass, pale as seed on the watermelon sky. You couldn't see the sun yet: just the land where he meant to breakfast. Jude could understand that: a watermelon would go down excellent well. In fact, his mother had one in the pantry, all carved into quarters. He meshed his lips by grass-tips, tempted by the cows to start on those.

Just as he thought this, though, the sound of real shears outdid him. He raised his head west, where the boles were black but the tops of the yews were fire. There, snipping among new graves, was an old woman, bowed like a snowdrop, a face propped on her shoulder.

She stopped snipping. 'Alright?' she said, not in the least surprised. Her voice was disarmingly clear. Till now, Jude might have fancied himself charmed. Now the charm changed, became conscious—no more than utterance. 'I knew you would come,' she said.

'Hi there,' said Jude, still sitting. She grinned. She was the kind that could not smile but only grin. It was a humourless grin, more like a grimace, imagining its disguise secure, though nothing more transparent. Two rows of yellowy teeth showed, loose-arranged, divided in the upper tier by an eloquent gap. The hair was white, curling at the shoulder like infants' fingers. The nose was horse-ish, eyes vacant, her dress, new-ageish, long and leaf-bedizened. This last was of course an unforgivable error, and yet—and yet—in that snatched glance, to his great surprise, Jude saw youth, saw beauty. Where exactly did he see it? The luxuriant whiteness of the hair, far blueness of the eye, cold as the time of morning? Hard to say, but time had worn her well. She might have been twenty, were it not clear she was at least sixty-five. Then again, time being so kind, perhaps she was eighty. Jude had not seen anyone so potentially immortal, except perhaps Harper; though, as this could represent no achievement on Harper's part, rather a slice of good-fortune, so Jude was not about to give the woman any undue credit either. The best one could say about her—which was much—was that she was *fantastic*. To this length

Jude was prepared to stoop. He picked up the scythe, pushed back the cloak. Impressed but underawed, he wandered over, past doors of various kinds. A cellar-door bottomed a stairwell. A yellow door leaned by the stairwell rails. A thin door stood sentry on four steps to the tower, and an arched, dwarfish door sat in the belfry, as if made for the gargoyles. Paying respects to each, Jude sauntered by, to lean, flirtatious, on a grave.

'Morning,' he said. He leant the scythe on a neighbouring cross.

'Morning.' She continued snipping. All at once it looked as if she didn't want to be bothered.

'You haven't any idea of the time?' Jude looked high about him, as if the tower had a clock.

The woman straightened up, stripped a garden-glove, shook a finger. 'Almost six,' she said airily, eyeing as much of the eastern sky as the tower allowed.

'Oh really? I'm late.'

'Oh really?' she echoed, with the interest left out. She grinned again, exhaling.

Mental, thought Jude to himself, ceasing to lean. He looked at the belfry door. Carved arches framed it with six diminishments. The seventh was the door, which consisted of ten boards bound across, with a small lock on the left hand, and round iron handle. He was about to go to inspect it when the woman became inexplicably chatty. 'Just trimming the edges, see.' She started snipping again.

'Yes.' He looked back and forward.

'Can't use the mower a while yet—for the neighbours' sake.' She waved a disparaging glove; a petrol-mower appeared by the dwarfish door, such as Jude was wont to wreak upon the Kroner lawn.

'Oh really?

'I beg your pardon?'

'Oh really.' Jude turned his head.

'Strimmer I can use a little sooner.' Sure enough, like a flaming sword, a strimmer stood by the western gate. Jude considered these factors. She was a woman of means.

'Hm.'

She looked up at his face. ''Cause it's a bit quieter, look,' she rejoined, almost yearningly.

Jude chose to humour her. 'But these are the quietest of all,' he said, indicating the shears. She went back to work. Again there was quiet but for the *snip snip* of the tool. Even the birds seemed half-asleep. Only a pigeon cooed, and jackdaws flapped about the tower.

'Yours is quieter still,' she said, jerking at the scythe. 'Silent, like.'

Now Jude was heedless. 'Possibly.'

She did not break stride. 'Like that I can get a bit done before sun-up. Eagh—it's warm work, this

256

weather, if you wait till noon. But that will change today.' She straightened again.

'Why so?' Jude put a hand on an angel, companionable now.

'Oh, come off!' Suddenly alert, she took the extraordinary liberty of half-chucking, half-pinching his chin. 'You know the rhyme—red sky in morning—'

'—Somewhat insensitive?' It was Jude's turn to smile.

She was quiet. The grin lost volume but retained its surface area, like a parachute spread upon the earth.

'Tut, that's not a rhyme.'

'No. Speaking of rhymes, I hear the anchor's missing.'

A thrush came to a nearby stone and sang. Jude could see its bill, close-up, wide-open, and the pummel of breast. Such power in stuff so frail. Watch it too long and the song became a rapture: all the graveyard was included.

'Astonishing,' he said.

'A queer thing,' said the woman, queerly.

'Oh really?'

'Beg pardon?'

'Was it?'

'Yes.' The woman stared, open mouthed. Slowly the grin appeared; the eyes remained staring at Jude as if he were playing some elaborate game. 'That's an old one isn't it?' she said at length.

'The anchor?'

'The rhyme.'

'A tired one, certainly.'

'There's another verse associated with that, isn't there?'

'I'm sure.'

'You know it?'

'Associated how?'

'Both were inscribed at Folly Hall, they say. I forget whether it was a plaque or scutcheon or something. Perhaps on a sundial. In any case, there's a portrait of Sir Brabbant of the Hall—Lord knows where it is now. They say he is leaning on his desk, with fishing tackle and whatnot spread over it. A couple of elaborate-looking fishing hooks. All of those indicate his interest in fishing, see.'

'An excellent indication.'

'At the foot of the desk is the anchor. Eanswithe's.'

'Okay.'

'And in one hand is a roll, a scroll, you know. With a ribbon bow.'

'Naturally.'

'And the scroll is said to represent the prophecy.'

'Oh is it!'

'In the background, under another painting, there's a plaque with four lines of verse on it. Unfortunately you can't read them. At least, that's what they say.'

'Well, are they to be trusted?'

The woman regarded Jude steadily. 'Usually,' she said.

'What's the other painting of?'

'A skull, a quill, and a crow.'

'Crumbs.'

'Hence, you see, the association. With the second rhyme.'

'Which is?'

'Do you know it? Not many people know it,' she said, whimsically. She was bent now, face to the grave as if reckoning gold. With the reverence of age for the toys of youth, she began to murmur:

> *At the croaking of the crow*
> *Lark shall not her matin know*
> *Nightingale shall cease to sing*
> *Till the grave give up a King*

'I see,' said Jude, increasingly irritated. 'So smaller, more melodic, birdlife are briefly threatened by our old skulking scavenger, the crow, until the king—not a penguin, presumably, possibly a *fisher*—comes back, to reclaim top billing, as it were.'

The Lie snorted, showing his teeth to the morning.

'Which, when you think that, by the late seventeenth-century—nipping our ditty, so to speak, in its earliest-possible bud—England had already shown a violent caprice in the business of kings, may be prophetic, but is hardly startling.'

'No, they're still quite common. We've a few living here.' She gestured to the belfry.

'*Startling.*'

'Aren't they just!'

Jude ploughed on. 'More radical, though less prophetic, were to suggest the king were finally, *irrevocably*, dead. You see prophecy, as a genre, is hopelessly reliant on returns.'

'No no, they don't migrate. Quite the contrary.'

'I'm talking about the *King*.'

The woman smiled, wanting to appear in on the joke. 'Ah yes, the King,' she said. 'But which one?'

'Yes, there are so many of them,' said Jude, slapping a stone again, 'but only one God. Hardly seems fair.'

'On whom?'

'Quite.' Jude cast a glance upward. 'Either way, we don't have to concern ourselves with it for a while.'

'Why?'

'The nightingales will have migrated by now.'

'They do, normally, by Michaelmas. But it's been an Indian summer.'

'And besides, they're declining—along with their shrubbery and *coppice*.'

'It's the wet springs. They don't like it.'

'As are your *larks*, content neither with monopoly nor *habitat-schemes*.'

'It's the cereals, see: all autumn-sowing now. Spring comes round and the crop's too thick for nesting. Inhibits reproduction. Autumn's no time for mating.' Fixing meaningful eyes on Jude, she went back to her work. 'What I don't understand,' she continued, 'is who would want to steal an anchor?' She spoke as if the anchor were in a painting, as if they were all in a painting. She wasn't about to hurry with the snipping either.

'Someone with a grudge.'

'Against whom?'

'Ooh, anything really. Larks, kings, *nightingales*. It hardly seems to matter.'

The woman said nothing.

'Kings and nightingales I *get*,' continued Jude, 'but *larks* have done no harm. Apart from get up to a few pranks obviously.'

There was mechanical laughter all round. The Lie in particular chortled in his joy.

'None at all.'

'More singed against than singing.'

'Yes.' The woman cocked her head. 'Let me show you something.' He followed her over the grass, behind the church to the yellow door: the one beside the rails around the cellar. The rails were black, topped with winged lances. The door was a small battered five-board affair, faded, bruised and weedy. Two thick black hinge-clasps were bolted across three of the boards, ending in similar lances, only here the wings were curled, more like a *fleur-de-lys*. Underneath the upper, a note in plastic sheet was posted. It was smudged but legible.

Meal Common Churchyard Care

Please take your debris away.

The churchyard is maintained by a dedicated band of elderly volunteers. Try to make our work easier by taking your rubbish away. Remember everything left behind has to be taken away. Remember we generously give of our time.

Thank you for your co-operation.

Somehow the church could not avoid the sermon, even—especially—in a maintenance note. Jude removed the note from its sheath, pondered the title, changed the *M* for a *P*, another *m* for an *e*, a *C* for a *D* and added a comma and a couple of exclamation marks. Otherwise it was perfect. There remained but to cross *co-ope* and the final *n*.

He chuckled. Poised between the two left-hand boards, at waist-height, was a hole with a key in. The woman turned the key, stooped and entered. Even Jude had to stoop, placing his hand on the webbed wood. The hinges squeaked to yield, but boards urged solidarity. 'This way,' he heard and he stepped inside.

He was still chuckling at his brilliance when he realised he could hardly see. Light of the faintest kind strained through cracks. The flick of a switch revealed a stone and cement storeroom, buttressing the northwest of the nave. The roof was wood-boarded and low, and the air held all the must and dank which church and storage can contrive. It was filled with bric-a-brac: shelf and box, desk and sill, nook and cold cranny embrowned with care and equipment. It was only a matter of time before everything disintegrated; but then wasn't that so often the way? Jude looked round, as if calculating. What irrelevances were consigned here? If the ground opened and swallowed the room, would it not be *as you were*? The room itself was like the tossed remains of the earth, piled by some careless mole. Overground, underground, it was all the same to him.

The woman barged through a facing door, even smaller than the first. Once again, Jude was pleased with the sensation of stooping. 'It's over here, what I've to show,' she shuffled, and they broke into church-light, broad and dim, with pangs in the eastern glass.

'I'm just glad they left us Him,' she said. This side the belfry door, on the north corner of a column, hung a tapestry depicting Christ. There was the chin, with traditional wisp; there the raised hand, two fingers prised; there, the colourless robes, gone the colour of all cloth. Both cloth and robes were torn. Large eyes spoke spirit, bones spoke hunger. It was all there, recognisable. But at which stage was he? Fasting in the desert? Blessing last bread in remembrance of Him? Perhaps He was saying *Do you sleep! Could you not watch one hour?* One thing was different than usual. His lips were pouted like Jude's; plump, downturned, like a bird's bill.

'There's your King,' said the woman, quietly triumphant. She looked proudly at Jude and the tapestry, like one who has succeeded in a delicate introduction. Sure enough, the caption under the frame read:

Christ: The Man of Sorrows.

This early-medieval tapestry is a jewel of the area, removed from Folly Hall in 1955 at the construction of the reservoir. It is thought to date back to the twelfth-century and comes in a mystical tradition which emphasises Christ's humanity and humility.

'And God at once.'

Jude hardly heard. He was staring at the portrait, feeling like he'd seen that face before. Maybe in a book somewhere, or a picture upon somebody's shelf.

'A man of sorrows,' he said.

'*Shall the grave give up a King*,' she insisted.

Jude came to. '*Ah!* so it's using a *metaphor!*'

'Yes. Hah-hah.' The laugh started small and enlarged in the arches. 'So bully to the thieves, you see. They barked up the wrong tree.'

'Or dug the wrong grave.' Jude looked sideways. 'Either way it's doggerel.'

'What grave?'

Jude wafted at the caption. 'Assuming all this is halfway accurate—and it is a gross assumption—then your metaphor is a dead one. The grave has given Him up already. Which,' he puffed, 'is what I'm inclined to do.' Jude was quiet, grinding his jawbone. He sensed her disappointment.

The woman eyed the Christ. 'Of course,' she said, 'you know what they're saying?'

'It wouldn't surprise me.'

'It wasn't taken by a human hand.'

'Ha!' Now Jude's voice was loud. 'Oh is *that* what they're saying? And which inhuman, or exhumed, hand—presumably joined to an equally impossible *body*—are they holding responsible?'

The woman rested lightly on the pillar. 'Those Langlys were a strange crew, if memory serves them. A long-haired, illegible lot.' She motioned eastward where the window grew a crown. Unnumberable flagstones lapped the pews, unnumberable because it was too dark to differentiate them, especially in the aisles and corners. 'They made that road there so no sound would reach them when they cast the bells.' She dropped her voice. 'Had to be silent, see. Or the sound wouldn't stay. That's why these roads are mazy. The sound gets lost in them.'

'Yes. Among other things.'

'The tin and copper was all local, see. From the mines. They melted it in a wood-burn furnace, two thousand seven hundred degrees *fahrenheit*.' She leered. Jude stirred a finger in an open collection box; it too was all coppers. 'Poured it to the loam-mould, just as you'd pour water. They even made the mould itself—with mud from the Meal.'

'Crumbs. Gods have walked among us.'

'It was a real cottage industry. Clockmakers too, you know. Brass was rife roundabout, 'count of the zinc and copper. Mostly longcase clocks, but lanterns too. Some of the clocks had extras added. They might tell high-tide at the docks, for instance. With mottos. *Ex His Una Tibi. Dum Numeras Amittis. Ego Redibo, Tu Nunquam.* Things like that.'

'Speaking of which I should be numbering myself.'

'Yes, yes, I have to ring the bells at seven. Michaelmas isn't it, today? Langly bells have always rung for Michaelmas. I'm sure there's a tradition associated with that.' She looked vague for a moment, then left off, as if she were not fooling anyone. 'Yes, they made all sorts, did the Langlys. Bells were just a branch o' their arts.' She scratched a bit of dirt off the tapestry frame, then stood, admiring her handiwork. 'The anchor, of course,' she said, still admiring. 'Is a different thing altogether.'

'Where was it?'

'In the Hall as well, wasn't it?'

'I mean where did you keep it?'

She turned toward the porch, as if to go that way. 'A gift, they say, from Queen Bess to the Brabberts. Plunder actually.' She gazed at Jude like one highly disturbed. 'From St. Eanswithe's.'

'The convent?'

267

'It was dissolved, you see. Fifteen thirty-six. Dear-o-dear. There's a gap in the account, isn't there? I suppose that's the meaning of sacrifice.' She nodded to a plaque commemorating deaths of World Wars. Seventeen Mealers: eleven from the First, six from the Second. 'Just ask them. Tuh. We lose more than we ever can win. And how could it be otherwise?' She tapped toward the porch.

Jude looked back to the storage room. A flare touched the east windows, like a birth in heaven. 'There's always storage,' he said, following.

'That's the solution to everything, isn't it?' It was hard to tell if she took him in earnest. 'Or perhaps we should say the dis-solution. Hee hee. Yes, the funny thing about the anchor—ironic I suppose you'd call it—it was the only thing that floated.'

'Apart from the Man of Sorrows.'

'Yes. Apart from Him.'

She drew the door and staggered in the porch.

'My Lord!' she said. 'The anchor.'

And there it was, as it had apparently been, as it had never gone. A wide-faced woman, with swept, wavy hair, broad shoulders, sailors arms. The left arm was folded on her bosom; the right held the anchor ring, at the virgin zone. From the ring, the anchor dove through a cross-beam, to the hem of her skirt, for all the world like the sign of woman. Or *ankh* for that matter. The whole was in pale stone, green-stained down the left. Lichen had been scratched from the surface.

'It's back. It's. Yes, it really is the same. A little tarnished, but. I was here only yesterday. It wasn't there then. It's—what—well I—. How extraordinary!'

They looked it up and down, but plainly it was intact, and it was there, and there wasn't much more to be said. Plainly, too, it was time to leave. The woman followed Jude above the pews, past *The Man of Sorrows*, and once more they were in the storeroom. They barged back through it, kicking at cardboard and plastic, planks and lawnmowers, compost and flowerpots, brackets, brushes, rollers, plinths, newspapers, nails. Jude scuffed at one of the newspapers, slashed by a grid-metal doormat. *Church Could Face Closure* it announced. *St. Swithen's Flock Hits Record Low*. Straightening the corner with a deft backheel, Jude saw a picture of the church he was standing in. *St. Swithen's*, read the caption: *Last legs*. It was the local *Glum Leaves*, even more local than the *Minerva*. Jude kicked it careless in the shins; the woman added insult with a strong application of welly. 'That's all it's good for,' she muttered, savaging it underfoot.

Jude stood in the graveyard again, fingers trim at his pockets. He summoned breaths, watched the cow-parsley, accused the heavy yews. He had forgotten, he was still wearing the cloak, the mask,

269

tucked back on his hair. The woman hadn't even mentioned it.

'Oh I see,' said the woman, wiping curls of paper from her wellies. 'You were talking about *mourning*, with a *u*. Very facetious.' She smacked her palms together and they wandered back to the graves. Warmth was rising from the ground. Jude took it all in: strimmer, mower and scythe. Even that thrush was still around, on the mower-handle.

The woman looked at it, side-on. 'You're declining too, aren't you?'

'Aren't we all.'

Without moving, her eyes transferred to Jude.

'Oh, why do you say that?'

'Oh, because I'm going downhill.' Jude made as if to descend the path.

'I'd hardly call that a hill.'

'No, no, I was using a *metaphor*.'

'A metaphor for what?'

Jude was stumped. 'A dark night of the soul?' he suggested.

'Oh you mean *inner-demons*?'

'Yes.' Jude threw himself into it. '*Yes. Inner-demons.*'

'Well you're too young for that.'

'Metaphors?'

'No, there's enough real ones around.' She picked up the shears. 'But he'll tell you more of that than I.'

'Who?'

Jude, who had turned north to face her, spun like a striker on a fivepence, touching a cross with a forefinger. A man hove in view like a ship from out at sea. He stood under a yew in the corner, head down, folded all in blue. It was dark under the yew, and the blue almost black. The beard was black too, and the monkish fringe. Only the nose spoke from the dark, like a candle on a grave.

Still, it was strange Jude had not seen him. 'Who's he?' he repeated, superfluously, struck in the stomach. It was not fear of the man; the man was a buffoon: *The Man Who Would Be King* to be exact. But it was that old chestnut again: *presence*. Scarier than absence every time. Still, fear quickly gave way to loathing, as it always did. They went back a long way, Jude and *The Man Who Would Be King*. Had they not had run-ins? Had *The Man Who Would Be King* not given irresponsible prompts when Jude was on the point of speaking? Had not actions been misrepresented, words taken out of context, sadness mistaken for aloofness, and silence, snobbery? Which, of course, was exactly what they were, but that was not for a *Man*, still less one *Who Would Be King*, to presume, far less *infer*. Jude was bored with inference, tired of interpretation, deeply disinterested in psychology and its psychopathic subscribers, among whom he counted *The Man Who Would Be King*.

Jude followed this thread. 'No, what your psychology fails to grasp,' he reflected, 'is its sheer *pettiness*. The fact that it says what everyone knows but can't be bothered to say. Even when, through some statistical anomaly, it hits upon a right reason, it is scuppered by the pompous, quasi-systematic vocabulary which couches it. Where it would reveal to us an awful truth, it succeeds merely in poking out our eyes. No, psychology has had its day. Like all facts, it turns out a fashion, and a crimped, gimpish, Viennese one at that.'

'Well, I'm with you there,' said the old dame. She had paused, crabbed, with open shears, and was looking at Jude with a staring, sidelong eye. 'I never held by it. Mad Jen they call me, matter of fact. But I don't pay mind. It's all a question of degree.'

'Exactly,' said Jude. '*Exactly.*' He marvelled at the apposition. 'That's what they don't get—that's what the *world* don't get'—and he slapped a tomb: 'a question of *degree*.'

'Most people haven't learned to die.' Her voice was precise in the grass. She poked it like a snake, with an economy of thought. 'It's not the dying, you see,' she continued, gesturing with a welly at the graves. 'It's the learning. Takes a long time, the learning. I should know.' And she chuckled repeatedly, before changing tack. 'But they want it all at once—dropping in the ointment. What do they know of degree? They can't fall quickly enough.'

'Well it's just as we've always maintained. *Harper and I.*' Ordinarily, here, Jude would have dared his audience to ask who Harper was, thereby exposing an unforgivable ignorance. All it would take was a flexed stare. But with the old woman it would have been a wasted effort. She unconditionally accepted Harper's pertinence— which was more than could be said for most—and the validity of his maintained position, despite not yet knowing what that position was. In some ways, Jude reflected, she was his ideal audience. 'Just as they *cling* to the unconscious, so they all— *desperately*—want to die. If only so as to be absolved of responsibility.'

'There's a prime example,' said the woman with surprising directness. She poked her shears toward *The Man Who Would Be King.*

'A prime example I suppose I'll have to acknowledge.'

Jude's mind moved but his legs were still. At length they picked up where the mind left off and deposited him near enough to attract attention.

'Josh!' exclaimed *The Man Who Would Be King.* He looked up slowly, with a fixed smile. He was saying by it, he had known Jude was there.

'Hull*o*,' said Jude, saying by it, he knew he knew. 'How are you?'

'Oh, you know...'

'Nice day for it.'

'No, I don't think so.' The man's cheeks were red as his nose.

'Oh really?'

'Not for me.' He smiled through his pain.

'Oh, I'm sorry.'

'Heh, oh it's nothing. Just the usual thing. A little pain, a little *sorra*, heh, then all is over. But fancy seeing you here!'

'I was just thinking the same.'

'I'm not sure I'd have recognised you if you hadn't come up.'

'Oh, I would have.'

'I'm sorry?'

'I would have.'

'Heh, right answer! It's been a while though, hasn't it?'

'Actually, I saw you last week, in the *copsewood,* at Bullish lake. I would have said hello, but when I rounded the corner to where you were, you'd gone.'

The Man Who Would Be King shook his head.

'You looked a bit different though.'

'Nope. Heh.' He shook his head again.

'No, I'm sure. I was about twenty yards away. I rounded a clump and you'd taken a fork.'

'I haven't been there for yonks. Bad associations, you see.'

'If it wasn't you, it was your brother.'

He shook his head, slower this time. A sad look reigned.

'Strange. I was convinced it was you. Do you have a brother?'

'I suppose I do, heh.' He sniffed.

'Clean-shaven, perhaps younger than you?'

'In a sense.'

'How do you know he wasn't there?'

'Because he's here. You're standing on him actually.' He smiled a smile of pity.

'Oh. I'm sorry.' Jude raised his *all-stars* from the turf, one then the other. The trouble was, the grave being ill-marked, it was at least two steps in any direction to neutral ground and, by the time he had stepped back, then sideways, he had planted four heavy feet over the heart. Turning round he read *Requiescat In Pace*. And beneath it: *Here Lies A Man Whose Heart Was In The Right Place*.

'Crumbs,' said Jude. 'No wonder he died.'

'He's been dead for ten years.'

'Oh. I see.' Jude was beginning to dislike *The Man Who Would Be King* all over again. 'Is it the anniversary?'

'Funny word for it, mmm? No. I'm here to ring the bells. For Michaelmas. Kind of a charity event, heh. Have you heard about the anchor? It's surfaced, so to speak.'

'Yes.'

'You don't seem surprised.'

'I'm not. I suppose I anticipated it.' Jude looked carefully aside. 'What could be more predictable,' he said, 'than something that was lost being found. That was, after all, why it was lost in the first place. Loss,' he concluded, 'is an *attention-seeker*.'

'Nifty bit of psychology.'

'No. A reason to *scorn* psychology.'

'Hm. Food for thought. Actually that ties in with a quote I've got prepared. "How come they to dig up fish-bones, shells, beams, iron-works, many fathoms underground, and anchors in mountains far remote from all seas?" Eh?' *The Man Who Would Be King* wagged his eyebrows. 'I suppose your response would be: because that's where they were most likely to be found. Heh. Heh-heh.'

Jude said nothing. He was faintly outraged.

'Yup, the "Anatomy of Melancholy". There's one for you. Bit of a heavy tome, but some hidden gems. Or perhaps it's just me. I'm a little "melancholic" myself from time to time.' *The Man Who Would Be King* let out a sigh. 'Still, if it's attention they're after, they've succeeded. That's where I come in, actually. Couldn't have timed it better, with the bell-ringing an' all. Photo-ops all round.' He jerked a thumb behind him. Across the lane was a van with *Minerva* on the side. 'Few journos coming, from the Minerva, Herald, Chronicle and whatnot. Do a little panegyric on the anchor, church heritage, that kind of thing. Plus a stern word for the thieves. Just because they've put it back, they don't get off scot free.' His head fell to one side. 'Of course, they may plead a little leniency.'

'It all seems so well *timed*.'

'Weell, you know what they say: 'the early bird,' mmm?' *The Man Who Would Be King* rubbed his hands together. 'We want it in the evening editions—'specially for Michaelmas, hmm? Ties in well, with the bell tradition.'

'Yes, good publicity.'

'That's the world we live in, yup? And we'll do a few pics with Jenny, if she's willing.' As he said it, a car roared up the road and braked at the entrance. *The Man Who Would Be King* watched it come, chin in the air. 'But in the meantime,' he said, still watching. 'You're trespassing—technically speaking. They've closed off the church for the time being.' He looked kindly at Jude, pointing to a policeman at the eastern gate.

Jude pointed to the woman. 'It didn't stop her.'

'Oh, Jenny has dispensations. Come to think about it, I don't expect she knows.'

'Oh, she does. Perhaps she came that way.' Jude regarded the western gate.

'You didn't, though. I've been here a while.'

'You're very involved.'

'I'm on the Heritage Committee. I like my history and culture and all that, though I couldn't really call myself a believer.' *The Man Who Would Be King* wrinkled his nose. 'More of an agnostic, really. A humanist, me.'

'Where's the vicar?'

'Oh, there isn't one at the moment. They had someone, Reverend Russell, but he resigned last month, not long after arriving. Couldn't *rustle* up sufficient interest, heh.'

'I knew the Reverend Hannah had retired.'

'You know what they say: if you can't take the heat.' *The Man Who Would Be King* mopped his brow with a handkerchief.

'Are they not getting another?'

'In all honesty, it's not all that relevant to the modern generations. Sad but true. Can't stand in the way of progress, hup.' He sniffed. 'It will probably have to close, or be rebranded as it were. We're thinking of a charity. A little philanthropic thing. Peace, Positivity, Pathos—that's our slogan. Otherwise. Well, there's always luxury residences.'

Somehow the conversation had turned nasty. Jude wasn't sure whose fault it was, but then again, he had a very good idea.

'How did they get in?' he asked, uninterested.

'That's what we're trying to work out. No windows smashed. Doors all locked. Jenny and her crew are the only ones with keys at the moment. Since the, heh, Russell affair.'

'Who found it?'

'No one, technically. Someone phoned the papers. They got on to me, seeing as I made a hue and cry when it was stolen.' *The Man Who Would Be King* folded his arms, and looked about resignedly. 'Yup,' he said, then turned back to Jude. 'Strange crime, *innit?*' He wiggled his eyebrows and crooked his knees like a policeman.

'Very.' Jude thought a space, then started to the grave for his scythe. The dialogue needed abridging.

'What are you doing here anyway?'

'Going through that gate.' Jude pointed to the western gate.

'Must get that taped up,' observed *The Man Who Would Be King*. 'They do say, don't they, that a criminal often returns to the scene of the crime.'

'That is because *they*—witness or criminal, it's all the same, as they will gleefully assert—are obsessed with obsession. They think it makes for a good story. Desperately trying to convince themselves the detective story is *actually* the modern-day romance.'

'I tend to think there's a bit of a detective in all of us. Don't you, Josh? Is there a bit of detective in ya? Eh—whaddaya think?'

Jude thought, with his eyes in the yews. 'No, I—I despise detection.'

'Many people despise what they fear.'

'But only a few despise properly a trite diagnosis.'

'Heh. Good one. Nice to see you again Josh. Nice outfit, heh. Josh Harley, in't it?'

'Yes, nice to see you.'

'How's Harpie getting on?'

'Fine.' Jude was stalking down the path, removing the strimmer, opening, closing the gate, waving, cutting a left past the eastern-gate, just as a cavalcade of journalists drove up and emptied into the churchyard. The policeman watched him to the end of the road. He turned the bend, climbed the steep drive to The Manor, stole through Grouse's open door, helped himself to brandy, bade good morning the snoring Grouse, trespassed over grounds, took a hid stile in his stride, melted through field, down ditchful of nettles, up pained other side, leapt fence and pressed through holly hedge—straight into Harper's garden.

*

'There's no one there.'

'So I saw.'

'Gone to Wales.'

'WALES!' cried Magnus. 'What the hell's in Wales?'

'Auntie Jean.'

'Quentin's gone to Wales?'

No, said Harper. Quentin was in town, doing drafts, audits, analyses? Something of that nature. He stared at Francisco's lines, absorbing them into Marcellus'.

'Quentin is forever analysing,' grumbled Jude. 'And his technique is to gaze intently at the object of analysis, as if it will discover itself through sheer force of empathy.' With his famous left foot Jude bent a pass round the semicircle. 'Unlike Bjørn's, of course, which is simply to stare for a *very long time*, and expect it to discover itself through sheer boredom. Which of course—and, again, unlike Quentin's—works every time.' Jude looked a defiantly short distance—at his *all-stars* on the step's edge. 'And the irony is, Quentin's a total *mole!* Wielding veils and sunglasses as if it made any difference.'

Magnus looked a defiantly long distance—a defiance, unlike Jude's, borne of abstraction—until *The Man Who Would Be King*'s car dipped under the hill. Then he strode back to his bike and allowed himself to drift downhill, one hand touched to the brake, and the front-light wavering. As threats went, *The Man Who Would Be King* was a broad front. His was a slow pressure, applied at the margins. He waited for you to present yourself to him, trussed up for Crimbo dinner. It didn't do to agitate—to think—about a man like that for any time, or that's exactly where you end. His threat lay in threat itself, in all its opacity. He was never going to blow your house down, hunt your carcass, shoot you at ten paces. *The Man Who Would Be King* was an ideas man. He had big ambitions, national reach, connections in the media. Magnus was interested in the tangible. His experiments were on pumpkins and tulips. No astrophysicist, his science was essentially a local one. Everything else was rumours, and they flew. You just had to cast your eye at the papers. Examples gross as earth. People in arms, armies in transit, travellers evicted just for travelling. Here an exploded bus, all petal and no stamen. Over there, somebody's head, fixed to a fencepost, with a white dunce-cap and snowman's eyes. There were fundamentalists crawling from corners, and *culture* was the word on everyone's lips. The police had no answer but gas and gunfire, like a fool-child crying *Because!* to every *Why?* Plus immigration was an 'issue'—which cut both ways. People arrived in crates and containers, packed in trucks and loaded in lorries. Some were full of corpses, others of cannibals. One truck contained nothing but babies. It was a scam whichever way you looked at it. Some walked straight through the tunnel, distracted the guards with old ruses and slipped into the country. Some had been deported but they came right back. All had their perspectives; all were obstructed in abstract ways. Who were they to have perspectives?

They could take their perspectives and put them to the wheel. Mobs were formed. Houses were burned. Sceptical people were hounded all over. Old fashioned appearances were out. Hoods were suspicious. Veils kicked up a storm. Sikhs were rolled in blankets, Hindus were laughed at. Vicars were blindfolded and forced to eat cake—or perhaps they were complicit. Meanwhile, the scholars had gone into overdrive, creating reams of isms which blew about the streets, to the tune of a thousand accusations. It was messy. Not only were racists pilloried but dentists as well. A flautist was assaulted outside a philharmonic hall. People were rooting through their neighbours' dustbins, then taking all the rubbish and posting it back through other people's letter-boxes. Roadworks were going on everywhere and never being finished. You could see right down beneath the tar into the wet clay, clogged with debris: magazines, bottles, bits of plastic, some deposited recently, some sixty years since, when the pipes were laid.

Images flashed on the idle eye like the reels of early cinema, gaps and bars between them, crowded into animation. Magnus was up early, had seen the morning papers, quiet on Pale pavements, awaiting the spark of sun. They were full of panic. *Water Shortage Hits Crisis Point* said one. *Driest summer on record puts strain on resources. Foot and Mouth 'Impossible to Isolate'* said a second:

Farmers told to 'expect epidemic'. They all loved a subtitle. *Livestock Burns On The Levels* said a local. 'I suppose that's my doing too!' said Magnus, biking away. The Haverley Levels—they were only twenty miles. From the top of Broody he could see the smoke, but in Pale it seemed another world. Bakery trucks growled on the roads. Someone lay drunk on the Cathedral lawn. Stalls were being stocked with self-help material. By the time the sun warmed the tar, Magnus was out of town.

Now he was riding the hills. He pushed a pedal, flew through avenues. 'Fantastic!' he cried. 'Keep your epidemics! Stow your frigging resources! Here comes the dawn, to whip your sleep like a conjuror strips the table!' It was true. Dawn was stealing in, nipping needles from the pine. Wind rushed under, blew a smile about him. He hurtled to a plain of rutted knolls, rutting and knolling like a benign affliction. It was the Broody Sumps, once copper-mines, now pleasure-ground for potholers. But the Sumps were not safe, as the signs advised. Many of the ruts concealed sinkholes or *swallets* under cover of dock or nettle.

'Is that right?' said Jude, thoughtful. He scraped a sole. 'Hmmm. Sinkholes, eh? Ruts, say you?' He jabbed a finger into Harper's ribs. '*Under cover of dock or nettle.*' He grimaced like a goat, contracted his muscles, shrank to dwarfish dimensions. 'Dock or nettle,' he repeated. '*Dock* or *nettle...*'

Harper planted a slow foot studs-up on Jude's shin.

'No seriously, dock? *Or nettle?*'

'I'm going to have to think about that one.'

'Sweat it.'

Magnus braked on a knoll, and wiped the sweat away. It was hot already. Sheep-bells plotted the distances. Otherwise all was still. No, not *all*. He listened hard; he stared down. There was a movement as of bowels. All at once, in the rut-bottom, spittle spurted from a hole. He started. He squatted to wait. Five minutes more, and the movement repeated. He walked to another rut, with the same result. A burble, a gulp, a release of fluid. He left his bike, walked round the ruts in a quarter-mile radius. It became a symphony: the Sumps themselves, gurgling like a maternity ward.

This bore scrutiny. Magnus trotted down the original rut and parted the nettles. 'Water,' he said, touching the excrement. Sediment had collected round the hole. Some kind of calcic deposit. The Sumps were a thousand feet high, a few miles from the major reservoirs. Why were they big with water? He wiped his hand, kicked a warning sign, ploughed back up the slope. There wasn't time for this. He straddled the bike, leaned forward, skimmed folds like a ski-jumper.

'Where's Drake?'

Magnus shook his head. 'Nothing doing.' he said robotically. 'He called me at Claudine's. He's in Milton Keynes, of all places! Hah! Hungover as only a Drake can be!' Magnus shrugged. He didn't look bothered.

'There's always me, I suppose. Haff-a-haff. A kind of impact substitute, you might say.'

They looked up and sideways. Feet apart, with the sun between them like an expanding football—over which they would occasionally practise a laboured stepover—stood the Lie, whose sepia stripes might have been the illusion of light. A dog was calm beside him.

'BENJAMIN McCORMACK KEPPERLY-LIE!' said Magnus.' That walking PRODIGALITY.'

The Lie hesitated, looked a moment at Jude. White lashes flickered. Slowly, like a bird's wing, his jaw began to wag.

'Haff haff haff,' he said, sniffing, almost silent. 'That's me.'

'Well of course it is!' roared Jude.

'I suppose it is really, isn't it?'

'Ha!'

'Ohohohono.'

'DAMN RIGHT IT IS!' Magnus grinned humourlessly, staring east. The Lie narrowed his eyes, placed a finger on his upper lip. He had been strolling with his dog down Bonfire Lane, as quiet and long a lane as you could wish to know, connecting Latterly to Coal Hill, Coal Hill to the lake. Suddenly Beau began to roam, briskly back and forth, as if checking for mines. Actually he was vetting a host of frogs, splayed along the road, showing a remarkable, but Lie-like, restraint.

The Lie did not know what to make of this. He circled about, as if shielding a football from Jude before turning him, all too easily, to go through on goal—only to realise that he wasn't fast enough to avoid the retaliatory tackle, and so resorted to shielding, and then turning him again, until it began to seem that life was a constant process of shielding and turning. Finally he tottered in, grinning like a crab, to blaze high wide and handsome, or flap with an air shot and overbalance in a puddle, soaking his tracksuit trousers and Juventus shirt, gawping and hoarsely laughing.

From somewhere ahead and westward, a shot quaked and died. Geese took wing above the lake. The Lie knew a gunshot when he heard one. He shielded the ball, turned his frog. Again he sidewayed, again shielded, turned his frog. By this method, meticulously applied, he negotiated the whole eleven. He didn't like it though. It spelled trouble of one sort or another. It was warm for September. He listened to the cracking of branches. His blue eyes searched the rolling fields leftward. Then he disappeared between high hedgerows.

Magnus left the main-road, and took hedged lanes to Upper Dovecombe. Braced above the saddle he slalomed up from the decimated forest and pulled into the forestry track. In the west, night and storm were indistinguishable. East, over scrub and brush, was the Bircher Chimney, legacy of the lead mines. As he watched it, a howl leapt from its mouth and bounded round the forest. 'Weird shit,' he said to himself. 'Worthy of study.' But in mind's eye he saw the sun, under horizon, set to speak like an actor in the wings. With his own wings he flew down Dovecombe hill, through footpathed fields, across the main-road to the lakeside, west of Farnham's Bridge.

Here the grass was long. Deer slipped through it, losing the dew. Locking bike to fence he passed down a path, narrow as a man, high-hedged and crossed with thorns. It made for a thick atmosphere. In ten minutes he hit the Dovecombe road, not far from the Mallard Bank, now a steep mass of mud. Cutting across the road, he stole along the sidewater, shrunk to a puddle. Nearby were the remains of the Coot Bridge Station. Across the road, in the reservoir proper, he saw the Ossly bridge and, like some ocean growth, the greenstained ruins of Folly Hall. Further out, crags that once were houses, where you only rolled one die, if any. The lake was hardly ten feet deep. Fifty odd years since its death, Ossly was rising up, with the grave rags dragging. A deathly silence hung over all. Which trauma compared with resurrection? You could clear the passages, but it took much longer to uncake the voice.

Beyond Eanswithe's Peninsula, Magnus recrossed the road and headed for the boathouse. The way lay through pathless fields of sleeping geese, and he shrank among them like a night-nurse through the army. He trod no necks, broke no beaks, displaced no plume, as if himself the spirit of sleep. The sky was lightening but the field was dark. He had made it as far as the field-middle, when a shot cracked the air, and he was stopped in his tracks, hand hanging, dance redundant, like a scarecrow in snow. All at once the ground rose around him. Masses and blizzards of them blundered up, effing and blinding and batting their arms. It was nothing but pounding and screeching and the waking terror. Vast figures struck grand attitudes, as if the sky were a marble pantheon. Magnus was stone, air still cleft with an arm. He looked like something from Magritte or de Chirico. The grey field, the strip of hedge, and the geese frozen like the Christmases past.

The geese fled. Magnus checked his watch. *6:25.* A little late, but he'd make it. He trotted through field, over gate to the boathouse. No one was about. The lake was fifty yards from the shore proper. All the boats were high and dry, except one. At the water's edge a rowing-boat was moored to a post. He trod cracked mud to the reaches and untied it. It was the same boat he'd borrowed a couple of months ago, oars clipped and a couple of inches of water in the bottom. There was a dismantled fishing rod under the seat, and, strangest of all, what appeared to be a bad imitation of a crocodile-mask. Magnus snorted, settled in, pushed off along the surface.

Harper tapped a pocket-watch. 'Six thirty,' he said. 'It's the sun's move.'

'And with that, he comes,' said Magnus, straining fingers in the rays. 'Stretching over the board!' He looked approving.

'He should be warned,' said Jude. 'It's touch-piece, move-piece.'

'He knows the rules. He INVENTED them.' Magnus stalked along the Gods, rolling his shoulders like a magician moving a coin.

Jude stole a glance. 'There's an actor who won't brook direction.'

Harper took a breath and carried the camera to Station *A*. He wanted to get this over with. Jude went with him. They set the camera. All Jude had to do was start and stop it. He watched Harper climb onto pedestal 3, looking to the lake, and his finger touched the button.

Action. Marcellus spins about.

Marcellus:
Who's there?

Cut. The camera went back to Magnus, on the amphitheatre, taking in arch and road both. It looked like a delicate balance. Harper bent over the pedestal, straining down under the arch. Jude gone in the underpass. *Action.* Jude's voice booming:

Horatio:
No. *Answer* me. *Un*fold *yourself.*

Marcellus:
Long live the King!

Unbeknown to camera, Jude began scrambling up the bank on the arch's other side, through the Pump House grounds. He pushed through the hedge, jumped the fence, and landed on the dam road. *Marcellus is still leaning over the railing when Horatio climbs up and surprises him at his shoulder. They embrace.* They shout to reach the microphone.

Horatio:
Marcellus!

Marcellus:
Horatio!

291

Horatio:
A piece of him!

Cut. Magnus wandered to the Outlet Tower. *Camera to D. Horatio gazing to Dimly. Zoom on his profile. King can be seen approaching on the wall, sun on shoulder. Action and voiceover.*

Marcellus [*sotto*]:
Horatio says it's but our fantasy,
And will not let belief take hold of him,
Touching this dreaded sight twice seen of us.
When this same star that's westward from the
*   pole,*
Had made his course t'illume that part of
*   heaven*
Where now it burns, the bell then beating one—

Cut. St Swithen's tolls for Michaelmas morning. *King stops. Camera to A. Wide angle, takes in Pedestals 1-3. Set time delay. Marcellus to Pedestal 3. King walks. Action. Marcellus turns slowly.*

Marcellus [*alto*]:
Look where it comes again!
In the same figure like the King that's dead!
You're a scholar! Speak to it, Horatio!

Cut. Camera to C. Set time delay. Run to position. Action. King in foreground, Pedestal 1, back to camera. Beyond, a piece of Horatio, a sliver of Marcellus.

Horatio:
What are you?! That usurp this time of night!

They watch each other, calm, inexpressive, sun and storm in faces. *Cut. Camera to A. Wide angle again. King turns round. Action. King walks away.*

Horatio:
Stay! Speak!

Cut. Jude and Harper run to the camera, training it on Magnus. *Action. King walks as far as Outlet Tower. Cut.*

'Here's the problem with your theatre sans audience,' observes Jude. 'You're never sure no one is watching you. Lost in a vast forest, trees crashing silently all around, you cling to dialectics as to—bike-spoke reflectors.'

There was no one around. Jude trailed away, knuckles dragging in case anyone was watching. Spying a Water Board van at the Meal Common junction, and pleased with the excuse, he crossed the road, walked right through Raquel Dullet's garden, without—to his considerable surprise—

catching sight, at an upstairs window, of Raquel Dullet in a state of undress—which was to say, without catching sight, at an upstairs window, of Raquel Dullet—climbed a wall, shuffled an aspen, slipped a fence, leapt barbed-wire, strolled through the yard of Caulton's freezer factory, scaled lattice, jumped again and landed in a strait way, bordered with hedges. The van was oblivious.

'Excellent,' he said, striding down the path, still followed by the cloud. He took Harper's note from his pocket. *Act 1, Scene 1*, said the note:

> *6:30 am, the amphitheatre, Michaelmas. Arrive precisely when you mean to.*

That was all. Jude flicked it disdainfully and looked ahead, bouncing down the bumps to a pool of nettles. Left was a stile and, beyond, a belt of fields. Ahead was a footbridge, leading to field, road and reservoir. Between, under, around, the Glum went trickling, little more than stream. 'Nn, old Glum,' said Jude, 'creeping on the earth like a *creeping thing.*' He threw a stick to its windings. Roads were best avoided, but then fields were too. If roads meant guards, fields meant farmers. A man could easily find his theatrics curtailed. A man could actually break a leg.

'Footbridge, or *stile?*' he asked Harper.

294

'Hmm?'

'What I said.'

It was touch and go but Jude took the stile, aiming to follow the Glum and cross it later on a short stone slab. He entered the established fields. Down they bent, bowing low where the Glum drew line. Gravity was the order of the day. You could tread such necks to the bottom of the world. Visibility was poor. Fuzz was at the edges. Jude went into the shades, field on field, hedge on hedge, cow on cow, surpassing all with unlikely agility. All the while, the Glum sallied at his right, like a humble brown Panza to his squat Quixote. Hunchbacked, thick-thighed, feet flapping at angles, Jude felt a flying giant, mowing dew from air, cloak casting counties into night. The upslopes steamed, but it was still dark in the gulley, lit with lines and twice as cold. Jude walked cool in his own breath-clouds. But there was nothing unusual about that. Onwards he went, by post and hollow, weed and ivy, gap, gate, and hollow again, till he came upon that stone bridge, jammed between the banks.

The sun was not yet up. The west was blue, but the east was wounded. Jude pulled up into shapelier airs. Sweat stood on his brow—slid between shoulder blades. The field was lined, scantly, with yellow barley; to the left, slick fences. It was the sewage works: the kind of place you couldn't find if you wanted to, but if you didn't, would always chance on. He followed one of the lines, rehearsing his own, till a gap in the next hedge framed the Pump House, like a pot of gold. 'Nya, the Pump House,' he murmured:

This, I take it,
Is the main motive of our preparations
The source of this our watch, and the chief head
Of this post-haste *and rummage in the land.*

He vanished through the gap. The land was dry as bone. The Pump House stood in a circle of its own power and Jude walked to it, seemingly magnetised but actually quite voluntarily. The west was all shadow, but the east all rouge. Climbing gentle slopes from the Pump House to the dam-bank, a fence formed horizon, slashing the rouge with eyeline. Jude thought about Sarah Kent.

'I'll slash her rouge any time she likes.'

'And dam her bank to boot.'

It was a peculiar feature of the Pump-House grounds that, within its fence, like a sore thumb in the dead-middle, stood a legal stile, fed by legal footpath but barbed with wire. To walk that path, to climb that stile, even to dismount that stile—these were common joys, with civil laws to back them. But to set foot on the other side the stile—that was trespass. Jude walked that path now in full

296

possession of his pleasures. Jude was relentless where stiles were concerned. Magnus said they were function in its purest form; but Jude knew different. A stile went well beyond function. A stile was a state of mind. A point of honour. You could get high just tangling with it. Consciously common, yet exultantly individual, he straddled that stile. For a second, the scythe-blade caught on the crossbeam—detached—then, crabbed and culpable, he hit the ground, sinking to the Pump House like blood to the impression. The east was cut, but west was crust and tannin. To a cowering eye, it looked alarmingly like the Langly Bell, impossibly grand and the stone tongue swinging. Jude cowered, looked back, bristling. He saw the sky's frightening dome, vast and savage on his shoulder. Sweat mowed him like a lawn.

All-stars crunching the grasses, Jude watched the Pump House rising before him—and how different in appearance! It was true that Jude was surprised by very little—and appearance was hardly *revelation*—yet that did not stop him being *annoyed*. He immediately set to work forestalling the Pump House's expectations. Appearance—the forerunner of *presence*—was a presumption at the best of times. Jude lost no time letting the Pump House know it. Striding near, he saw the wall on one side had been removed. Where had been pumps and dials was an array of furniture and accessories:

imitation-marble tables, chairs, sedans, lampstands, candelabra, stand-alone ashtrays, dumb waiters and Lazy Susans, even a sundial, all ornate, most of them done in hard materials, and harder lines. On the tables were wine-glasses, flute glasses, brandy glasses, also cut-glass decanters and bowls. There were awnings, tarpaulins, screens, and a dish to reflect light. Mops, buckets, plastic barrels loitered at the sides. Around and above all, leaking pipes swooped and ran, water fleeced freely the walls, and a large crack had opened in the far corner under the ceiling. It was a work in progress. In the midst of it all, in a large marble armchair, at a marble chess-table, was Hole, hand idle on the stone.

'Hole,' said Jude. 'I expected as much.'

''Arlow,' said Hole. 'I foreseen it.' He sniggered. Streamlets stopped the echoes.

'Lounging, like Antonius Block, with his concupiscent chessboard.'

'Dressed as Death. But who's the tenor of yer metaphor, what I want to know?'

'Funnily enough, Antonius Block was asking the same question.'

''Ee should 'ave answered it.' Hole let an air-rifle wink from his lap. It was the first time Jude had looked a gun in the face. Of course, guns had always been there. But he hadn't actually had to stare down their barrels.

He looked back up at Hole. 'A man in touch, I see, with the base of his power.'

'There's a definition o' Death.'

'A friendless sybarite,' continued Jude. 'Sprawled self-congratulatorily on the factory floor—which, in his grand delusion, he conceives to be imposing and *impossible* theatre. There's another.'

'End's the same.'

'Ah, the *end*: last resort of the witless. With whom Death is first among equals.'

'Too right, boy. The great leveller. Movin' and shakin' what wit can only watch.'

'So I see.' Jude leaned, nonchalant, on a square chair. 'Doing a spot of refurbishment?'

'It's kind of furbishin' itself.'

'Well, a house takes after its occupant.'

'I call it the War Rooms.'

'Wet Dreams?'

Hole sneered into chins. 'Fuckin' tropical innit? Real fuckin' Mousetrap.' From the pipes above him, a spurt lurched forth, spattered on his head, set thick attacks on the chess-table, pooling in the squares. Excepting the black checks, the table was pale. The board was set into the surface, and the pieces, huge. Hole's hand attended the King like a liveryman. The other reached behind him, whipped up an open umbrella, with the PPP emblazon. The water pummelled it, ran down the sides, hid Hole in a gleaming curtain.

'Oh it's like that is it? Percatum. Plaga. Penitentia.'

'Poor Piece of Piss.'

Jude looked aside. 'Presumption. *Precocity. Preposterousness.*'

'Pussies. Pricks. Pillocks.'

'Preening precious *pedantry.*'

'Peter Piper an' 'is fuckin' Peck o' Peppers.'

They chuckled in unison. Hole tossed the umbrella, squinted up at the vapours. 'Na, bit of a waste isn't it?' he continued. 'On the one hand, there's a hosepipe ban, bath ban, fuggin' handwashing ban.' His hand formed a crown. 'On the other, this.'

'That will change today,' said Jude with the boredom of certainty. '*Apparently.*'

Hole continued staring at the table. Water rode between the lines, cleared the spaces, nudged the feet of pawns. The sound grew louder as you listened. Hole grew stiller. Only a finger inched between the royals.

Eventually he said: 'Ice you's on's so thin, 'Arley; move but a li'l an' you're through.'

'I know. I can't move today without trampling a grave.' Jude jerked the cloak across his shoulder. 'I only need jump to hit a six-gun salute.'

'Always was a wit, weren't you, 'Arle? Always popular. Draggin' wiv ya your *cortege.*' The same finger lifted from water, pointed at the sky like cannon. Turning, Jude saw the cloud which had tracked him building to a front. 'You'll be missed.'

'Only by those who haven't grasped a word I said.'

'Ferget graspin' 'Arle. Long as they 'member 'em.' Hole really had it in for the table-side. 'An', mark me, they will.'

Jude was susceptible to flattery, even at the point of a gun. 'Possibly.' He blushed in the cut-glass. 'Though not due to any exertions of their own.'

'Got the air o' destiny about ya. Gon' make a name fer yerself.'

'Yes yes.' Jude recovered. The world's obsession with prophecy was as dull as vain.

'Funny, in't it? It's an endless old universe out there, and 'ere we are, the two of us, in this unlikely scenario at this godforsaken fuckin' time.' The cloud moved, sombre. It looked like a whale consuming the world. 'It's centrifugal, my man. We gets sucked together. Embrace or 'splode, but we cancel each other.'

'No, I won't have your tired dichotomies.'

'Oh but you must.' Hole winked his gun again, motioned to the table, as if 'his power made that jovial scene'. 'Sit yerself down, I got another 'un fer ya.'

Jude looked slightly left, widely right. Stains spread on the walls. The cloud was a bucket at his shoulder. He was sceptical of chess. More specifically, he was sceptical of Quentin's, Harper's, above all Bjørn's, enthusiasm for chess, which was, like all enthusiasms, wildly disproportionate to the object. *Nimzo-Indians* refuted him; *zugzwangs* bamboozled; *en passants* passed him by. It was true, certain attacks were rugged, healthy affairs. The *Crab Opening* was to be applauded. The *Lizard Attack* was hilarious. About the *Fried Fox Variation* he felt frankly ambivalent. But defences in general were despicably premeditated. The Spanish was too square, French too *nuanced*, and the English was insistently eccentric. The *Sicilian Dragon* was the only defence Jude was prepared to tolerate, if only because it was actually an attack. A man could fall victim to the *Dragon* while retaining a measure of respect for his opponent, end up guffawing on the sharp end of his *fianchetto*. A *fianchetto* was amusing all round, inviting comparisons with ballet. Jude had nothing against ballet. Fran Peters did it, and that was fine with him. He had been to a ballet once, at the Kirov in Moscow. He had fallen asleep.

There was little chance of that now. Pipe-water washed him as he made his way to table. He placed the scythe on an awkward armchair, drew up another, placed his rear in a puddle. Hole watched him from white eyes. The lashes looked heavy with liner. Perhaps it was the dawn.

'Trespassin', int you. Laws are tough on that, the minute, what with the arson an' whatnot.' The idle hand toyed with a radio. 'I could 'ave the police 'ere 'fore you could even retort, witty as you are.'

'I lost my way.'

'That's it, though, int it, 'bout trespass? Int about motive. 'S'about crossin' a line. You're either on that side, or on this side. Black and white, see.'

'Clearly. Who but a knob would trespass with *motive?*'

''Specially in that get-up. 'Specially with a camera filmin' 'im.' Hole indicated two new cameras. They were screwed to soffits at the open corners of the building, one bent on them, one on the fields. 'Caught you crossin' that stile. Sneakin' over the lawn. Film ya some more, if you like.'

'No thankyou.'

'We got some backdrops, props and whatnot. Could be a real old session.'

Jude was appalled.

Hole continued, undeterred. 'See, when I said this was a *scenario,* I chose my words carefully. But I'm willin' ta waive all that.' Hole waved before him, as if brushing off flies. Behind him Jude saw some monitors, half draped in tarpaulin. One showed a stile; on another, part-covered, were Hole and Jude, Hole waving, Jude with back to camera. 'After all, I'm a water-man, aren' I? Heh. Win, an' you can 'ave our li'l film.' He drew a circle in the

303

air, which the screen repeated. 'Keep it fer private viewin'.'

'No,' said Jude, abstractly. 'I don't think I want it.' He was wondering if the gun was real.

'Shame, considerin' what yer enemies could do wiv it.'

'Isn't it.'

'I'm puttin' up your continued liberty. What you puttin' up, 'Arle?'

Having what was far better than motive, namely, *opportunity*, Jude decided to play along. Feeling in his cloak pocket, he produced the fish-hook and placed it on the table.

'This,' he said.

'Heh. She's a beauty. You gon' catch me out?'

'Well, something smells fishy.'

'A man 'demns 'imself by his own mouth, they say. Where d'ya get it?'

'From Nemmins' actually. This morning.'

'Brought it where?'

'Fourpoints *Farm*.'

'Ye're lyin'.'

Jude gazed at Hole, all coy transparency.

''Arley, you're a fuckin' nut! What were you doin' at Fourpoints, by Christ?'

'Oh, having breakfast. You see, Nemmins took it from *me.*'

''Ee's a big fuckin' baby, innee? So you was jus' takin' back what's rightly yours?'

304

Jude pondered. 'There's a difference,' he said at last, 'between *rights* and *inheritance*. People just keep *giving* me things.' He nudged the hook. 'No matter how many times I give them away.'

Hole pondered this too, tongue on one side. 'Not me,' he said smiling. 'Got ta win what I gives.'

'I hope you don't play like Bjorn Bjornsen,' said Jude.

''Ow's that?'

'Bjorn doesn't beat people. He waits for them to die.'

'Oh, I int that kind. You can call me *pro-active*.' Hole sniggered again, putting gum to lips. He pushed his King's pawn.

Jude's competitive instincts roused. 'I see you're white,' he queried.

'Like I said. No one's shade, am I.'

Jude parried with the Queen's knight's pawn. Jude liked a knight. He liked its deviance.

'Now whatcha doin', pokin' where ya dunt belong?'

'A little scoping out.'

Hole swung out his bishop. 'That's my domain, see.'

Jude took his own bishop. Cool as you like he cut a *fianchetto*. Floods kissed the episcopal feet. 'Debated waters,' he said. You could hardly hear for piss.

305

'I got backing.' Hole chewed away. 'Out chugged the Queen like a steamer. 'I'm the law.'

'And eager to prove it.'

'I got initiative.'

'The illusion of movement.'

'My, 'ow you could do wiv 'at now.'

Jude thought for a while. The situation was an unpromising one. 'Your threats,' he said, 'are as tiresome as your pleasantries.'

'But you got to face 'em.'

'I'm not sure I have. I refuse the obsession with Nemesis.'

'Maybe. But it's still your move.'

'I refuse your amateur psychology, and, after all, *all* psychology is amateur. Denial is not always acquiescence.'

'You came 'ere a-purpose, 'Arle. What's yer purpose?'

'I'm going over that *stile*.' Jude pointed where he came.

'You just came from there.'

'I thought I'd tackle it from another perspective.'

Hole drummed his fingers. 'Saw yer friend Crow t'other day. Snoopin' too. You've a penchant fer it.'

Jude cradled his head. He could hardly see the pieces for water. But the air was close, the shower a relief.

'Yes, Magnus is relentlessly *improving*,' he said. 'He's his own sworn *apprentice*: perpetually developing his Nimzovitchian *system*. Hooks and crampons, pipes and shafts, bells and whistles—all pawns in his pedagogical game.' He air-flicked at a pawn.

'I see.'

'Yes, it's all about plots with Magnus. Meal. Marching. Dovecombe. Fire. Water. Big cats, rare birds—he uncovers it all.'

'Was that wise?' said Harper, squinting to his right.

'Well, I'm not convinced by wisdom. The only thing I value less is secrecy.'

'I'm not sure Magnus will agree.'

'Magnus will do well to ignore it completely. In fact, he may turn it to his advantage. Secrecy is overrated—by none moreso than itself. Something it makes laughably transparent every minute of the day.' Harper went back to the camera. Magnus' features were coming into focus. The lined eyes, the grin, the glimpse of dodo.

'You don't understand,' continued Jude, twitching his mouth. 'That *all these things are ridiculous. Juvenile.* Taken *far too seriously.*'

'What kind of system?'

'Oh, Magnus is forever *probing*. It's all theoretical of course.'

'Not when he's probing my patch.'

'Especially then.' Jude hovered on a knight.

Hole lifted his rifle. 'See, my theories, 'Arley—' he began and a pellet flew into the wall, dropping plaster from the brick. The report was no sooner sounded than absorbed. '—'Ave practical applications.'

'Ha!' Jude turned round, took in the patch, the scraps, the streaming ruin. 'No, you're right! I forgot about the *applications*.' Back he manoeuvred in his enormous chair.

'That's the difference 'twixt us. You's brainy, 'Arle, but you an't got a *plan*. An't got *ends in mind*.'

'Because I scorn your *ends in mind*.'

'Can't 'ave both ways, 'Arle. See, you score, even as you scorn.'

'You're mistaken. My scorn is all means.'

'Like the sound of one 'and clappin'.'

'More like a standing ovation.'

'Must be an echo then.'

'No.' Jude breezed a hand round the room. 'Dead in the water.'

Hole chuckled. 'We're doin' laps.'

'Self-comparisons.'

This time Hole inhaled. 'S'always *touché*, all *tactics* wiv you. An't got no *plot*, 'Arle.'

'I scorn your plot, its desperate *naivité*. Constantly suspending its disbelief.'

'Got ta think moves ahead. Got to get *strategy*.'

'So keen to *outwit*. Like a man who laughs too long.'

'Glass 'ouses, 'Arle. You outwit yeself.'

'Let him without sin.'

'Glass 'ouses again.'

Jude gazed round the building. Windows were shattered, shards strewed the ground, walls were pressed with water. The whole thing was a sick luxury, fat potentate, rotten parliament, grown upon the poor. 'Glass houses,' he said. 'Built on sand.' He chuckled.

'Wrong! She's founded deep!'

'Up to her neck?'

Hole glowed like carbon. 'She's clean,' he said quietly.

'I scorn your *cleanliness*.'

There was a scuffle: bricks slid away where the wall was shot. In the context it hardly registered. The sound was crushed like a lit match, gone before it came.

'Careful there.' It was Hole's turn to admire. The confluent channels formed a pool about them, as if the lake itself were moving house. ''Ell hath no fury,' he said quietly. 'An' she's womanly in moods.'

Jude continued watching the wall. Something was building. It was as if the whole House were about to slide. The walls would tear away, someone call *Cut, that's the wrap!*

Nothing changed. The bricks lay piled. Dust rose, dispersed in spray. Then, all gingerly, a fox came crawling to the rift in the wall. It crouched, looking at them, nose over the trench.

Hole reached for his rifle. 'What'd'I say?' he said quietly.

'A green-eyed monster.'

Hole looked at Jude, presenting his rifle to the wall. 'You got to be jealous to survive, 'Arle.' He squinted, turned back, but the fox was gone.

'Unlucky. For you, obviously.'

'Luck ain't it. It's plans, 'Arle. I got 'em, Crow got 'em. Usin' brains fer gains. You and yer ginger familiar there—you live from day ta day.'

'But we live.'

'For a day.'

'No more do you.'

'It's in our 'ands, Crow's an' mine.'

'I scorn your porous plans, your building and destroying, in fictional crevices and imaginary crags. The merest glance sees through them.'

'Glance away, 'Arle. But you may not be so lucky as your friend.'

'And then again, I may.'

Hole put the rifle on the table. He leant back, looped a bird-leg round the arm. 'Always liked you, 'Arle. You're 'ard—like me. Dunt fuck around.'

Jude said nothing.

'Know 'oo yer friends are. Any doubts—you're rid of 'em!'

'The percentage game.'

'We could use someone like you.'

'I'm sure.'

'Could show you things.'

'No thanks. I'm straight.' Jude's southpaw reached for the pawn. It paused, calculating.

'Dunt be a fool, 'Arle. Could show you wonders.'

Jude looked up, as if from reverie. In the side of his eye he saw the fox, loping to stile in the purple west. A cub and vixen tiptoed behind. The adults were scabes-ridden, but the cub looked healthy. They disappeared under the stile. On the screen behind, they disappeared again. 'No,' he said. 'I don't think you could.' The paw flicked the pawn for last deliberations.

'How so sure?'

'Because I have anticipated *everything*.' It turned to the knight.

'Touch piece, move piece, 'Arley, my boy.'

'And?'

'You already touched that pawn.'

'No I didn't.'

'Heh, but you did.'

'I didn't fucking touch it.'

'Fuckin' saw your flick.'

Jude huffed audibly. The spout renewed hostilities with the table. He watched in slow-motion the sticks of water.

'You're deranged.' The paw touched spout, cut the flood on the knuckles.

'Jus' observant.'

Palm turned, spout smacked the wrist. 'Then see: I wash my hand.'

Hole took up the rifle. 'Smells like resignin'.'

'Must be the stalemate.' The right joined it. They cupped, instantly filled. Spillage wrapped softly the rims, ran down wrists and arms.

'Fool's mate, 'Arley, soon as you push that pawn.'

Jude dropped the water and it scattered.

'What if I don't push it?'

'No alternative.'

Jude scratched behind his ear. 'What, so you're going to murder me?' He looked like a person making provisions. 'Think about it. *You're going to murder me.* Is it worth going to jail for? More importantly, is it worth being a *murderer* for? Because once you're a murderer, you're a murderer. For *eternity.*' He stabbed a finger on the board. 'Only oblivion could wring it from you, and oblivion is hopelessly theoretical. You know that, you're the credulous kind.'

'No alternative.'

'You make your own alternatives.'

312

'Each way, the King is dead.'

'What if the game is abandoned? Rain stopped play?'

'Ain't an option.'

'Abandoning is always an option. Especially in catastrophe.' Jude rose, pushing out his chair. He wasn't sure if Hole was a psychopath. He wasn't convinced he would use the gun. And if he was, and if he did, then Jude would die.

'I said it ain't no option.'

'It's already done.' Jude turned an arching back.

Hole raised the hook. 'Then she's mine.'

Jude slouched away, trailing his scythe. 'I suppose so,' he said.

'Got ourselves a whopper, ant we?'

Jude left the building, straight through the absent wall.

'And you're the conscience caught 'im!'

But Jude was out of sight, going over *that stile*. Cloak and scythe he shepherded but he caught his sleeve going over—ripped it on the barbs. 'Fuck,' he said, straddling the beam. Then he grew stubborn. If there was a stile, there was a right of way. Wherever you were, you merely had to say you had lost it. What were they going to do— deport him? He couldn't see Hole for mist. Unhooking his sleeve, he stepped down, gave the building a berth, walked yellow lawns to the spillway. Was that Hole's face at the window? He

313

couldn't care less. He jumped down and rolled up
the chute, hair flapping in his face, all the way up
the shallow gradations whose rise you barely
noticed, level by level, crack by weed, to the
underpass.

'Who's there?' said Harper.

'Friend to this ground.'

The two embraced as if after some ordeal.

Magnus hit the first pedestal. He came to a halt,
foot beside foot. Back was cowled. Shawl clasped
about him. Teeth spoke of knives. It had been a
long journey—only rehearsal for what was coming.
You could see Magnus was ready. He looked like
the crow they called him, hooded in resources.
Prompted by stopped feet, the voiceover:

Horatio:
If you have uphoarded *in your life*
Extorted treasure in the womb of earth,
For which—they say—*you spirits oft walk in*
                                  death,
Speak of it.

Nothing. Just the man on the outcrop, world closing
round him. The sky was a bronzed ocean. The sun
shot straight into it, storm answered with an axe.
Harper turned off the camera, edged it right. It was
a wide angle, zoomed-out, taking all four pedestals
and, each side, a deal of wall. Harper nodded to

314

Jude, who assumed the third pedestal like an ominous bird a-wing. He pointed to the second pedestal and the King began crossing. Thirty feet up, with the same sure step that conquered the wall, he trod the inch-wide railing. Harper climbed down, exhaling. He had to act swift but smoothly; he could not afford to pique his actors. He went precisely over the road, took up the tripod, brought it back like a trophy. Over wall he went, down-slithered to theatre and roamed semicircle to the middle. Here was the cross for *Camera 2*. Out sprawled the legs and he checked the lens. Magnus reached the middle outcrop. Harper set the time delay, crept back up like a wolf from the fold. Up dam, cross flagstones and over the wall. He had six seconds. Jude watched him, side-eyed, suspicious, braced like a surfer on the board. But Harper was deft, full of empathy. Up he leapt with the gingerest leap, brushing only the cloak back—and if even this enraged, Jude did not lash out for fear of falling. As it was he bent him further to the feet, coiled as any spring.

The camera clicked. A heron flew up, framed against the storm, dangling like clothes from its hanger of wings.

Horatio [*alto*]:
It's here!

315

Hairs hit faces. There was a flapping of cloaks and cowls. Forth went Jude's and backward Magnus'. Over eight feet of rail they fronted; one defiant, the other, implacable. Behind Jude, hand on his arm, was Harper, thin and shawlless. In these postures they stayed—against the sky, bound to wall, three fine railings between. Three seconds, then the camera stopped.

For a moment they were still, summoning courage. Then Magnus put foot on the railing and Harper descended. Over wall, down dam and round the endless curves. Back he brought the trophy to the cross of *Camera 1*. It was dim work and hard. Camera was a weight in the wind; tripod a vengeful umbrella. Again he checked the lens, again he set the timer. Clouds were claiming the sun. Soon the light would fail. Magnus was with Jude now, leering down, face to face, toe to toe, almost nose to nose on the pedestal. It was stone versus scissors. Jude's form flew forward. Magnus' fanned back. A fraction of daylight showed Jude onside. He was crouched like a prop over the ball, waiting for impact. Harper saw it all, toiling as in a tunnel— wind at his side, leaning on the sun. How slow could he go? Thighs blurred but the body was still. Hands hardly left the waist. Now he was a gull in high pressures. One had to adjust, allow for digression. It was all about context, taking each on its terms. He aimed right, to the pedestal's edge.

316

Even as he rose a gale force threw him. Wind warped his flight, like wood in a century of sun. He distinctly remembered Magnus' hand, an *all-star* worse for wear, Jude's fearful eye like algae on the water. He veered east, took the pedestal in his stride, straddled shadow-like in the back of Jude. But not a hem he touched, and the *click* they imagined was lost in torrents.

Marcellus:
IT'S HERE!

You had to roar just to hear yourself speak. Harper roared and the blast bore it, perhaps camera caught it. The enraged Jude raised a fist to strike—whom he wasn't sure, for the threat was general. The arm was cocked, the fingers bunched. He stopped. Might this not be more dangerous still? With supreme restraint, he reined his punches. There he stood, elbow pinched, facing one way then the other. Magnus didn't move. Neither did Harper, a head away. He merely counted three.

Again he breathed. Again he descended, Jude quivering above. Putting out a hand, Magnus passed Jude on the south side. The hand was large but calm. Jude remembered it too: veined and assuring, spread like a starfish. No grip nor grab, but it pushed him gently. What pleasure there was in that push: to know that the worst that could

317

happen was a scrap with the pavement. A tug, a tussle, a badly grazed elbow. All power to badly grazed elbows! Put them to the wheel, for they have built character.

Jude took great delight in tottering backwards. 'Wha! Ahah!' he yelled and flapped his arms. *All-stars* gripped stone and slid. He grinned feverish. Then he did a sparrow-hop and landed on his feet. It was a five foot jump and he made the most of it, crouching to the land and dusting himself down. Harper checked the lens, set the timer and fled. Back he came, bundling Jude. Up they climbed, looked ino sun still laughing. Make the most of the moment. The world is gone dark now and sun sealed away. Magnus is behind you, inching over rail. Thunder shakes the dam and the camera sees him go—over the plinth to the wall's end. Slow as you like he descends, moves over mud and enters the waiting boat, a King over the water.

Marcellus:
It's gone!

And their faces change. It's hard to see your neighbour. Anyone had thought it was night. Pouring up from under comes an army: dozens then scores, in Water Board blue. They scale the walls, swarm the dam, press breathless at the pedestals, poking fun. The camera catches all of them,

318

attempting the stage both left and right. There is no room for bashfulness, no last attention to dress. Supplied by the spillway, they are packing the spaces, front and rear: a cussed audience, intent on accountability. The world looks like a forge. Lightning flashes, rain is relentless: it drops a solid curtain. Crowding the road, both sides they come, till the scene can't take any more. Horatio and Marcellus go under. The camera is made the fly to wanton boys. It rides the waves of shoulders, by Moore, past Walsh, to the plastered faces of Hole and Nemmins. They laugh at it, scold it, raise it like a baby and never once look at the boat on the water, its cargo of shreds and patches.

Wrap.

Printed in Great Britain
by Amazon

84852354R00193